To Don
Best Wishes
Tony Auel

Tony Aued

The Blame Game

Blair Adams

An FBI Thriller

Tony Aued

Tony Aued

Other Novels by Tony Aued

The Package

The Abduction

The Vegas Connection

All titles available through Amazon.com.
Also in independent Booksellers.

Tony Aued

For my Parents

Prologue

Blair Adams and her partner Brandon Booth solved one of the most talked about cases in recent FBI history with the capture of man who killed the Chief Justice of the United States. They were also able to track down the two brothers that had parlayed their gambling empire into purchasing a key casino in Las Vegas. The case of the Vegas Connection uncovered the gambling syndicate that the Ellis brothers formed and led three members of Congress to resign in shame.

The opportunity to move back to southern California and her new assignment with the Los Angeles Bureau was exactly as she wished. Blair and her partner Booth became very close during their time together in Vegas and now she had some personal decisions to make. She hadn't been close to anyone since the death of her husband. How this new partnership evolved would only take time to tell.

Steve Orrison the Bureau Chief in Los Angeles made sure his two top Special Agents were involved in many of the new cases that came their way. Steve had a great track record and had his eye on a corner office in the J. Edgar Hoover Building in Washington.

Frank Fitzgerald had just been appointed the Director of the Federal Bureau of Investigation and his acrimonious relationship with the CIA Director would affect the political atmosphere in the White House.

President Morgan and his administration were seeking a second term and the recent polls had shown the election too close to call. Morgan was making every move possible to be reelected and his team had argued on what path to take during recent world events. How would a major problem affect his reelection and the chances for him to stay in office?

Terrorists groups had wanted the peace around the world to end. The war in Afghanistan and Iraq were over and the United States was concentrating on problem at home. This caused a major drop in the need for weapons and purveyors of war needed action to increase their profits. The FBI was diligent in its on-going efforts to protect the national interest and the CIA wanted to regain its prominence in the eyes of the country. What action each agency takes was yet to be seen.

One

Good afternoon this is your captain Leonard Herrmann. Thank you for choosing Asian Air. This is flight 792 departing from Seoul, Korea and headed to Los Angeles, California. I along with your flight crew on Asian Air look forward to serving you. Our flight pattern will be taking us across the Pacific at a cruising altitude of 30,000 feet and an average speed of 912km/hr. The Boeing 747-400 is equipped with the latest navigation enhancements and we will be coming around to make sure you're as comfortable as possible. The thirteen hour flight will take us over the southern coast of Japan and then we will fly directly over the Hawaiian Islands before arriving on the west coast of the United States.

There was a lot of excitement on the plane. Many of the passengers had been at the Olympic trials and the United States had done very well taking the bulk of the medals. Everyone was looking forward to the upcoming summer games in London. Because it was the first time the trials had been held in South Korea the United States wanted to make sure that the Government of the new President saw the support that the U.S. sent.

There were many media members and two officials from the U.S. Olympic committee along with the athletes'.

The US Olympic Swimming team along with the distinguished Senator Harding from Ohio had been seated in first class.

The swim team was one of the brightest groups that the country had fielded for the trials since the 2004 games. The clean sweep of the World games in Seoul was a fine tune-up for the coming summer Olympics in London.

Jenny Sinclair had just gotten her two young children seated and each had their books and hand held game devices for the long flight. She hoped that they would settle down and maybe sleep most of the time. Jenny was thrilled that she could bring her two children to watch their uncle, Brandon, who was one of the premiere swimmers on the team. This was the first time she had been able to see her brother in world competition. She was very proud of him.

The plane taxied onto to the runway and was third in line for takeoff. Captain Herrmann was a veteran pilot with the airlines and had made this trip many times. Once they were in the air he knew the flight crew would be bringing passengers a small food basket with crackers and cheese products along with a drink cart to deliver refreshments. Herrmann was a tall man with light brown hair that showed slightly under his Captain's cap. He always attracted female passenger's attention when he boarded the plane. The Captain was married and met his wife ten years ago on a similar flight. His wife, Sue was a flight attendant on Asian Air and routinely flew on the trans-Atlantic route. He maneuvered around in his seat as he gave final instructions to his co-pilot. It was always a smooth ride flying west to east usually with head winds that often allowed you an earlier arrival.

The captain gave the final announcement that they would be taking off on runway number four and the flight attendants were covering the specifics of passenger safety as they stood in main aisle's demonstrating seat belt and flotation devices.

It would be a long flight and many people had brought pillows and some even had their sleeping mask ready.

Jenny settled the kids in their seats and the take-off went smoothly. She was twenty six and recently divorced. She had a silky white complexion and dark brown eyes. People said she looked just like her mother. Being of Korean and American heritage seemed to blend the best features of both cultures. Jenny was the eldest of two children in her family. He brother Brandon was the captain of the U.S. swim team. Brandon, came back to check on his sister and her two children. He wanted to see her and the kids after they leveled off and gave them each a picture and souvenirs he had from the medals ceremony. Jenny was very proud of her brother's accomplishments and the kids were excited as other passengers started asking for his autograph. The kids were nine and six and now realized how cool it was that he was their uncle.

"It's going to be a long flight Sis. I thought the kids could play with these video games that I brought along." Jenny appreciated his thoughtfulness. She hugged her brother and they smiled at each other before he headed back to his seat up front.

The flight path took the plane over the Pacific Ocean and would cross over the southern tip of the Hawaiian Islands. Some people that were awake watched as they made their way over Kiholo Bay on the western side of the Island. They could make out the big island and Maui pretty well although it was now dark outside. The lights on the islands below created an outline of their shore and were bright against the dark Pacific Ocean.

The flight was pretty smooth and with the western tail winds was ahead of schedule by close to thirty minutes. They had been in the air for close to ten hours and most of the people had either fallen asleep or now were quietly reading.

Kyungai Yun was the lead flight attendant and her team had been awarded the highest recognition last year for their work. She passed through the cabin and noticed one of the swim team members looking for something.

"Can I help you," she asked.

Brandon Thomas was leaning out of his seat attempting to find something that he had dropped on the floor. He turned and looked up at the pretty dark haired stewardess and smiled. "Guess I dropped one of my medals and can't find it. I didn't want to wake my friend who is sleeping but it has to be here!"

Yun motioned that she would look on the floor for him. As she stooped down she spotted it. "Here it is," she said. The shinning gold medal had slid behind the seat he was in and almost impossible for him to see. It got caught on the back of the seat belt and hung a few inches off the floor. She reached under the seat and retrieved the medal and handed it to Brandon. He was pleased and thanked her in Korean. "사의를 표하다."

Yun was surprised that he spoke her native language. She answered him in Korean and they both exchanged a warm smile. As she walked back down the aisle she had a grin on her face. Yun had been with Asian Air for ten years and had found that many American fliers were not very friendly. They often demanded many items from the crew and were mostly rude. The exchange with the young swimmer from the United States was a pleasant surprise.

Brandon was always a gentleman. His parents hadn't been able to make the trip to Seoul but his older sister, Jenny, attended the games with her two young children.

His sister was seated in the back with the kids and he had gone back there twice to see how they were doing. He wanted to give the gold medal to his mother when he got home.

Brandon's father had served in the Marines and married a beautiful young girl when he was stationed in Korea.

Brandon's mother taught both him and Jenny how to speak Korean and he was very happy when they got to the games because everyone wanted to travel around with him. His knowledge of the language made everything so much easier. After a solid performance in the games he was interviewed by a local reporter and when he answered the questions in Korean he immediately became a local favorite.

Although he was young, he handled himself in a very mature manner. Many of the women said what a handsome young man he was. Like many swimmers he had broad shoulders and short cropped hair. His features were mixed with those of his mother's heritage and his father's. He was very popular in college which was a far cry from his high school experience. He was bullied in high school because of his looks. High school kids could be so mean and being part Korean didn't help. Because his older sister had gone through much of the same things she helped him get through it. This experience made them very close.

The sun was now rising as the plane was in its last leg of the journey. They had left Korean airspace the previous day at two in the afternoon and would now be arriving in Los Angeles early Wednesday morning. The almost thirteen hour flight left many passengers restless. The attendants from Asian Air moved about the cabin offering passengers assistance with items that needed to tossed out or information on connecting flights. LAX was a collage of terminals and the international flights always had many people needing to catch another plane to their final destination.

The pilot, Leonard Herrmann, was a seasoned veteran of the airline and his crew was regarded as the best flight crew in the fleet. Yun headed into the flight deck to gather final instructions from the pilot for her crew. He confirmed their landing and gate arrival with the tower from LAX and she planned to make a general announcement to all.

Senator Harding moved up to talk to some members of the swim team and hoped to get a few extra photo ops in Los Angeles before they all headed their separate ways.

The Senator's family had taken an earlier flight but he wanted to make sure he would be photographed with the victorious team at the airport. He knew with two swimmers from Ohio State on the team that the pictures would play well with his constituents back home. After all it was an election year.

The coach had marveled at the stadium in Suwon and the reception that they received. He was telling Senator Harding that his team members were surprised at how friendly the locals were. Koreans were known to be a reserved people and their openness to the U.S. team was well welcomed. The Senator was talking to Brandon and the team coach as the plane made a wide bank to the right. He had to grab onto the back of a seat so he wouldn't fall. The announcement over the intercom advised everyone to return to their seats and buckle up. The view of the ocean lapping the shoreline of Southern California had many of the people leaning and some taking photos. The pilot came on and informed everyone that they would be making their final approach into LAX and everyone needed to be in their seats and buckled in.

Just about then the plane shuddered and started shaking violently. All of a sudden the plane dropped and everyone seemed to let out a gasp in unison.

Was it just an air pocket that they hit? The pilot pulled the levers up and to the left and tried to level off. They were dropping fast and fear took over the mood in the plane.

Suddenly a fireball erupted on the left wing. People had fallen out of their seats and the crew attempted to tend to some people that had been hurt.

The quick decent sent people falling into the aisle. Passengers could now see that the wing on the left side was on fire. Panic occurred and the crew scrambled to calm people down. Yun got on the intercom and told everyone that they needed to remain calm.

There were screams and people grabbing onto each other as the plane jolted through the sky. Some passengers had fallen out of their seats and many were hurt in the dramatic fall in the sky.

Brandon crawled down the aisle trying to get to his sister and her two children. He knew that he had to help them. The plane was thrashing back and forth and he could see Jenny now holding her young son. His sister was crying as he made his way to her. The four of them now held onto each other as they tried to calm the kids.

The pilot and co-pilot pulled the gears and steering mechanism as hard as possible to right the falling bird. The nose was finally pulling up and they were no longer in a downward fall. The pilot appeared to get the plane leveled off and Yun got back on the intercom to address the situation. People were still on the floor and many were hurt or crying. "Please everyone, we will be okay," Yun stated. "The pilot had just contacted the tower at LAX and we received emergency clearance to land." Confusion and panic was still the order in the cabin as you could hear people praying. There were passengers to be cared for and the crew had their work cut out for them. Yun again grabbed the microphone and asked for everyone to remain calm. "We will be okay," she said.

That was the last thing they heard. The plane was only a few hundred feet off the coastline south of Newport Beach when it broke apart.

People along the shoreline were stunned. The explosion could be heard for miles. Many described the scene as a fire ball caroming through the sky and then a blast that sent pieces of the plane soaring through the air. The channel that opened to the Marinas and homes along that stretch of shoreline were bursting with tourist and pleasure crafts.

Many of them headed to the spot where the plane has disintegrated over the Pacific Ocean hoping to help in some way.

It would be hopeless. Over three hundred people were on flight 792 from Seoul that day.

Calls went out immediately to the NTSB and Coast Guard. Air Traffic control at LAX then notified local law enforcement agencies and the FBI office in Los Angeles. The tower at LAX reported that the captain had called in an emergency just minutes before the explosion but seemed to feel he could still guide the plane to safety. FAA inspectors noted that a jumbo jet of that type could have safely landed and an engine fire wouldn't cause that type of an incident. Asian Air officials noted that they had never lost a plane. Reporters clamored for answers as the news broke. Airline officials didn't answer questions regarding an emergency landing they had to make in British Columbia April of 2012.

The blame game would just be starting.

Two

The day after the crash the FBI office in L.A. was given the lead on the investigation. The NTSB confirmed that it was a bomb that caused the crash. The Navy Special Service team from San Diego assigned a Seal team to search the Ocean floor for evidence. They had recovered pieces of the bomb off the coast discovered by the Seal's divers. News media outlets hadn't been told that it was a bomb that brought the plane down. The Bureau wanted more information before releasing that fact. There was also the recovery of the passengers from flight 792. It was a delicate operation and important to recover the bodies of those lost. Many families needed closure and funerals would be important to accomplish this.

Morning papers headlines showed the plane with the Olympic Team loading in Seoul before takeoff. The Asian Air crash was a great shock to the whole world. It created quite a commotion in the FBI offices in Los Angeles. Steve Orrison, the Bureau Chief, summoned his team to the large meeting room in the building on Wilshire Boulevard.

There was a lot of action in the office and phones were ringing off the hook. The Associated Press was calling for comments and the Bureau was being buried with calls from officials in Washington and the Olympic Committee.

CNN was running pictures of the Olympic Team and Senator Harding with the story being covered 24/7. The Bureau Chief wanted to get his key people together to sort out the events and direct plans for the upcoming investigation.

The FBI Los Angeles team had completed a great year with the capture of all the suspects in a major corruption case. The two Special Agents Blair Adams and Brandon Booth, were given the highest praise from the President and the outgoing Director gave each of them special commendations. The trial had made headlines worldwide with the two brothers, Omar and Salem Ellis, getting life sentences for their role in the death of Justice Leonard. Assad Jacoby received the death penalty for the actual killing of the Chief Justice. It was Blair and Booth that captured Assad that helped solve the case.

The team of agents knew their role would be crucial in the investigation of the bombing of Flight 792 from Seoul. Steve had been the Bureau Chief in Los Angeles two years now and was very comfortable with his staff. Blair Adams and Brandon Booth were his two top Special Agents. They were a strong team and Steve relied upon their expertise. The Bureau Chief had made a solid impression with his team in the two years on the job in Los Angeles and they were a well oiled machine working together on many fronts. Drug trafficking was an important problem with the proximity of Mexico and many international flights arriving into LAX daily. His agents covered Southern California, parts of Arizona and worked closely with the Nevada Bureau.

The new Director of the Bureau, Frank Fitzgerald would be addressing the agents via Tela-conference in the meeting room. Steve had known the new Director from his previous position in Seattle when Fitzgerald was then the Assistant Director of the FBI.

It was back in Seattle that Steve's team captured the head of a drug ring that operated out of western Canada. That was a big break for his career and prompted his move to Los Angeles.

The Los Angeles Bureau along with those of New York and Washington were the three top positions in the field. Fitzgerald knew the importance of his teams and the LA Bureau was one of the best.

Frank Fitzgerald had been with the agency for close to twenty-five years and his close relationship with the President and the outgoing Director made him the logical choice to succeed John Martin. Success in Washington was measured in the size of your budget and Frank had made sure the Bureau's percentage grew during his tenure as the Assistant Director. Frank's physical appearance gave one the immediate feeling of confidence. He had a stout neck; wide shoulders and a chiseled chin that let you know he was in charge. He was six foot five inches tall, sandy blond hair and deep blue eyes. Fitzgerald was an imposing figure, especially when he appeared on a television screen. He often towered over others in meetings. Fitzgerald came from a large family in Michigan. He was an athletic star in high school and received a football scholarship from Notre Dame. It was there where he decided to major in criminology.

Although his sports career was average he graduated at the top of his class and was awarded a fellowship to Cornell University. He originally thought about a career in the legal profession. He met and married his sweetheart while finishing his studies at Cornell. Frank once worked with an FBI agent helping him get ready for upcoming testimony in a possible terrorist case.
The aspects of that work seemed to hold great interest to him.

This experience led him to seek a position with the Bureau. Once he was hired he was glad that he made the change in career paths. His first assignment was a position in Arizona. Due to his bi-lingual skills and legal background the assignment was a natural. His rise through the ranks took him across the country to many locations including a stint in Puerto Rico where he headed a group of agents working to stop the flow of illegal drugs. With all these successes he was reassigned to the Bureau's headquarters at 935 Pennsylvania Ave., Washington, D.C. Frank worked closely with the President and Director on the National task force to stop the growing tide of drug usage in the country. His expertise also covered the gang problem that went hand-in-hand with drugs. A few years ago he was promoted to the Assistant Director of the Bureau and responsible for all the agents and office budgets in the country. His nomination to the position of Director of the FBI won endorsements from both sides of the aisle.

Frank told Steve was that he would be coming to Los Angeles soon and wanted to see some progress. Key detailed information on the bomb type and facts about every crew member on Asian Air flight number 792 would be number one.

The FBI's Strategic Information Center was sending material to the LA office. This was a full-court press if there ever was one. The briefing room was standing room only. The crime board was already started with photos of the downed plane, the airport in South Korea and a map of the flight path it had taken. Steve made sure that everyone knew all the details of the events leading up to the plane crash.

The FAA hadn't released their finding yet but the Bureau had their preliminary report. The blast was caused by a bomb that had been hidden in the wing of the 747-400 jumbo-jet-liner.

The chemical make-up of the bomb had not been determined yet and due to the unknown origin it was only speculation that they were working off of.

It wasn't clear if the fire on the wing was set on purpose to happen before the bomb went off but it was clear that the plane had been sabotaged. Many question remained. Why did they wait to activate the bomb so close to landing? Was the bomb activated by someone on board or remotely? There was no sign of a timer mechanism found yet. The FAA team, along with the Bureau's people was working on that.

The screen in the conference room came alive and the Director opened with a short statement. "We lost many American lives in the crash of flight 792 from Seoul. The President and people of the United States demand answers. We will be working along with Homeland Security to uncover those answers.
You all are to cooperate in every way possible with other national and local agencies. If you have a questions contact your Bureau Chief. I have given Mr. Orrison directives on this investigation and expect each one of you to work 24/7 until this is solved."

The message was short and to the point. Steve stood in front of the room and addressed the group. "I know we have many things on our plate however, this plane crash takes precedence. When we say we will work 24/7 to resolve this we mean each of you assigned to this will report directly to me as we proceed. We will utilize all of our expertise and resources to get the job done. You are not to discuss any aspect of this case with anyone. Not your wife, husband or girlfriend. If you do you will be reassigned. Do you understand?"

Agents nodded their heads.

"If not we still have opening in Fargo!"

The agents looked around and no one was smiling. This was as serious of a situation that many of them would be involved.

Mr. Fitzgerald was still on the screen and listening to the directions Steve was giving his agents. Although the CIA and Department of Homeland Security were involved in the operation, the Director would make sure everyone knew the FBI would be taking the lead. In law-enforcement circles the Bureau was the seven-hundred pound gorilla in relation to other agencies.

Steve continued. "I have set up three teams to work directly with me and our counterparts in the FAA as well as the CIA. They will be two other teams working with members of the local authorities. We don't need heroes or hot-shots on this. Special Agents Blair Adams and Brandon Booth will be the team leaders.

No one was surprised to hear that special Agents Adams and Booth would be in charge of the lead group.

After all they were instrumental in capturing the assassin of the Chief Justice last year. Since then they have enjoyed many plum assignments.

Steve Orrison turned toward the screen and signaled the meeting back to the Director for final orders. No one in the room had personally meet Frank Fitzgerald except for Steve. His hard nose approach told them not to relax. The Director covered key names and instructions to this group of agents. Steve added important information along with the name of the members of the FAA they would be working with.

They heard the names of their CIA counterparts working in Seoul and others operating in Russia. Josh Smith along with Rusty Nelson would be the main operatives in Korea on the case.

They would also utilize their National Terrorism group. It was and would always be the FBI's authority to investigate domestic cases. The Central Intelligence Agency was to handle the aspects of the case in International venues.

Fitzgerald made his last point. "When I say work directly with the members of our sister agency, I don't mean were working for them!" He emphatically clutched his fist as he made this statement. "Son-of-a-bitch this is our investigation. We defend this country and it is our turf this happened on. The other agency needs to be working on the angle from the Republic of Korea and what happened there. They will report to me and not the other way around!" The agents in the room all nodded in approval. They knew one agency telling another the truth about their investigation was counterintuitive. The last message confirmed what they had heard about the new Director. He worked hard and expected you to do the same. He also expected you to take no bullshit from anyone. The Bureau was his life and he's not a politician. The meeting concluded and Steve motioned to Booth and Blair to follow him to his office.

Steve confided to Booth and Blair that the Director was headed to LA. "He wants to get the lay of the land on this," he told them.

"We need to get on this and find out what the FAA can tell us today. They have the black box but I'm not sure it will help. From the recording we heard from the flight tower at LAX everything went dead after they gave the pilot his clearance and runway information."

The two agents reassured their boss that they would get right on it. When they were walking to the elevator Blair looked at Booth and asked.

"Did I hear him right? Are we supposed to work with the FAA too? I thought another team got that assignment."

"Yes, you heard him right. Yes, we will work with the FAA and yes he gave that assignment to another group." Booth continued walking into the elevator and Blair just followed.

"So we will do it! I got it." The two Special Agents would follow their directives and head to Newport Beach to being their investigation.

Three

The country lost a prominent Senator and sports lost one of the greatest assemblies of swimmers in history. The U.S. Olympic Team along with the International Olympic Committee was outraged and many were in a state of shock. The plane held 333 passengers along with a flight crew of twelve people headquartered from Seoul. The CIA was investigating each member of the flight crew and also tracking data on all the passengers. The flight manifest showed that 75 people were citizens of the Republic of Korea and another 50 people were from a variety of countries along the Asian rim. The bulk of the remaining passengers were from the United States and Canada. It would take a long time to gather the details necessary of those passengers. Every agency was affording the Bureau with the information that was being requested. That was very unusual but this case was unusual.

The CIA had agents checking on everyone in Seoul who worked on the plane while it was on the ground. The records were not as thorough as they had hoped. They had their lead agents tracking everyone down and looking into backgrounds. One of the many things that bothered them was the timing of the bomb. A few minutes off and the plane would have landed. Was it to suppose to explode on the ground? Had the bomb gone off too soon?

There were two levels of agents operating in Seoul.

One was a covert group that operated specifically in all matters of the agency. The second group was a black ops group that only the Director had knowledge of. How this would all play out wasn't quite clear. The only thing for sure was that this investigation would become a Washington tug match between the FBI and CIA before it was all over. The Director of the CIA, Robert Chiarini was appointed by President Morgan and had been a key political ally. He was in his position for a few years and played the political game very well. Frank Fitzgerald was recently appointed to replace John Martin and would have to fight every step in the investigation.

Senator Harding's family had been on an earlier flight and although his wife was grief stricken she was glad that her husband suggested that she and the three children to take the earlier flight home. Harding said he had wanted to spend some time in LA and she knew the kids would be going back to school soon. He always thought about them, she would tell her friends and the press. That is why when the opportunity came up to go to Korea he decided to take them all along. This would be a great opportunity for the kids he told her. The President was holding a Cabinet meeting and demanded that his team get quick answers to this disaster. After losing a Senator and Chief Justice last year he knew the country was weary with events of national mourning.

The bureaucracy of Washington was like a pretzel. It was impossible to tell where things started or ended. It was sure to be a conflict between two agencies and the President was concerned about that.

Both men reported to the new Director of Homeland Security, John Martin and the CIA felt he would lean favorably toward his old position in the FBI. President Morgan wanted answers and he wanted them now!

This would become a major international incident pretty fast with disastrous results.

The North Koreans were denying any knowledge of the bombing. By now usually someone was claiming responsibility even if they didn't do it. So far, all the leads were coming up empty.

Fitzgerald informed the group gathered that he would soon fly to Los Angeles to get firsthand knowledge of the operation. John Martin acknowledged that this was a good move. The Director of the CIA nodded but then added. "This is a case of National Security and an act of terrorism. Our agency should be in the forefront of the investigation." The two men started arguing about control of the investigation when John Martin yelled, "Enough!"

The room became quiet and John turned to them, "Officially what happens on U.S. soil is under the FBI's jurisdiction, outside our borders the CIA is in charge. However in this endeavor we must work together and as fast as possible. This will escalate very fast if we don't resolve it." Both men settled down and seemed to be in agreement.

Chiarini turned to one of key aides and whispered in his ear. "Get Tony Kim on the phone now. I want him to handle this as quickly as possible." The aide left the meeting excusing himself on the pretense of needing to take an important call.

The call to get Tony Kim involved was going to be the ace-in-the-hole for the CIA Director. Chiarini controlled a rogue group of agents under the moniker of Silverstone. This group came to light under the command of his predecessor and had been order to be dissolved. Chiarini agreed to do this but still kept a small group that would be under his control. He had continued to utilize the underground bunker that was built by his predecessor to house his top secret operation. The location was known to only a handful of people.

Tony Kim was his top deep cover agent. He was operating in North Korea without anyone aware of his presence. The Director, like his predecessors, had this clandestine group that only he and a few of his closest allies knew of. Politics and power was always the pursuit in Washington and this event would escalate that.

President Morgan had returned and moved around the room.

He conferred with other Cabinet members that accompanied him. His mood was somber and it wasn't too often that you saw him like that. His shoulders were drooped and he had a pensive look on his face. Many people had commented on how much he had aged in just three years in office. His face had a deep crease along the bridge of his forehead and his hair had turned gray along the edges.

Morgan leaned against the desk as his team stopped to listen to what he was about to say.

"I don't understand it. Why hadn't we heard something from some radical group? Every group from Al-Qaida to Iran or Belgrade would have normally tried to take credit for this."They knew he was right. Peace between nations was bad for the weapons industry and if they could cause a break in the peace their business would flourish. Every radical group would love to send the U.S. into another conflict.

This was also an election year and questions remained on how this incident will play with the public. People expected quick answers and there were calls from Senators and Representatives for action. Many people had a stake to claim and politics was a vehicle that was driven by events both negative and positive news.

The other party candidate would wait only a short time to question the resolve of the sitting President. Everyone in the room knew the dire aspects of both the bombing and the affect on the public's perception of its leaders.

People were arriving at the Thomas' home on Oak
Drive. Mr. and Mrs. Thomas were surrounded by family
members and friends wanting to console them in this time of
great loss. How could this have happened? Just yesterday
they were celebrating Brandon's victories in Seoul.

Mr. Thomas had stayed up all night watching feeds on
the satellite channel from Seoul and spotted Brandon three
times during the closing ceremonies.

He had taped all the action from the World games, and
now that was all they had left. The disaster of flight 792 took
both their children and their only two grandchildren. It was a
fate no one should have to endure.

Mrs. Thomas had been sedated by their family
physician. She was hysterical when she received the news
and shaking badly. Mr. Thomas was still stunned. There was
no one that seemed able to come up with words that seemed
to be appropriate. People held hands and talked in low
volume as Aunts and Uncles set out trays of food and desserts
that were being dropped off at the home. Mr. Thomas's sister,
Eugenia, along with her two daughters greeted guests and
thanked them as they handed her platters of meats and
vegetables. They were setting them on the kitchen table for
guests to munch on. There must have been fifty people in the
house and many were former teachers and local swim team
members of Brandon.

Jenny's former husband had dropped by and talked to
Mr. Thomas about arrangements for his ex-wife and two
children. The two men shook hands as he left. It was so sad
to see them together this way. Although Jenny and her
husband had been divorced for a few years it seemed to an
amicable arrangement. The family would never be the same.

The Thomas house was set back off the street with a
long winding driveway that was packed with cars.

The small town of Mason, Ohio was so proud of their native son Brandon and now mourned his death along with the other members of the Thomas family. People would demand answers. The President needed to respond. They would be waiting and watching for his reaction.

The television was on in the family room with groups of people watching. Reporters that were covering the events broadcasted the news and were now listing the names of the passengers along with the flight crew that were killed in the crash.

Other reporters were telling the story of events from the stadium in Suwon, Korea. It was the stadium that had been the scene of the celebration just two days ago.

American journalists had been showing taped telecast of the team's victories in Korea and showing photos of each Olympian. Stories were circulating on the background and home life of the members of the team and local news teams were interviewing family and friends all around the country. The tragic loss of so many people was magnified by the loss of the Olympic team and a prominent Senator.

Mrs. Harding had declined a television on-air interview from her home in Cincinnati. She knew that her husband's office would handle any request that the press would need. Her only statement earlier was that her husband always cared for her and the kids. Her main thoughts were how to best protect her two children during this time. The Senator had married late in life and had two young children. Their privacy was Mrs. Harding's main concern now.

Senator Harding came from a long line of political office holders. His great-grandfather was Warren G. Harding the 29th President of the United States. Senator Harding like his great-grandfather was a staunch conservative.

Although historians didn't give President Harding's term high marks he did accomplish many things including fighting for the civil rights of African-Americans. President Harding died in office on a long political trip out west of exhaustion and pneumonia in 1923. The Senator's father before him also served in the House of Representatives and his grandfather had been the Governor of Ohio. This long line of public servants had now ended with the crash of flight of 792.

The Senator's staff was making every attempt to keep Mrs. Harding's wishes of privacy during this first day of the tragedy. His Chief of Staff handled the request from the Cincinnati Enquirer as well as the television stations around the world and the desire for an interview.

The Harding family had a large home in Cincinnati near the Xavier University Campus. It was in a gated community and keeping the press away was easy.

President Morgan had called the Senator's wife earlier and offered her anything that her family needed in this time of great sorrow. Morgan and Harding were on different sides of many political battles however they had great respect for each other and Morgan respected him as solid family man. Senator Harding had been in the Senate for three terms and head of the House Ways and Means Committee. He was popular with his constituents and his re-election was a foregone conclusion. The Republican Party would now look for a new candidate to put before the voters this fall. The prospect of losing the seat to the Democrats was now a concern of his Party.

The man that appeared on every television screen looked worried and more somber than anyone had ever seen before. How he would make this important speech might affect both his future and that of his country.

He stood in the Oval Office wearing a dark gray suit with a red and blue striped tie. His short cropped hair and olive skin stood out sharply against the background of the massive desk and American flags that draped both sides of the screen.

The *Resolute Desk* that he stood behind was in the center of the Oval Office. It was originally given to President Rutherford B. Hayes in 1880 as a gift from Queen Victoria. It was built from timbers of the British Arctic Exploration ship *Resolute*. Although it had been used in various parts of the White House it wasn't in the Oval Office until Jackie Kennedy moved it in there in 1961 for the President.

The *Resolute* desk is a large, nineteenth-century partner's desk that has been used by every President since it was brought back into the Oval Office by President Carter. President Johnson had put it in the Smithsonian Museum after President Kennedy was assassinated.

"My Fellow American's. It is with heavy hearts that we here in this great nation today mourn the loss of so many people. Our thoughts and prayers go out to each and every family member. I guarantee the commitment of our great nation to resolve and hold accountable those responsible for this evil deed. I am working with members of the armed forces and my cabinet on this issue and we will answer this attack on our great country. I offer my condolences to Mrs. Harding and her two children, and promise his service to this country will be remembered. To the families of the United States Olympic Team, God Bless you in your loss today. May you know that we stand together to honor your fallen heroes. To the flight crew and family members of the people on-board Asian Air flight 792 we will bring to justice those responsible for this tragedy."

People were glued to their television screen from living rooms to bars and restaurants across the country.

They were nodding as the President stood firmly in charge and promising to hold the nation responsible for this bombing. Many people were waiting to see if he had any specifics as to who might have done this.

"I have talked to President Lee Myung-bak of The Republic of South Korea and we have issued a joint warning to whomever we find responsible for this action. I have requested the key members of both the House and Senate to convene both chambers tomorrow for a vote if necessary on our response."

This statement brought both cheers from many observers and worried feelings on many families at home. Did this mean war? What did the President mean by our necessary response?

Most felt that his actions were just what were needed in this time of crisis. They were felling comfortable when he stated that he had his Cabinet and would have the House and Senate involved in this decision.
Newspapers prepared to scrap their headlines for the news that the President had just delivered to the Nation.

Reaction from both Parties was positive. The Democrats were standing tall behind the strong language the President had used. The Republicans were putting their own spin on things but supporting the President as long as he keeps them involved in the decision.

Like many politicians each man and woman wanted to be the center of the conversation however none offered any real resolution.

Talk was cheap and in Washington there was a lot of cheap talk.

Four

It was now past mid-night in Seoul and most of the population was fast asleep. Joshua Eli Smith had just entered his apartment. It had been a long day. He had just come from Seoul with his counterpart, Rusty Nelson, when he received the news of the crash. The phone call detailed the urgency of the situation. He needed to contact Rusty right away. They had been meeting with a key contact that Josh knew in Seoul. Due to the nature of problems between the North Koreans and the United States they would have to gather Intel as soon as possible for the Director of the CIA. Josh Smith was a key CIA Agent and would be very important in this investigation. He had an asset that would be very valuable in this regard.

The CIA had many operatives along the Korean Peninsula. Josh had been assigned as a covert Agent there since 2010. He was a slender man that fit in nicely with the population. So many Americans were large people and stood out from the norm. Josh had been with the Agency for close to ten years and his expertise was in Pacific Rim Nations. He was Thirty Three and single although quite a ladies' man. He had dark hair and blue eyes. His knowledge of the language also helped him stay under the radar.

His cover was that he operated in Suwon as an Import and Export merchant and had a small but lively business in the shopping district.

He spent a lot of time in the big market district and operated a small warehouse there. He loved Korean delicacies especially Kimchi and Pork Bellies.

Josh had a hobby that also allowed him to gather a lot of material. He loved taking pictures and was very good at it. He often used his hobby to gain access to spots that were helpful in his investigations.

Suwon was the perfect place for him to headquarter. It is the provincial capital of Gyeonggdi-do, South Korea. It is a major city of over a million inhabitants. Suwon location being so close to Seoul was also important. It was approximately 30 kilometers (19 Miles) south of Seoul and just a forty-five minute train ride. He had left Rusty at the train station just an hour ago.

The train was the fastest form of transportation in Korea. The landscape was aglow with the huge flashing billboards calling to the throngs of daily travelers. With so much night life in Seoul there was always something going on. Josh's cover allowed him many trips there and the short distance to Seoul made for quick rides. The train station was a short walk from his apartment.

Rusty Nelson was a CIA counter-terrorism agent and a fifteen year veteran of the agency. Rusty and Josh were very different. Rusty started his career as a pilot in the Air Force and served in Iraq during the invasion under the first President Bush. Rusty was older than Josh and did not speak the language as well as he did. Although he was a CIA agent he reported directly to the Director of Homeland Security and was often torn between his two bosses. Keeping the Director of the CIA in the loop was always important but so was that of the Director of Homeland Security. You didn't want to get trapped in-between the two men when they were playing politics.

On the trip to Seoul he was working on a project for the agency along with Josh. They were planning to infiltrate a group shipping knock-off goods to the States. Josh had the tie-in with his business cover in Suwon to get them into this group. Rusty hated this type of work but went along with the orders from his Director.

Rusty Nelson was paradox. He was well traveled and had an extensive knowledge of terror suspects operating in Seoul. He also didn't like having to work with another agent. He was strong and built like a football player. Rusty stood six foot two and weighed close to two hundred pounds. His short reddish-blond hair and size made him stand out in the crowd. He didn't care because he had tremendous skills in hand-to-hand combat and held a black belt. Everyone who worked with Rusty knew he had a short temper and you never wanted to cross him.

Working on the sales of knock-offs was something he didn't give a shit about. If a bunch of women bought bullshit bags and clothes from the Koreans it was just too damn bad for them. He tried to beg off the assignment but his Director needed him in case there were other things being smuggled into the States along with the fashion accessories.

Phone calls would soon come in to all the agents operating along the Korean Peninsula. Whatever they were working on would be on the back-burner. This situation would take precedence.

The call to Tony Kim meant that he would return to the states. Tony was their version of Jason Bourne. He was highly intelligent and an expert in martial arts. He was a key black ops CIA operative. Tony worked in secrecy, both in the states as well as Korea. Kim got direct orders from his Director and had another agenda. He wasn't working in conjunction with anyone else.

His presence in the states would offer him more opportunities to gather Intel than other agents. He also would not hesitate to use any force necessary. His cover was unknown even to other agents operating in the field. Kim was five foot ten and being of Korean nationality he fit in here as well as in California. He was born in Los Angeles. His parents were from The Republic of Korea and came to the United States just before he was born. He kept a residence in Venice Beach under an alias with a second apartment in Seoul.

He had many contacts both in the States and Korea. Tony did not work with anyone else on assignments. He was a loaner and kept to himself. When Chiarini was ordered to disband Silverstone he erased all knowledge of the remaining agents that he kept under his control. The Director planned to use them only when it was of dire situation and this was one of those instances. Tony Kim would be the wild card in this investigation.

Josh Smith and Rusty Nelson had been out late last night at the Pre-Lantern Festival in Hwaseong. They met their contact along the walls of the fortress there. The cover of attending the celebration allowed them the opportunity to meet with Josh's asset to gather key information on the investigation of counterfeit goods coming into the US. Now the crash of flight 792 would change everything. Reaction to the plane being blown up rippled across the world. Many Nations' leaders called the President and offered both condolences and support to find the terrorist who perpetrated this deed. People were positioning themselves against this event due to the great loss of civilian lives. This brought back memories Pan Am Flight 103 over Lockerbie, Scotland. That plane crashed over land and killed eleven people on the ground along with all the passengers on-board. The captured terrorist in 1988 had stated that the plane was supposed to crash over the ocean. Was this the same type of incident? Could the same group be involved twenty-four years later?

Blair Adams was reading the latest report from her I
Phone to her partner Brandon Booth as he kept on driving on
Highway 10 toward Santa Monica. They would jump off
Highway 10 and take the 405 all the way to the 55 which went
into Newport Beach. Los Angeles was a jungle of highways
that snaked through the cities along the coast.

They were meeting with the rescue crew that found the
black box and key investigators from the FAA.

The information they got first hand would help in the
possible identification of the explosives and maybe lead them
to the country of origin. This was a remote possibility but
they had to start somewhere.

Newport Beach was off the Pacific Coast Highway and
close to Balboa Island. It was expensive real-estate. It was
from Balboa Island that the FAA had worked with Navy Seals
on the recovery of fragments from the plane. The homes and
apartments that lined the Marina were all in the million dollar
range. It was also the home for many tourist attractions
including whale watching boats that went out from the
Marina daily into the Pacific in hopes of catching the view of a
Gray or Blue Whale's tail rising out of the ocean. You could
also take a passenger ferry to Catalina Island from one of the
many seafaring boats that operated out of the harbor.

The two agents planned on picking up one of the FAA
inspectors at John Wayne Airport located just off highway 55.
He would accompany them to the meeting with the rescue
crew at the Harbor Patrol building in the Marina. Blair said
that they needed to make sure both the FAA and Harbor
patrol knew they were in charge of the investigation. He
agreed. It would be important to set the ground rules.

Blair and Booth were a solid team and worked well
together. Their first operation was in Vegas and they bonded
as the chase for suspects took them through the California

mountains and finally to the coastal area. What they didn't know was that a CIA operative was planning to foil their investigation.

Five

Blair Adams had been through lot of changes in a short time. There were times that she would think back to when her husband Hunter was alive and how they enjoyed walking along the beach holding hands when he returned from a mission. It seemed like a lifetime away since he was killed by a sniper in Iraq. How much she had changed. She valued her friends and family more than ever. Now she was a seasoned FBI agent and a damn good one. She had earned the respect of the members of the LA Bureau in her recent cases and the Director knew she was a valuable asset. At five-foot-four and blond she wanted to be thought of as more than a pretty face. She always made sure she was dressed professionally and handled business like any agent. She had deep blue eyes and wore her hair short. Her jaw line was sharp and it gave her features a distinguished look. Blair was a health addict. She belonged to a local gym and trained daily. She also liked hanging out at Muscle Beach in Santa Monica. She would work out with some of the guys that liked to hang on the rings and perform circus type acts. One summer she joined the team of trapeze flyers on the Santa Monica Pier. She became very skilled and performed in one of their shows. She said it was great exercise and the precision timing helped keep her in top condition. It was also great fun and a departure from her every day activities at the agency.

She never wanted to be taken for granted nor have people assume she was eye-candy.

It was a big mistake to ever call her cute. After her appointment the original plan was to have her become a spokesperson for the FBI and help in recruiting. All that changed when she became involved in the Vegas case. She teamed up with Special Agent Brandon Booth and their success led to their permanent partnership. During one case a suspect smiled when she cornered him in an alley. "Well what a pretty thing you are," he had said. "Guess this is what you might call speed dating." He laughed and started moving toward her. That was his second mistake. Her martial arts training had him on the ground begging for help in less than ten seconds. Booth arrived just as she had him handcuffed and reading him his rights. Booth didn't quite know what to make of her statement when he heard her say.

"Guess the dates over."

Since her relocation to California everything had been pretty normal except that her car was broken into one night at the apartment complex. It was strange nothing had been taken just the passenger window broken and stuff messed up in her back seat. Booth helped her look into it but they never came up with anything. There was always a concern that someone might still be trying to hurt her especially since she was instrumental in helping to foil a terrorists plot in New York last year. The Bureau had checked her car for prints but none were found. They never bother to check her apartment because it never seemed to have been compromised.

Her partner Brandon Booth came from a much different background. His parents were killed in an auto accident when he was young and he bounced around in the foster care system for years.

Booth was closed about his experience and never opened up to anyone about the trauma he went through as a kid. He was tall and handsome and fit the description of the silent type. It was his partnership with Blair that opened him up for the first time.

He and Blair were good together and other agents noticed that they seemed to have a special relationship. Agents spent a lot of time working together and it was important that they got along well. Steve made them permanent partners after their adventure in Vegas. They made a great team and worked closely during the chase for the assassin of the Chief Justice last year.

The drive down the 405 to highway 55 was never fun. It was even worse at this time of day. Bumper-to-bumper traffic from Los Angeles to San Diego and points south made it hell. They had just passed the Howard Hughes Plaza on the right and Booth quickly moved to the speed lane and pushed the pedal to the floor. He was doing close to 75 when a new Ford Escape driven by a white haired little lady moved across the double solid white lines into the commuter lane. "Shit lady! What the hell's wrong with you?" Booth was hollering and shaking his fist.

Blair grabbed the handle on the dash above the glove box and held on tight.

"This crazy old lady just jumped across the double line and now is doing 50." Booth was pissed and trying not to ram the back of the ladies car.

Blair pulled open the glove box and put the blue bubble siren on the dash. "You okay," she asked before turning it on. Booth didn't answer but just waved at her. When she hit the button on the machine and it started flashing blue and red the Escape in front of them started to swerve and went from the speed lane over three lanes almost causing a huge pile-up. Booth accelerated past the freeway action and cars started to get out of their way. He didn't say anything for about ten minutes. "You know were not suppose to do that," he told her.

"Well it was either get her out of the way or drive you to Sinai-Grace after your heart attack." He just nodded and continued driving.

If they only knew what other dangers lie ahead.

Tony Kim had just arrived in Newport Beach aboard a private jet. He headed out of John Wayne International Airport to a car waiting for him. The man behind the wheel took off as soon as Kim jumped in. He handed Kim a folder and pulled out of the parking lot almost hitting a black Impala that was turning in.

Blair turned to Booth, "Shit that's the second accident we almost had on this trip. I'm driving on the way back." Booth just looked at her.

"That shit head almost hit me. I'm on my side of the road and he swerved into our lane." He was not happy and almost being hit a second time didn't help. "Did you get that license plate number?"

"No, it was a silver car, an S Class and there must be a thousand of those here."

The two agents proceeded to park at the terminal and went in to meet their guest.

The airport terminal was just off highway 55 and the road led directly into Newport Beach. The driver of the S Class that just missed hitting Booth turned to his passenger and asked, "Where to?"

"Head to the Sea Foam restaurant it's on Ocean Boulevard. I have a meeting with the man that has the information I need to complete my mission."

The driver nodded and headed up the highway toward the Ocean and the Sea Foam restaurant. Tony Kim didn't have much else to say.

As they continued Tony Kim was going through the folder that the driver had handed him. They continued heading toward Newport Beach.

Tony would meet there with a contact that had information from the FAA on the crash.

The folder he read had the names of the key FBI personnel that were assigned to the bombing of flight 792. He looked at the two pictures that were included. One was of Blair Adams and the other was Brandon Booth. It wasn't the first time Kim had looked at the picture of Blair Adams, nor would it be the last. The attachment had their record and pertinent information. It would be all the material he would need to lead them in a circle while he investigated the bombing and found those responsible. The CIA wasn't going to have some hot shot Bureau team get all the glory on this one, state side or otherwise.

A black Lexus was parked along Ocean Boulevard in front of the Sea Foam Restaurant on the corner of Ocean and Balboa Highway. The passenger was waiting for someone. The silver Mercedes S Class pulled behind the Lexus and only Kim got out and headed into the Sea Foam. The passenger from the Lexus soon followed him. They sat in a booth along the far right side away from the entrance. The man from the Lexus handed Kim a folder and Tony slid an envelope across the table. As the man started to run his fingers through the one-hundred dollar bills Kim said, "It's all there. Count it after!"

Kim slid out of the booth and headed back out of the restaurant. He waved his car back and jumped in.

"Did you take care of it?" He asked.

"I did exactly what you ordered me to."

"Good." Tony smiled as he gave the driver his next instructions.

They pulled around the corner where they still had a good view of the front of the restaurant. They sat in the car and waited for a few minutes. The contact that Tony had been with came back out of the restaurant and got into his Lexus.

He could be seen thumbing through the envelope that Tony had given him.

So many people were greedy and everyone always had a price. The man smiled and slid his key into the ignition.

The noise was deafening. There was a white-hot flash then an orange fireball erupted from the front of the Lexus. The blast shattered windows in the restaurant and shops along Ocean Boulevard. The car lifted off the pavement as a second blast erupted from the fuel tank. Glass peppered the area and chunks of metal rained down on the pavement. Flames rose from the hood of the Lexus and people ran in every direction. The car parked right behind the Lexus also exploded. Chaos had resulted outside as people ran in every direction away from the flames. Some people had their cell phones out taking pictures of the action from across the street. Soon a siren was heard in the distance. The Lexus was consumed in flames and on-lookers could see what looked like a body in the front seat now engulfed in the blaze. A charcoal gray cloud of smoke consumed the area.

Tony Kim watched for a few seconds with a smile on his face. "Good job," Kim said to the man sitting next to him. "Now let's get the hell out of here!"

They headed south on Ocean Boulevard and Tony opened the packet. It contained details from the FAA and the findings were clear, the bomb was Russian made. The markings were found by a Navy Seal dive team and the folder included many details on the FAA inspectors assigned to the investigation as well as the two FBI agents that they were meeting with. His next task was to get the bomb fragments and Tony was always successful on missions.

"I've got what I need. Head to Pier 86, it's on the south channel. I'll grab the Sea Ray and head up the coast." Tony was planning to intercept the FBI team before they got back to Los Angeles. Little did Blair and Booth know that they were being set-up!

Six
_____

The Sea Ray slowly pulled out of the slip from Pier 86 and throttled down. Tony didn't want create a wake in the channel. The buoys in the channel marked the way and Tony Kim knew the route well. It was a route that he had taken many times when he was in California. The dark gray lower half of the boat along with the white top side blended in well with the other water craft. The thirty five foot 330 Sundance model came with an expansive cabin, wet bar and gourmet galley. He often would spend weeks on the craft and it had everything needed for comfortable trips. Tony used the vessel to travel up and down the coast often while he was home in Venice Beach.

He had the slip in the Newport Beach Harbor for years. Although he lived in Venice Beach the Marina in Newport was a great jumping off spot to head south to Mexico or west toward Santa Catalina Island. But today he was headed north along the California. He planned to run along the coast up toward Long Beach. Once he was past Point Verde he could then duck into the channel at Marina del Rey. The ride along the shore line of the southern California coastline was beautiful. You would see schools of dolphin and in the spring an occasional Grey Whale. Many sailboats and cabin cruisers skirted the shore as people could be seen sunning on decks and fishing in coves along the way. Tony kept his mission at the forefront of his thoughts.

He had used a friend's boat dock in the Marina there when he needed. The call to his friend told him that the guy was out of town and the dock wasn't being used. Tony had one thing to complete before trying to get the bomb fragments. It was important not appear obvious to others along the way. He sailed a little further out than usual so as not to gather any attention.

The two FBI Special Agents picked-up their guest from the FAA and headed out of John Wayne International airport. Booth and Blair were in the front seat while the FAA inspector climbed in the back. He had a package under his arm that he had been holding onto tightly. Blair was talking to the inspector as Booth drove toward the Harbor Masters office in Newport Beach.

"What's in the package?" Blair asked.

"I brought a copy of the report from the dive team. They sent one to my Chief and we need to confirm the pieces found match their report. The fragments of the bomb that the Navy Seal team found had Russian markings. We always knew the Russians were sending weapons to the North Koreans," he said. "We're still not sure who is responsible for the bombing but this information narrows the field."
Blair nodded knowing that a very critical part of the case would be who was to blame for the bombing of flight 792. She asked, "Were they able to make out anything else that might help distinguish this device?"

"No, they found seven pieces that allowed us to be able to put them together and make out the markings."

Booth listened to the discussion as he continued to drive. He asked, "That was pretty fast work finding those pieces."

"Yes, the Seals had one of the best teams on it."

"I'm sure your Chief told you the importance of keeping all of this close to the vest. We don't need to let anything slip."

The inspector wiggled in his seat and then cleared his throat. "Well we had to tell the Director of Homeland Security and of course our Chief told his key commanders."

Booth gritted his teeth and was clenching the steering wheel. His tone was deliberate, "How many commanders would there have been in that meeting?"

The inspector didn't answer him.
Booth was ready to pull over. "I said, how many?"

The inspector now felt threatened. "Um, it's about six or maybe seven all together."

Booth was irritated and raised his voice, "Anyone else!"

The inspector could tell Booth was pissed. He didn't answer.

Booth turned his head toward the back seat. "Really, we need to know if anyone else was at this grand secret meeting."

"Booth, give him a few minutes to answer you." Blair was concerned that the FAA inspector was about ready to jump out of the car.

"We have our job to do, and our priorities may be different than yours," The inspector finally stated.

"Well I hate to be the first to inform you but keeping our investigation out of the newspaper is one of the top priorities. Now anyone else that you can think of that might have this information?"

A few minutes passed then he said, "Maybe a few more agencies because the President was informed during a Cabinet meeting."

"Shit! That's great! Guess everybody knows now. In his anger the car swerved to the right almost clipping the blue Ford van next to them.

"Look out!" Blair yelled.

Booth was still hollering, "It will probably be in the New York Times tomorrow. This is Great, some secret information!"
He wasn't happy and the FAA inspector slouched in the back seat. Information in Washington always seemed to find a leak somewhere. With so many people involved and everyone with their own agenda, who knows who else will know?

The inspector was quiet and held onto his report even tighter. "I'm just following orders." He said.

Blair glared at her partner. "We understand," she said. "We all have our responsibilities. Don't worry, it will be okay."

They pulled into the Marina and the FAA inspector was quick to jump out of the car. Blair hurried behind him. "Wait, we need to go in together." He turned around and looked very nervous.

"I'm not sure your partner feels the same way. I'm just doing my job. We don't report to the FBI." He was now determined not to be bullied by the FBI.

Blair touched his arm and looked into his eyes. "We all have a job to do and sometimes the pressure gets pretty tough. Booth is okay and he knows you did what you had to." It was hard for him to resist her smile and gentle touch on his arm. He smiled at her and said, "Your right. We'll do this together."

By the time Booth caught up to both of them he had calmed down. "Sorry about that, but this investigation is so critical none of us can afford a mistake. Just too many times when we think we're on to something someone leaks it." They all headed into the Marina to find the Harbor Master and check out the evidence.

The Navy Seal team had brought up the fragments and they were being guarded in the Harbor Masters safe. The FAA inspector and Booth and Blair were to confirm the findings and bring the pieces back to the Bureau office.

The Sea Ray pulled into the harbor at Marina del Rey and bobbed in the water as it slowed to five knots.
Tony Kim planned on using a slip along the channel near Admiralty Way.

He docked his boat there when he was state side and living in Venice Beach. Tony had a Condo on the top floor of the Sea Horse Resort just off Washington Boulevard. The boat slip was just three miles from his place.

His informant gave him the home address of the two FBI agents that were meeting with the FAA in Newport Beach. Blair Adams' apartment was in Marina del Rey and about a mile-and-half from Admiralty Way. Tony planned to check out her place first. He had been there once before and knew this trip was to place a recording device in her place. He needed to know everything possible that the two agents that the FBI had on the investigation. He planned to check out Brandon Booth's place next. Tony would do anything to throw them off the track. His orders were clear. Succeed and get the hell out.

Chiarini and his team met in their underground headquarters located just south of Falls Church, Virginia. In 2013 after the Iranian attack in the Persian Gulf, the Director added equipment to be able to correspond with the new satellite that NASA had put into orbit. This was all done without congressional or Presidential approval. Now the CIA operated a second command center that only they knew existed.

Chiarini planned to utilize it to the fullest to finally get an upper hand on the FBI. He could also circumvent any order from the Oval Office from this location.

Seven

President Morgan sat behind the large Resolute desk in the Oval Office and addressed the men gathered. The Head of Homeland Security and Secretary of State were concerned about the potential conflict between the FBI and CIA and the head of the National Security Administration wanted it settled now. It was important to get all the players together before anything went wrong. Once the short briefing was completed they brought in the heads of the FBI and CIA into the meeting. It was obvious that the President wasn't happy. He addressed them, "Gentlemen, we want to make this perfectly clear. You are both to work together to solve this investigation and keep us apprised of how your teams are proceeding. There has been too much bullshit about who is in charge."

It was common knowledge that the FBI and CIA were always at odds. Neither would give the other agency any assistance. This was always a thorn of contention. If they operated better together many felt more could be accomplished.

The President's message was directed at Frank and Robert. It was firm and to the point. The President didn't mince his words. "What are your next moves?" He looked at both of them as they stood in the middle of the Oval Office. Fitzgerald was the first to speak. "Sir, every agency inside the beltway has a stake in this and keeping them at bay will be a problem."

"I understand, Frank. I will handle the situation here. What I need is the two of you working together on this investigation. I shouldn't have to explain the potential ramifications."

"Yes Sir," Frank answered. He filled them in on his plans to travel to the Los Angeles Bureau office and oversee the investigation from there. He detailed that his team was meeting with FAA inspectors and would bring the bomb fragments in for further inspection. Chiarini just listened. Once Frank had completed his information, he then moved closer to the front of the desk. The President looked surprised but just leaned back in his chair.

"Sir, I have the best opportunity to resolve this as quickly as possible. My men have already gathered key Intel in Seoul about a group that is linked to Russian agents operating in North Korea. I am confident that we will have names by tomorrow and these agents will give us the information we need. I am also looking into the Russian markings on the fragments found in the water from the plane's wreckage."

Frank was visibly upset. "So much for working together," he quipped. "The investigations at the Marina in Newport Beach and bomb fragments are being handled by my people. Do I have to remind you that California is not in your jurisdiction?" Frank moved closer to Robert.

The President stood. "Both of you sit down." He had raised his voice and pointed to the couch across the room. This surprised everyone in the room. Morgan was usually a calm organized man and almost never raised his voice. It was clear the pressure of the events were weighing heavily on him. He was now standing. His fist was clenched and he pounded on his desk. Pointing at Robert he said, "You are not to, and I mean not to be involved in any activity on US soil unless directed by me. Am I clear?"

Chiarini nodded.

"Sir, what I meant was that combined with the information you gave us about the Russian marking on the bomb fragments we might tie it to this group in North Korea."

It was clear that the two men had the same agenda and working together would be almost impossible. Again the President, still standing, added. "Either you work together or I will find someone else to handle the assignment." The two men now crouching a little nodded. Frank and Robert agreed to keep each other abreast of their investigation. In turn Robert restated that his team will only operate outside the US borders on this issue. In his mind he knew Tony Kim was already on the case. He didn't worry about that. Kim was a smart agent and operated without any CIA identification, especially on missions such as this. Fitzgerald looked at Chiarini and asked, "Robert could you tell me more about the Russian agents that your agents have leads on."

"There isn't too much to tell you yet, Frank. There are two Russians that we have been tracking for the past twelve months. One of them has been seen meeting with a high ranking government official. There isn't enough to bring them in but our team is tracking their every move."

"Thanks for that," Frank answered. "I have two of my best agents meeting with the FAA and their people. Once we have reconstructed the bomb fragments we might be able to tell more about its origin."

"Better! This is what I expect from both of you." President Morgan had moved to the large blue chair that sat at the end of the two couches that faced each other in the middle of the Oval Office. "Gentlemen the nation depends on us, and I'm depending on both of you to bring this to a positive conclusion. We expect that some radical group is going to take credit for this soon so we need to work fast. I won't let either you blame the other guy for your lack of progress." Everyone agreed and said they would keep each other updated.

The President addressed them one more time. "The Vice-President is being sent to Seoul this evening. I will address the American people later today about the progress we've made. I need your information as soon as possible to be able to calm the nation."

The gravity of the situation was clear. Someone has to be blamed for this deed and the President needed evidence to do that. President Morgan wasn't going to name any group without strong verifiable evidence.

The meeting in the Oval Office lasted about forty-five minutes and the men left with their orders. The spin machine in Washington wouldn't wait too long to start second guessing the President and his administration. After all it was an election year and the polls had the challenger almost even with the President. How would the next few hours and the press conference later that day affect them was still up for grabs.

Blair was studying the bomb fragments that the Seal team had brought up on the ocean recovery mission. It was clear that the markings were Russian. There were seven pieces with various Russian letters on them. Once they were put together it read, ВЗРЫВЧАТОЕ ВЕЩЕСТВО, and that was clearly Russian for explosives. The first four letters of each word were embossed on pieces of the shell casing. One piece about four inches long had ATOE, on it and another piece about two inches long had CTB on it. Preliminary findings were that they were composition of C4 explosives. Not terribly high tech for this type of mission.

The FAA along with the FBI forensic team there had been working on the words for about three hours when they came up with their findings. Although they knew it was Russian markings there wasn't any indication as to who was responsible.

No one had come forward claiming responsibility for the action. This was unusual, because some group always seemed to claim it was them just to make a statement of disgust for the United States.

"Booth, we need to get all these pieces back to headquarters. I'm sure the forensic team needs to do more investigating so they can maybe date the pieces. That might help narrow where it came from and possibly who it belonged to."

"Did you all get all the information and pictures you need before we head back to Los Angeles," Booth asked.

"Yes, I got everything."

Everyone agreed and knew that the forensic team in LA would have to do some carbon dating along with other tracking tools to determine more data on the pieces. The FAA man that Blair and Booth had picked up said he would catch a ride back to John Wayne International with one of their officers. Booth knew after his confrontation that the guy probably didn't want to be in the car with him again.

"Okay, if everyone is good, we will box up the fragments and take them back with us." Booth had a metal case that they brought with them. He handed it to his partner. They watched as Blair lifted the metal container and put on a pair of surgical gloves. She proceeded to place the seven pieces in the metal box and once she was finished she sealed the box with a tag. It was dated and she initialed it. "Booth, sign this too." She was handling the only evidence from the bombing and didn't want to make any mistake. He initialed the tag and had the FAA inspector also do the same. They headed out to their car and Booth carried the case. Once it was secured in the trunk they got in and headed out of the lot.

Tony Kim had finished casing Blair's apartment in Marina del Rey. He carefully made sure he left no fingerprints and put everything back into place.

It wasn't his first time in there. His Director had him trailing her ever since she and her partner broke the casino case wide open. The last time he saw Blair was when he watched her from the Pier as she strolled the beach. He made one more attempt to find out more and broke into her car but didn't get much. Robert Chiarini always wanted to know everything about his competition and the FBI was his number one target. The listening device he placed in the large floor lamp in the corner of the room should catch anything that was said. He inserted a small camera in the air vent that was over the couch. The angle would show anyone entering the apartment and had a clear view of eighty percent of the room. His final step was to put the small digital receiver into the phone that sat on the kitchen counter top. He knew many people only used their cell phones now-a-days but since she had a land line he would bug it anyway.

Her apartment complex was off of Via Marina and just across from where his boat was docked. It was easy to get to. Tony strolled by the guard with a beach towel that he took from his boat and draped it over his shoulder. He just looked like another resident headed for the beach. The Mariner's Village had over one thousand units and the buildings ran all the way back to the channel and across from the marina. Tony easily made his way down the stairs from the units on Captain's Row where her apartment was located.

He left the apartment clean and made sure that there was no sign of an intruder. It was almost too easy he thought. On the way back to his boat he called Chiarini to let him know his progress. The Director was in his second command center and anxious to hear the progress from Kim. The wall of monitor's beamed views from space back to the center and Chiarini could track the action that was taking place.

"Sir, I'm going to head to Santa Monica and the other agents place," he said. "Once I'm done there my next mission is to get the evidence from the plane crash.

I have their car plate number and plan on creating a diversion on the highway that should allow me to get the evidence you want."

"Make sure you're not spotted or photographed. We can't be found out." Chiarini remembered the Presidents last words. Get the job done or he will get someone else to do it. The CIA wasn't going to be told how to handle their business. Not by this President and surely not the FBI. Hell, the President might be out of a job come November anyway. Chiarini laughed as he hung up the phone.

Eight

   The ride back to LA along highway 5 to the 405 wasn't quite so congested. It was now close to eight and traffic was much lighter than on the trip down to Newport Beach. Blair had suggested that she drive but Booth told her to relax and he was fine. They had grabbed a sandwich and coke in the Marina before they left and planned to drive straight back to the office. The evidence had to be delivered to the FBI forensic team in the lab. Maybe with their special equipment and tools they can find out more detailed information.
They pulled out of the marina and Booth and headed to the highway. He turned toward Blair and asked, "Why did you want to move to California?"

   "As a kid my parents brought me to Southern California several times on vacation. Guess that is where I got the urge to move out here. Hunter was gone on the first mission to Iraq and I told him that I would find us a place along the beach. He was all for it too."

   Booth knew the story about Hunter being killed in Iraq and didn't want to go that route. Guys really never know how to approach the subject.

   "So you came out here with your parents as a kid."
   "Yes."
   "What kind of things did you get to see?"

"Oh, my dad was the coolest. He had everything planned out and we went to Disney Land, Long Beach and the Queen Mary, and all the attractions in Los Angeles. He took my mom and me to see the Dodgers play the Braves one afternoon and I got a Dodger cap. He wasn't too happy about that because he loved the Braves and hated the Dodgers. I just liked the colors."

Booth wished he had similar memories but loved listening to Blair tell stories about growing up.

"Have you ever been to a Dodger game?" She asked.

"No," He answered. "I never seemed to have that much time. Once I got transferred here it was always something that the job needed."

"Well then we have to go sometime. Blair knew Booth liked sports and wasn't sure if he liked baseball. I really like baseball, mainly because my dad took me to every ballpark in the country. He always called me his little kid. We really had a lot of fun."

"That sounds great," Booth answered. "I like baseball too.

We should check out the schedule to see when the Braves are coming to town." He smiled at her as she asked, "You hungry?"

"Starving!"

The two partners were relaxed and Booth grabbed his sandwich. "This Turkey BLT looks great."

"Can I grab your drink for you?" Blair asked.

"Thanks just put it in the cup holder." Booth was headed north on the 405 and traffic was starting to bunch up. They had just got in the speed lane and were going close to eighty miles an hour. "We can make good time on the way back," he said.

Just then a car coming out of what seemed to be
nowhere was flying down the middle lane and cut over two
lanes. Booth saw it out of the rear view mirror and started to
tell Blair to see if she could make out the plate number.
The vehicle came charging at them hitting the rear quarter
panel of their car sending it into a wild spin.
Booth tried grabbed the steering wheel with both hands
hoping to get control of the spin when they plowed into the
guard rail and bounced off into another vehicle. The
sandwich flew off his lap and coke spilled everywhere.

Blair screamed. They had bounced off the guard rail a
second time as a small truck rammed them from behind. The
sounds of steel crashing and glass breaking were everywhere.
They spun around hitting the guard rail at least two more
times and then a Toyota Rav 4 crashed into their trunk. The
air bags deployed causing both passengers to be bolted back
into their seats as the vehicle continued to be rammed by
another truck. Smoke poured out of the front of their car and
the awful smell of burning rubber filled the air. You could
hear screeching tires in the distance as people tried to avoid
the collision.

A large van crashed into the Toyota and that pushed
them back into the guard rail and the left front tire of Booth's
car climbing up on the center railing. Now their vehicle was
partially up in the air and in danger of being catapulted into
on-coming traffic on the south bound side of the freeway.
The sound of metal against metal was everywhere. They must
have hit or were hit by at least four other cars before it was all
over. Booth was slumped over the steering wheel and Blair
had been tossed into the dash and had a cut that was bleeding
over her right eye. She felt scrapes on her forehead from the
air bag and had been knocked around pretty good. Both
agents were out and people were starting to get out of the cars
to see how they could help.

California Interstate 405 was six lanes wide and now resembled more of a junk yard than a highway. Cars and trucks were all over and a Chrysler mini-van was upside down across the two center lanes. Traffic was blocked up for miles and sirens were heard from every direction.

Booth's head was laying on the steering wheel in the front and he was unconscious.

Blair was starting to come to and shook her head. She looked around and reached for her seat belt but it was locked and not coming out from the clasp. The hood had been pushed into the front cabin of the car and the dash was split in half. She struggled to get loose. She looked over at her partner but her view was somewhat blocked because of debris from the accident.

"Booth, Booth are you okay!" She called out to him but there was no answer. Blair shook her head to clear out the noise that was ringing in her ears from the impact. She finally was able to unhook her seat belt and tried to climb across the seat. She could see that Booth was unconscious and his head was bleeding. She reached him with her arm and was able to pull him back off the steering wheel by his shirt collar. He now was leaning back but she had to be careful. She had no idea how bad he may have been hurt. His driver's door was pushed in and she could see that he was trapped in the seat. There was no way for her to get to him from inside the car. Their car had ended up sideways across both left lanes of the 405 and up on the guard rail. This along with other damaged vehicles caused a major traffic jam on both the north and south bound sides. Steam was coming from many of the wrecked cars and fluid was pouring out all over the pavement. People were getting out of their cars. Three of the freeways six lanes were cluttered with damaged cars.

Two men were knocking on the passenger window of the car and Blair looked up to see them waving to her. She pushed against the door but it was stuck. There was no button to unlock the doors and blood had started to trickle into her eyes and she was having a hard time seeing clearly. One man was waving and had a frantic look on his face. She could tell he was yelling but what? The engine was still running in their car but making a terrible racket. She reached for the key and turned it off.

Just then she heard glass breaking and felt nuggets of glass flying into the front seat.

"You have to get out of there!"

Someone was yelling to her but she was disoriented. "My partner is hurt. We need help!"

The man that was yelling was now pulling open the rear door on the passenger side of the car. It made a loud screeching noise as the door slowly pulled opened.

"Your car is on fire! You have to get out now!" Sirens were coming from everywhere and other people were rushing to help the lady and her kids in the upside down van. Flames shot out from under Booth's car and Blair was being pulled out to safety.

That was the last thing she remembered about the accident. A man in a white coat was kneeling over her and a siren was blaring as she rocked back and forth on what appeared to be a gurney of some sort. She had a plastic mask over her face and the person was wiping her forehead with a sponge.

"Where am I? Where is Booth?" She tried to get up but the man held her down. She had an oxygen mask on and could feel the cool air flowing on her face as she pulled it loose.

"You were in a car accident and bleeding. You need to leave that on." Blair struggled with the mask.

An arriving rescue team used a Hurst tool to cut the posts flanking the windshield and put the jaws in place to pry the driver's door opened. They pulled Booth from the vehicle. Another driver had a fire extinguisher and helped just before it was engulfed in flames. Booth was placed on a stretcher.

Blair was still asking about Booth. "My partner, where is he?"

"They had to use the jaws-of-life to get him out of the car. Thank God a man in a truck had a fire extinguisher to put the fire out. He is being taken by another ambulance to the same hospital."

"Is he okay?"

"We're not sure. He was unconscious when we pulled him from the wreckage. Is there someone you need us to call for you?"

She couldn't think straight. "Yes! Yes, I've got to call my boss."

The ambulance attendant just smiled. Lady your boss will be okay. You've got to worry about yourself first. "Now let's put that mask back on."

"You don't understand it's very important. I have something very valuable in our car. I've got to call it in."

"Okay lady, what's the number?"

"My phone, it's in my purse. I have the number in my phone."

He reached around on the floor and picked up a purse. "Guess this is yours. It was next to you when you were pulled from the car."

"Yes."

The attendant handed her the purse and she searched for her cell phone. The call came into the Wilshire office directly to Steve's number.

"Steve, this is Blair. We've been in a car accident and Booth is being taken to the hospital." She was breathing hard and Steve was concerned about her.

"Where are you?"

"Where are we," she asked the attendant.

"On the 405. We will be getting off at the Howard Hughes Parkway. We are taking both of you to the Medical Center at the Hughes Plaza."

Steve said, "I heard what he said. Are you okay?"

"Yes I'm fine just a bump on my head. More important the case with the evidence was in the trunk and the car is in the pile-up on the highway."

"Let me talk to the guy in the ambulance," Steve said. Blair handed him the phone.

"Yes Sir, their car is at mile marker 243 on the north bound side of the 405.

You're not going to be able to get near there. They have the entire north bound side closed."

"How is she?"

"Bleeding from the right side of her head maybe needs a few stitches. She should have X-Rays; their car must have been hit quite a few times."

"Thanks let me talk to her."

He gave the phone back to Blair.

"Blair you have to let them do their thing. You're not any good to me if you're hurt. We should be there in less than thirty minutes."

"But sir, I got to check on Booth."

"I understand. By the time they have you checked out I will be there and check on him first thing. We'll jump on the helicopter. I'll drop off a team at the accident scene. Is everything in the trunk?"

"Yes Sir. We put the pieces in the metal case like you said. I'm so sorry."

"It's not your fault. Just take care of yourself first. We are on our way."

Blair slumped down on the gurney as the ambulance swerved to the right. They were getting off the freeway and heading up the ramp. The Medical Center was just off of Sepulveda Boulevard a little way down from the Hughes Shopping Plaza.

"Can you radio to the other ambulance to see how my friend is," she asked.

"Sure," the attendant answered.
She watched as he asked for an update on Booth's condition. He had a frown on his face as the person on the other end gave him details. "Okay thanks," he said then hung up.

"What is it?" Blair feared the worst.

"They are just pulling into the emergency entrance and won't know anything else until the trauma team evaluates him."

"You're not telling something. What is it?"

"There is nothing to tell you yet. You should know something when you get there."

The sounds of more sirens were now heard as they were slowing down. Blair was breathing hard and the attendant secured the oxygen mask back on her. "You're going to be okay," he said as the door flew open and two men started to pull the gurney out of the back of the vehicle. Tears welled up in her eyes as she laid back.

_____Nine

The meeting had been set-up with the contact in Seoul. Josh and Rusty planned to meet him at the old Palace at the Jongmyo Shrine. The Jongmyo is a Confucian shrine built for the memorial services of the kings and queens of the Jongmyo dynasty. It's expansive, impressive and quiet. The contact had wanted to meet there because he feared being seen with two Americans.

They made their way through the expansive palaces – pacing along the paths of ancient merchants and warlords. They were now close to a hillside looking down on markets and smelling meats, fresh fish and other fermenting foods. It was there where they were to meet.

"I'm concerned about this meeting," Josh told Rusty.

"Don't worry, I've been working with him for over a year now and his information is always reliable."
The meeting time had passed and Josh wasn't sure the man would show up. Just then Rusty poked him in the side, "Here he comes."

The man was short and looked to be about seventy years old. His long gray beard and dark cloak made him seem even more mysterious. He was using a walking stick that was very ornate and nodded as he passed.

"I'll follow in a few seconds then you come behind," Rusty said. "I don't want to spook him."

Josh waited about a minute and then headed out behind Rusty.

After one hundred yards or so he rounded the corner of the shrine and made his way into a small courtyard. He saw the man pointing up to the temple and Rusty nodding. He found a small stone bench that had shade and settled there as he watched the two men. The sun would be setting soon and when it did the winds always picked up. Josh hoped Rusty was getting the information they needed so they could head out of the shrine.

The two men separated and Rusty kept looking up to the top of the temple that the man had been pointing to. He went to his pocket and was making a call. Just then Josh's cell phone rang. He grabbed it quickly.

"Yes," he answered.

"He thinks someone is following him. He wants to move into the large courtyard that we passed near the entrance. Meet us there."

Josh waited a few seconds and got up from the bench. The shrine itself was made up of many buildings, both small and large. They were connected like houses in a secluded neighborhood. Small wooden ramps led from one structure to the next. Many of the units had sliding doors but also carried a sign in both Korean and English, "No entry."

The other courtyard was easily the size of a football field and held the largest of the structures. They were uniform in build and had rich colors of reds, bright aqua's and gold. The courtyard was covered in cobblestone and stretched out as though an enormous castle wall had fallen and remained perfectly intact.

There were iron hooks scattered out randomly along the walkway. Josh was wondered about their purpose. He looked up ahead and could see Rusty in a dark corner along the textured surface of the large temple. He waited and watched.

The men exchanged something, maybe a note book. Josh saw Rusty give the contact an envelope.

The two separated and Rusty continued along the colored path that led back to the entrance. Josh slowly walked along taking pictures with his camera.

Rusty stopped along the dirt path to admire an old tree. It sat on a small island, in the center of a pond. It looked almost petrified, yet still showing signs of life with bright green leaves. Josh moved closer to him, camera in hand pointed at the tree.

"Did he have what we needed?"

Rusty looked over at the tree. "This is really something. Must be pretty old, don't you think?"

Okay, Josh thought, "Guess I'll play along." "Amazing, the branches are all twisted, and some are held up by beams. It looks like a grown-up version of a Bonsai tree."

"You're right," Rusty said. He turned and held his hand out to Josh.

Josh shook his hand. They nodded to each other as two men just meeting for the first time. "So what's the plan?"

"Meet me back at the subway station." Rusty patted his coat to give Josh a signal. With that Rusty strolled off. Josh could see that Rusty had the small package in his coat pocket. Guess they had what they came for. Josh knew where they were to meet. It was near their train's departure ramp and it would be pretty crowded this time of day. He didn't want to look suspicious so he continued taking pictures. It was close to dusk and the mosquitoes had amassed a tireless army and started their attacks. Everyone knew they would be out this time of day so you always wore clothes that covered your extremities. If not they would bury their needle-snouts into your legs and crooks of your arms.

Josh moved around the large courtyard so as not to draw attention. He still had camera in hand and was taking random pictures.

Just then he saw the old man that Rusty had met with. He was acting strange.

The man kept looking around and had his backside toward the wall of the temple. Josh decided to follow him.

The man continued to moving along the temple walls and watching those around him. Josh aimed his camera and took telephoto pictures of him. The area he was standing in was near the gold colored mural on the temple wall. It was beautiful and embossed with bright red and aqua borders. Many people were taking pictures of the same mural and often asked others to take a picture of them against the wall. Josh watched the old man who was now almost at the end of the temple wall. He continued to look around as if he was waiting for someone. Josh wanted to make sure there wasn't a double cross in the works.

Just then he saw another man approaching Rusty's contact. He was much taller than the old man and moved in front of him. The shorter Asian man looked up toward the stranger and then the tall man blocked Josh's view. This stranger had a dark black handle bar mustache and wore a tan trench coat. He was at least six foot four inches tall and stocky built. With his view blocked of the older man Josh kept an eye on the two questioning if this was a second meeting of some sort. The view was blocked for what seemed to be just seconds. Josh moved in closer to see if the men exchanged anything.

All of a sudden the taller man turned and quickly walked away. Josh wanted to follow him but felt watching the contact that Rusty dealt with was his best option. He watched and saw the small Asian man all of a sudden slump against the wall of the temple. As he started over there the small man fell to the ground.

Two people came running over and Josh trotted up to see what had happened. He heard them talking in Korean and could make out most of their conversation. The man had been stabbed, they were saying.

He was bleeding badly. You could see a knife sticking out of his chest. The dark handle was covered in blood and the man was motionless on the ground. Josh moved in with the other people and felt the man's pulse. He was dead. Hopefully without anyone noticing Josh slid his hand into the man's jacket and retrieved the envelope Rusty had given him. He didn't want anything left that would tie back to them. The crowd was growing and two Korean police officers appeared pushing their way through the mass of people.

Josh slowly moved back away as the police officers were yelling to the crowd in Korean. "Did anyone see what happened? Who was near the man?" Josh didn't want to be remembered by anyone. He pulled back into the crowd and started back toward the entrance of the shrine. He had to call Rusty to warn him. He wondered if anyone could identify him. At least there were other Americans in the crowd. What was in the envelope Rusty gave the man? He figured it was money but would wait to check it out. He had to get Rusty on the phone right away.

Josh made his way toward the entrance and dialed Rusty's number. It rang five times and went to voicemail. He hung up and tried again but still no answer. He was now moving fast out of the palace area and surveying the landscape to see if the large stranger was anywhere around. He did not see him. He knew the man would stand out in a crowd of Koreans due to his size but he was nowhere to be seen. Josh dialed Rusty again and this time left a message. "Something went wrong at the meeting site. Call me right away!" He hoped he would hear from his partner soon. It didn't make any sense that Rusty wasn't answering his phone. Josh moved quickly out of the shrine and headed toward the subway station and their meeting place. There were places that had poor phone reception but he kept trying Rusty's phone as he headed toward their meeting spot.

Once Josh was away from the crowd he looked at the envelope that Rusty had given the old man. It had ten one hundred American dollars inside. Certainly a lot of money but the man wasn't killed for it. If so why did the big man leave the envelope in the man's jacket? Josh had more questions than answers.

Cars were all mangled along the 405 and a chopper had landed in the far right lane. Steve Orrison jumped out and headed toward the State Police Chief on the scene. They had called to let the troopers know that they would be landing at the accident site and if possible guard the car that Booth had driven. Steve gave them the license plate number and description. Once they had the evidence from the trunk they would head to the Medical Center.

There must have been over a dozen cars involved with major damage and Booth's car looked like it had been hit on every side. The troopers said that eight people in total had been taken to area hospitals. "A lady and her three kids were serious. We called the hospital to make sure they were prepared for all the trauma cases."

Steve asked about his agents.

They both have been taken to Hughes Medical Center and one, a guy in his thirties was serious. "Their vehicle burst into flames and we were lucky to get him out just in time. He was unconscious and we used the jaws-of-life to get him out of the front seat. He was bleeding from both his legs and chest." The Chief said, "It didn't look good. When we got here someone had pulled the lady from the passenger side of the car. She had a head injury and seemed dazed."

Steve was concerned about his two agents. He knew they had secured the package from the FAA and hoped it was still in their trunk.

The trooper also said that another man was seen limping away from the wreckage.

People didn't know if he had been hurt and was seeking help or running away. "Could have been a drunk driver taking off," the trooper said. "Kind of funny though, one passenger said he climbed over the vehicle you asked about."

Steve asked, "Did anyone get a description of him?"

"No, everything was moving so fast and when two cars burst into flames everyone started to run from the scene. We put an APB out hoping that someone had seen him or can help with his identification."

Booth's car was pinned against a large high cube van that had a local florist address on the side. It must have been a delivery vehicle. The driver had also been taken to the Medical Center. "Once we put the fire out it had consumed the engine area of the car. The dash was split in two and had started to melt because the flames were so hot." The officer stood along side of the fireman that was filling Steve in with the details.

The Chief said, "Lucky a man from another vehicle had a fire extinguisher and jumped into action, most likely saving your guy from burning to death."

As they studied the wreckage they could see the trunk was crushed and there was no way to get it opened. Steve asked, "Could we use the jaws to try to pry it loose?"

"Sure," the Chief responded. He headed toward the fire truck to make the request.

They worked on the wreckage for about ten minutes when the trunk finally gave way and popped opened. The package was pressed against the right hand side of the trunk sitting end on end. Steve reached in and pulled it out. "Thanks, Chief. This is very important to National security."

"Guess so," he answered.

Steve looked at the scene and asked, "Is there anyone that still needs to be transported to the hospital?"

The Chief was surprised but turned to ask his officers. "Do you still have anyone needed attention at the hospital?"

"Boss I got a lady that is feeling a lot of pain in her stomach and we think she should be taken in and checked."

"Bring her to us, we'll take her. I need to check on my people that are at Hughes Medical Center." Once they had the lady in the chopper it took off toward the Hughes Center.

When the information of the crash hit the hospital they immediately stopped all elective surgeries, moved trauma teams into position and were waiting for the sea of casualties to arrive. This was standard operating practice and ambulances were arriving at the front of the emergency center entrance. There were ambulances, police cruisers and one local fire truck all pulled into the emergency circle at the hospital. Steve and the FBI chopper landed on the roof and waited for a hospital team coming with a gurney to assist the lady that they brought from the accident scene.

Ten

The scene at the Hughes Medical Center was sheer chaos. There were heavy casualties that had been brought in from the accident. Many were slated for one of the Trauma teams to check out as well as people with broken bones, cuts and contusions and family members were all over the hallways. People were demanding answers and the staff was working to take care of everyone as fast as possible. Because it was a Friday there was always more action and today was no different. The trauma teams had two critically injured patients from the pile up on the 405 and another heart attack victim was being transported to them from the mall. Brandon Booth was in trauma room one and was being attended to by a team of surgeon's. They cut his clothes off and had an X-Ray machine scanning his legs and chest. A thoracic surgeon was called in due to a fear that his heart had been compromised when the dash jammed against him. Booth was still unconscious and they were working to stabilize him. He had an intravenous tube in his right arm and was on a breathing machine. He didn't have any exterior wounds but many times internal bleeding would be harder to find and treat. The surgeon and his team worked as quickly as possible to help him with more cases waiting outside. Each patient was being treated with the highest care.

Blair was being treated in the emergency room by one of the technicians.

She had a gash over her eye that would need stitches. They also knew she was confused upon arrival and was being checked for a concussion.

"Sorry, but I'm going to have stitch this," The intern told her.

Although she was a little glassy eyed she was worried about Booth. "I need to know how my partner is first."

"Which one is he?"

"He was in the car that they had to use the Jaws of Life to free him," she answered.

"Okay, I'll make a deal with you. Let me secure this gauze pad on your cut then I'll go check on him."

It seemed to be her only option. "Sure, I really appreciate it."

The intern was gone about ten minutes. She decided to get off the gurney and see if she could find something out herself.

Steve Orrison was coming down the hallway. "Blair, why are you walking around?" He had brought Kathy with him from the office.

"I'm so glad to see you." Blair started to ramble as the intern came around the corner.

"Hey, I thought we had a deal." He took her arm and led her back to the gurney. Steve and Kathy followed.

"This is my boss and friend," she told the young doctor. "They need to know about Booth too."

"Okay, I've got some information; however, you're going to need to talk to the team working on him to get details."

Steve, Kathy and Blair listened intently.

"They brought in a Thoracic surgeon because they were concerned about damage to his chest. He is being cared for by the best team we have and they should have more information for you once they have read the x-rays."

"Thanks," Blair said. "At least I know he's alive."

Steve looked at the intern and asked, "How about wonder woman here?"

Kathy and Blair laughed. "Yeah I'm some wonder woman alright. Your car is totaled, the evidence is possibly lost and I'm not exactly sure what happened."

"Well let me fill in some of the gaps," Steve offered. "The evidence case is safe and on its way back to the forensic team. The Police Chief stated that witnesses saw that a dark colored BMW cross three lanes of the 405 and appeared to aim right at you. The vehicle is being dusted for prints. It is one of about ten cars that will be towed off from the collision."

"What happened to the driver of that BMW?"

"Good question. People said they saw a man limping off from the scene. He also resembled the guy who was trying to get into your trunk. We're thinking that's the driver of the Beemer."

"What the hell is that all about," Blair asked.

"Not sure right now but there is an APB out with his description. Could have been a drunk and just lost control of his vehicle. He's going to need medical care because one lady said she saw that he was bleeding from his right leg and limping badly."

This news added a new mystery to the whole accident. The intern said, "Now you need to sit down and let me stitch your cut."

Blair moved to the center of the gurney and nodded okay. "Steve, please go see if there is any more information on Booth." She worried about her partner and felt it was her fault.

Kathy sat in the chair at the end the gurney and kept her company while she was being taken care of.

"I'll do everything I can so a scar won't show too much."

"I'm not worried about that, just do what you need to." Blair sat back as he took a needle and told her that he needed to numb the area first.

Steve walked to the emergency desk and asked for the head nurse. He introduced himself and explained what he needed. "One of my people is being worked on, I've been told in trauma one. I need to find out how he is and when can I see him."

The nurse was still looking at his chart and asked, "Are you a relative?"

"No." He pulled out his credentials and showed them to the nurse. "I need to see if he can fill in any other details from the accident. This is a case of National Emergency." Steve knew that statement always got action.

She got up from behind the desk and told him to wait right there. He watched as she headed down the hallway and disappeared through two large doors. She was gone for about ten minutes and he saw her headed back his way.

"He doing okay and stabilized. One problem is that he is still unconscious and isn't going to be of any help to tell you what he knows right now."

"When will I be able to talk to him?"

She glanced at her watch and said, "The attending trauma doctor said they will be moving him to a critical care room in about thirty minutes."

Steve thanked her and said he was going back to check on Blair. The nurse said she would come get Steve as soon as Booth is moved.

Washington was all consumed with the funeral of Senator Harding. His wife had wanted a private service in Cincinnati but the President convinced her that it was important to have it in D.C. He was the head of an influential committee on Capitol Hill and had many friends that wanted to pay their respects. He told Mrs. Harding that the Nation would handle everything. She finally agreed.

This was politics as much as anything else. Harding was a key member of the Republican Party and being a Democrat the President wanted to look as bi-partisan as possible. If his team headed the arrangements people could see that he was a genuine concerned leader and his press secretary could spin it any way necessary. November was around the corner and his opponent was closing in. Polls had the margin between the two candidates too close to call. President Morgan had his wife along with the Secretary of State making the plans and Mrs. Harding agreed to have her husband put to rest in Arlington National Cemetery, close to that of his Great Grandfather, President Harding. If there was anything Washington knew how to do, it was a grand funeral. Unfortunately they had too much practice lately.

Frank Fitzgerald contacted Robert Chiarini and they planned to get together to go over the progress of their joint investigations. They agreed to meet at one o'clock with the Director of Homeland Security. Fitzgerald had to update Chiarini on the evidence from the bombing and that a possible attempt had been made to seize it from the two agents. He planned to brag about the bomb fragments being safely in the LA Bureau's office. After the meeting Frank planned to grab the flight from Washington National Airport to Los Angeles. Chiarini was pissed that Tony Kim had failed to get the package before it arrived at FBI headquarters in LA. He couldn't let on that he had any idea what had happened. He also was not going to tell Fitzgerald about the incident in Seoul at the Palace with the CIA contact.

So much for working together!

One o'clock arrived and Robert sat in the large overstuffed chair in the outer Office of the Homeland Security Director. Fitzgerald was on his way up and the Director was on the phone with President Morgan. Frank Fitzgerald was just coming in the door when the Director walked into the outer office. "Hope you both have some details for me." Robert looked toward Frank and started his report. "My guys that are in The Republic of South Korea have a few leads that they are following. Nothing panned out yet but I'm sure we'll have something soon."

They both looked at Frank. "Well we have the pieces of the bomb that the Seal team found from the wreckage. It is being checked out as we speak in our forensic lab. We know the FAA confirmed that the markings are Russian and my team is checking to see if we can verify the date they were made. Maybe some old stuff."

The Homeland Security Director said, "Great."

"Well not so great," Frank continued. "Two of my agents were involved in a very suspicious crash while bringing the evidence in to the office." He looked at Robert as he explained. "Looks like someone wanted to derail them along the way and one of them might not make it."

Robert shot back, "What the hell Frank, it happened in California, that's not my turf. My people are only operating overseas as we agreed."

"Are you sure?" Frank answered.

The Director had his hands full with the two department heads. "Men, either we do this with full disclosure or we're headed back to the White House."

They both understood.

He said, "Let's lay it all out." All three men headed into his office.

_____Eleven

The events at the Palace in Seoul created a new concern for the CIA. Rusty's contact had been stabbed, but by who? Josh had gone to the train station to meet Rusty but he wasn't there. Had something happened to him? Rusty had the information that his contact had passed along and it could be critical to the investigation. It was missing too. Chiarini hadn't told either the President or Director what had happened in Seoul. He hoped that Josh would find Rusty and get the answers to this mystery. Calls to Rusty from headquarters weren't answered and it appeared that he disappeared off the grid.

Josh continued to search for Rusty in the usual places that he operated. Because Josh used his undercover role as an exporter he was able to move freely through the market places of Seoul. He planned to use a search for Russian goods to move through the warehouses. He questioned some of his contacts as he radioed to other agents joining the search. Josh told his contacts that he had a customer in the States that was looking for authentic Russian items. He thought that the man he saw with Rusty's contact just before the man fell to the ground was Russian. He was using that angle to help search for him.

Rusty Nelson lived in one of the finest hotels in Seoul. The Fraser Suites Insadong was centrally located and boasted of kitchenettes, satellite TV and an outstanding fitness center. It was much larger than the living quarters that Josh had in Sawon.

Josh had gone there first in his search but they hadn't seen Rusty since earlier in the day.

He had relayed his information to Chiarini and would continue the search. Robert made sure that Josh had extra help from the agency to track Rusty down. Robert Chiarini didn't convey any of this information to anyone. He would wait to see if his team could resolve it. The CIA always felt that they were above everyone and everything and Robert protected that idea. He was now waiting to hear from Tony Kim. He knew that the FBI had the pieces of the Russian bomb in their possession. Tony hadn't contacted Chiarini since the pile-up on the 405 that injured the two FBI agents.

Booth was groaning as the two orderlies were getting him in the bed. He was groggy and his head moved from side to side. The Critical Care Center at the Hughes Medical Center was on the fifth floor. Steve had been standing in the waiting room hoping the on-duty nurse would come and get him soon. Kathy O'Conner was waiting downstairs with Blair as they finished stitching her up. She would still need x-rays to make sure nothing was broken but other than the gash on her head she seemed okay.

"Mr. Orrison, I'll take you back to Mr. Booth's room but you can only stay a few minutes," the nurse said.

Steve followed her to room 536 and slowly walked in. Booth was lying in the bed, his left arm was in a cast and he was receiving oxygen and an IV was hooked up to his other arm. As Steve moved closer he could see Booth's eyes open slightly.

"You okay son?" Steve had his hand on Booth's chest and could feel him breathing deeply. He looked down at the cast on his broken arm and was now peering right over him.

"What? Blair, is Blair okay?"

Booth was coming out of an unconscious state and mumbling.

His eyes fluttered and were now opened. He looked at Steve with a glazed expression. His head rolled side-to-side and he asked again about Blair. Steve knew that the team of Booth and Blair had become close. He wasn't sure how close. Now after a horrific accident the only thing each one of them wanted to know was if the other one was okay.

"She's fine Booth. Downstairs getting a few stitches but otherwise okay. We're more worried about you now."
Booth tried to lift his head but Steve stopped him, "The doctor said you need to lay flat for a few days."

"What's wrong with me?"

"You're pretty lucky. Your left arm is broken and they put it in a cast. The Doctor said your breast bone is fractured. They are not sure if the air bag caused it or the collision. It could have been much worse. They said you will be better in no time but you have to lie still."

Booth now had his eyes wide opened and again tried to sit up. "You have to lay flat Booth, doctors orders."

The nurse appeared at the door to the room. "You need to let him get some rest now."

"I just need another minute."

"Okay, but I'll be back in a minute." She glanced at her watch and moved down the hallway.

"Can you remember anything about the accident?" Steve didn't have much hope of any clues from Booth but you never know.

"We were in the left lane and I was just about to grab my drink when I saw a dark colored car in the mirror crossing from the far right lane headed right at us. I tried to speed up but he hit the rear of my vehicle and spun us around. Not sure what happened after that."

Booth's story fit with the descriptions from others involved in the collision. Why would someone be aiming their car at his agents?

Were they being trailed from Newport and the meeting with the FAA?

More questions now consumed Steve about the incident.

"Okay your time is up." The nurse, a large woman, was standing in the doorway and pointing to her watch. "He needs to rest. You can come back in a few hours."

Steve leaned over Booth. "You're going to be okay. The doctor will come back and check on you but he said you'll be up and around in a few days. Take care, buddy." He walked out of the room and the nurse followed him out of the Critical Care unit. "I have another team member downstairs in emergency and she is going to want to come up here. I will try to hold her off for a little but it is critical that she see that he is okay."

"I understand. Check in with me and I'll bring her back. Try to wait as long as you can. We will give him something to sleep."

"I'm going to station a man up here just in case."

The nurse looked puzzled but said okay.

Steve thanked her. He moved back down the hall toward the elevators and to the emergency room to see how Blair was doing.

The meeting was breaking up in the office of the Homeland Security Chief when Robert's phone buzzed. He looked down and saw it was Tony Kim sending him a text. Kim was using one of the special burned phones that he only used when communicating with his boss.
Robert slid his phone back into his jacket pocket and continued to tell the other two men that as soon as he had some information he would let them know.

The offices of Homeland Security were located in the Nebraska Avenue Complex in Washington D.C. The agency was created after the 9/11 attacks and it enforced U.S. laws while investigating and gathering intelligence on national and international activities.

This group was involved in any activity that threatens the security of the nation. They had the greatest latitude of operating in both the domestic and international scenes. Neither Robert Chiarini nor Frank Fitzgerald liked that they had to report to the secretary of Homeland Security however that position had grown to the third largest cabinet position in the administration. Both men walked toward the entrance and stopped just outside on the steps leading out of the main building on Nebraska. "Let's make a deal," Frank said.

"I'm listening," answered Robert.
"Instead of fighting each other, let's handle this without involving either the Secretary or Director."

"Agreed," Robert said.

"Remember though, if you or your team gets in my way I'll crush you!" Frank smiled after saying that and strolled down the sixteen steps to the car that was waiting for him.

Robert stood at the top of the steps thinking, we'll see who crushes who.

Twelve

The text message was short. "I'm okay; a little banged up but failed to get the items we wanted. I have a few more ideas. Will let you know once they are implemented." Robert Chiarini was seated in the back seat as his driver headed down Pennsylvania Avenue past the White House. He would soon be on Pennsylvania and 9th across from the FBI Headquarters in the J. Edgar Hoover Building. He told the driver to take 7th all the way to highway 395 and across the George Mason Memorial Bridge. They would catch the Washington Memorial Parkway to Langley and CIA Headquarters. Before going there though he planned to head to Falls Church. It was there that he planned to meet with his key staff to devise the next stage of their plan.

Many CIA Directors often felt that their headquarters being in Virginia had both good and bad points. The good aspect was they were often out of the limelight and although they were only outside the beltway by a few miles, they usually didn't have press on their door step. The bad thing was the distance from all the action. When something of importance came up they had to travel across the bridge and maneuver through the congested traffic to get on the scene. The FBI building was just six blocks from the White House and always closer.

Robert Chiarini had been appointed to his position by President Morgan and had been seen as a key part of the administration. He wanted to keep it that way.

If his team can be successful in their quest to find those who were responsible for the bombing of flight 792 it would cement his position with the President.

He hoped that Tony Kim and the team on the ground in Seoul would have some positive news soon. If not he would take matters in his own hands.

Hughes Memorial Center was still bustling with many of the injured from the crash on the 405. Blair had been stitched and completed a battery of x-rays that proved to be negative. Kathy O'Conner had been with her while Steve contacted his office to see what progress was made on the bomb fragments. The forensic team confirmed the FAA finding that the markings were indeed Russian. The material of the shell matched ones that were captured during the Serbian War that ended in 1995. Could the bomb used been one sold on the black market in Europe? If so it only led to more questions, too many questions but few answers. Steve hoped that his teams of agents could get him some answers soon.

Kathy was walking down the hall pushing an empty wheel chair. Steve looked up to see Blair marching along side of her. "Why aren't you in the chair?"

Kathy answered, "I tried Boss but she won't have any part of it."

"I need to go see Booth," Blair announced.

"Okay, but first we need to get you a clean bill of health."

"I've got it right here. Doctor said there are no broken bones or fractures and just the cut on my forehead. I'm fine; just need to make sure Booth is okay too."

Everyone knew how hardheaded and determined she was to get her way. "I'll call upstairs and let them know were coming," Steve told her.

Kathy put the wheel chair along the wall where she had seen two other chairs sitting. The three of them walked to the desk in the emergency room and asked if they would call the main desk in the Critical Care Unit.

The duty nurse upstairs answered, "Mr. Booth was still sleeping and it would be best if he was left alone for a little while longer."

"I promise she will be up there only a few minutes," Steve told her.

"Well okay but just one person and she'll get one minute only."

Kathy said she would stay downstairs and help gather the reports from the witnesses that had been interviewed in the emergency room. Steve walked with Blair to the elevators and told her, "Booth is going to be fine. He has a broken arm that is in a cast and fractured breast bone that will need to heal. He'll be out of commission for a week or so but let's not get him excited."

The trip up to the 5th floor was quiet and Blair said very little. Once they checked in to the nurse's station the head nurse said she would take Blair to Booth's room. One of the men from the office had been stationed outside of the room. He asked Blair how she was doing. "I'm fine, just have to see Booth."

Blair stood outside of room 536 for a minute before going in. Booth was sleeping flat on his back and his left arm was across his hip. The cast went from his knuckles to the end of his forearm. He had a wet compress on his forehead and the IV drip going into his right arm. He didn't look good. Blair moved to his side and put her hand on his cheek. Tears welled in her eyes and she turned toward to door. The nurse had left and she was alone with him.

"I'm so sorry Booth. It's my fault; I should have seen that car coming at us." She again turned toward the doorway but it was clear.

Blair ran her hand along his chest and put her right hand under the covers. She leaned down and lifted the gown from his side and saw that he had been bandaged across his chest with what appeared to be a stretchy wrap.

He had bruises on his rib cage as well as on his face from the air bag deploying. She leaned in and kissed him on his right cheek. "I love you baby, get better soon."

Booth mumbled something inaudible but it seemed to her that he had a smile on his face. She wiped away her tears and patted him softly. "I'll be back later on." She turned and walked into the hallway.

The nurse was just coming back toward 536 and asked if Booth had said anything. "No he's sleeping so I didn't want to wake him. I'll be back in a few hours to sit with him."

"I understand that you are concerned but in the Critical Care Center you are not allowed to be in the patient's room for more than a few minutes at a time."

"Doesn't matter, I'll be back." She walked away leaving the nurse standing in the doorway.

Steve watched as Blair headed back toward him. "Let's go," she said.

He walked with her and waited until they were in the elevator before he asked, "Was he awake?"

"No, he looks pretty bad. His left side is bruised near his rib cage. I'm worried about him."

"I didn't think about his ribs," Steve said. "How did you know he was bruised?"

"I looked," she answered.

Steve didn't say anything else for a while. They got out of the elevator and found Kathy talking to another one of the people who was brought in from the accident.

"This is Manny Ramos he was in the truck that was behind Booth and Blair. Steve was glad that she stayed back and questioned people from the scene.

"Mr. Ramos, I'm so sorry that this all happened. Can you tell us what you saw?"

Ramos had been banged up pretty bad but was sitting on the side of the gurney. He looked up at Steve. "Yes, I was about twenty feet behind the car in front of me and we were all doing the speed limit when all of a sudden this dark colored car came out of nowhere and hit the back of the car. It spun into the guard rail and I couldn't stop fast enough. After we collided there must have been two or three other cars that plowed into us too."

"How about the person that was in the dark car that started the whole thing, can you describe him?"

"Oh yes. My truck was almost sideways and partially up on the rails when a man climbed over my hood and slid down next to the car that I had hit. He was kicking the trunk like a mad man."

"Kicking the trunk? You mean like he was angry?"

"Maybe, but then he seemed to try to pry it open. I don't know what he wanted. At first I thought he was with the police."

Steve looked over at Kathy and Blair.

"Why do think he wasn't now?"

"I saw he was bleeding from his leg and his shirt was torn."

"Thank you Mr. Ramos. You've been a great help. Here is my card, if you can think of anything else please call me. I'm going to have a man come over here and if you could try to describe the man kicking the trunk for him it would help. He will be drawing a composite from your description and maybe we can find that guy. My agents will get your information and if you need help with your insurance company let us know."

Steve and Blair walked away and Blair turned toward Steve. "What the hell was that about? Why was a man trying to get into our trunk?"

"Not sure but his story is consistent with others. We need a good description. Maybe Mr. Ramos is our best bet. After all, the guy was right in front of him."

Thirteen

Josh waited to hear from the team of agents that were waiting at Rusty's apartment. There was still no sign of him and it had been three hours since they left each other in the Palace courtyard. There was a second team of agents gathering information from the Palace courtyard on the man that had been stabbed. Josh needed to make sure he wasn't identified or that the local police weren't looking for him. The agents at the Palace had the information he needed and informed Josh that he had not been singled out from the incident. He continued his quest into Russian goods as a pretext to maybe finding the man that stabbed Rusty's contact. He feared that Rusty too had been attacked by the same man. The search of hospitals and clinics in the area turned up empty.

Josh was now in the market place hoping that some of his contacts might have any information on Russians that were operating in the vicinity. He was trying to check every possible place Rusty might have been taken to.

The warehouse where Rusty had been held was located at the far end of the market district. It was dark and Rusty felt his hands tied behind his back. He was on the floor and tied to a large beam in the center of the room. The ground was damp and he could see a dim light from the far end of the warehouse. Two men were talking in low deep voices and it was clear that they were speaking Russian.

Rusty tried to pull loose from the beam but they had a thick rope around his waist as well as his hands bound behind him. He had been out cold for a while and was still a little groggy. Blood dripped from the right side of his head where he must have been hit. He attempted to gather all the details that he could so that he might be able to escape.

A dark shadow approached from the dimly lit area in front of him. Rusty kept his head drooped down so that the man would think he was still passed out. The Russian called out to his partner.

"Он выходит еще холодная, сволочь. Давайте бросать немного воды на него." He was letting his partner know that their captive was out cold.

He kept watching as Rusty's head hung down. He walked back to the small office in the building. They were sure that their captive was still out cold. The men studied the material they had taken from the agent. It had their location as well as other key material that would foil the next stage of the attack.

Rusty peered out from his position and waited until the man was out of sight. He continued to try to free himself from the rope that had him held against the beam. Once he could maneuver a little he might be able to get his hands loose. The rope was thick and he started to kick his feet into the ground and was able to move around the beam. As he was moving he could see the spot where the thick rope was bound together. It was easy to get it a little loose and now he had the ability to free his hands. He reached down into his right side pocket with his finger tips and got hold of a small Swiss army knife that he kept in an inside pocket. He slowly pulled it out and started working on the binding that was around his wrist. Noise again came from the far end of the warehouse. He knew someone was again headed his way. The knife cut the plastic zip tie that bound his hands and he was partially free.

The huge Russian was now a few feet away and moving closer. The big man stooped down as Rusty hung his head down into his chest like he was still out. The man had a glass of water and splashed it into Rusty's face. He hollered in Russian, "Open your eyes American." He pulled Rusty's jacket with his right hand and was just a foot over him when Rusty grabbed him with both hands and slammed him headfirst into the beam knocking the big man out.

The Russian slumped partially over the top of Rusty and leaning against the beam. Rusty pulled the man to his side and searched his pockets. There was a switch blade in his coat pocket and it did the trick. Rusty was free and now had to get out of the warehouse. Right now his best bet was to escape. He could always come back with re-enforcements to take on the crew but now escaping was his only thought. The light at the end of the warehouse was dim but Rusty could see that a shadow reflected off the far wall. He bound the Russian that he had knocked out and stuffed a torn rag in his mouth. All of a sudden the voice from the office where Rusty had seen the huge Russian emerge from called out. It wasn't clear what he was yelling. Rusty only knew a little Russian and he thought for a second. The voice again called out. Rusty decided to take a chance and mumbled in a deep voice a garbled answer. He heard nothing for a few seconds then the voice hollered back. This time it seemed less agitated and the response was short. He listened for footsteps but none were heard. There was no time to waste. Rusty found a gun in the huge Russian's coat pocket and he held the Russian made Lugar in his right hand. It was about forty feet to the area that appeared to be an office of some sort. Rusty could see two men hovered over a large map and they seemed to be studying a map.

Rusty called out in a low deep voice the only phrase that he knew.

Мне нужно, чтобы получить что-то вне. He was telling the man that he needed to go outside for something.

The figures in the office didn't answer. Rusty was now only ten feet from the doorway and he could see from the opening that the men still hovered over the map that they was studying. The Lugar had a bullet in the chamber and Rusty was an exceptional marksman. He turned back for a second to insure that his captive was still bound to the beam. He hoped to take the man in the office alive. This man could be a key to the bombing of flight 792. Rusty wished he still had his cell phone but they must have taken it when he was captured. This was all seeming much too easy he thought. Just then the west wall of the warehouse made a screeching noise and someone was pulling a sliding door opened.

Rusty ducked back down and knew he had to get out of the building before more men arrived. As the doorway opened he could see a large gray vehicle come into view. He recognized it as a military version of the Hummer like the ones the army used in Iraq and Afghanistan. Now the men in the office were standing straight up and called out something to the arriving comrades. Rusty had slid along the side wall and made his way closest to the opened doorway. Whoever had pulled the door opened must have gotten back into the Hummer and proceeded to drive it into the warehouse. When the vehicle passed him Rusty ducked down and made his way out of the opening and took off running.

The warehouse was in the market district that had hundreds of merchants moving their items in and out for sale. It was a congested area that Rusty had been to just a couple of days ago with Josh. He was able to blend in with the throng of people that were filling their carts and wagons with merchandise to sell. He looked back several times knowing that it would be seconds when they realized that he had escaped.

Two men came running out of the warehouse just seconds after Rusty had made his way through the first layer of merchants.

They were brandishing guns and asking if anyone had seen a big man running from their warehouse. They said that they were chasing a thief. One man standing outside the building pointed toward the wide opening ahead where he saw a big American push his way through the crowd. The Russians were in fast pursuit of Rusty Nelson.

It wasn't unusual to see men running through this area of the market place. People milling around separated when the two Russians came charging through the crowded area. The initial walkway between warehouses and storage areas was about fifteen feet wide but quickly narrowed to less than ten feet. Once you went about a quarter-of-a-mile down that path it opened to a large market square where most merchants showed their wares. That is where Rusty was headed and the two Russians on his tail.

When you were as big as Rusty was and an American it was almost impossible to hide. He towered over the locals in the market place and because he was running and pushing his way through the crowd he caught everyone's attention. "Shit, where was it that Josh took me to?" He was talking aloud to himself as he pushed through the throng ahead of him. Just then it came into view. The open market with purses and handbags of all sorts was right in front of him. "That's the place."

When he and Josh were checking on counterfeit goods they found themselves in that market area. It was long and narrow but there was a rear entrance that went to the main thorough fare. The market place was indeed unique. The front of it had leather goods of all kinds and as you entered and made your way through it turned into a display of chickens, pigs and sheep.

Tony Aued

Other men were haggling over two roosters that one man was holding in the air yelling at the other two men. The aisle way was now less than two feet wide and Rusty had to duck just to make his way under the roosters that were squawking.
Pigs squealed as he pushed through and found he was now on the main street leading into the market.

This area was a round-a-bout full of cabs, rickshaws and vendors selling everything imaginable. A large fountain graced the center of the area and kids were wadded in it. Rusty waved at a local policeman that had been directing traffic and continued to jog down the side street ahead. He signaled to a cab that had just dropped off two ladies and it pulled up next to him. Rusty jumped in the back seat and gave the driver direction.

The two Russians had just made their way through the market place and were standing in the round-a-bout searching for their man. They asked people if they had seen a big American man running out of the market but no one noticed him. It was close to noon and the busiest time of the day. There were many people in the area and a lot of American tourists were wandering around. Rusty was gone.

Josh was talking to one of his contacts just outside of the main marketplace when he heard all the commotion. He saw the back of a large man climbing into a cab and turned to see two other large men questioning people in the square. He slid back out of view and made his way through the hanging goods to get closer to the men. He heard them asking about a big American. It had to be Rusty. The two men asking people had strong Russian accents and now turned back into the large market square pushing their way through the crowd.

Josh followed a safe distance behind. He called to a team that had kept watch at Rusty's apartment.

"I think he got away from whoever had him.

He will probably head your way. Let me know if you find him." Josh wanted to see where the Russians were headed.

Could they lead him to a secret hide-out?

Fourteen

Rusty made sure that he wasn't being followed and had the cab driver take him to a more affluent part of Seoul. The shops resembled those in Beverly Hills. The women that walked around were wearing high fashion clothes and the men were well dressed. He saw a Gucci store along with other more expensive stores along the sidewalk. He had the driver stop in front of a mall entrance and paid him. Although they had taken his gun and cell phone for some reason they left his wallet. At least he had money once he escaped out of the warehouse district.

He got out about a block from where a large crowd had gathered and music was blaring. There were loud speakers on tall stands along what appeared to be a stage set up in the street. This would be perfect in case someone had followed him. He made his way into the crowd and managed to squeeze up close to a runway of some sort that had beautiful young Korean women dancing along. Everyone around him cheered loudly as a middle aged man was dancing in the strangest form along the runway. It appeared as he had been riding a horse or mimicked riding one. His legs were flung side-to-side as he passed them. People screamed and cheered. The sign above the doorway nearby announced that PSY would be appearing today.

Who in the hell was PSY, he thought? Rusty turned away when a very cute young American girl and her Korean friend almost danced into his arms.

"Oh I'm so sorry," she said bumping into him.

"That's okay." Rusty was taken by their good looks and smiled at both of them. He checked the crowd to see if anyone was paying special attention to him. He decided to engage in a conversation with the young American. "So how are you both doing? Are you both here to see the singer?"

"Of course, aren't you?" The little blond asked.

"No I was just shopping and saw the crowd. I really don't know who this singer is."

"Heck mister, PSY almost danced in your lap." The American girl couldn't have been more than eighteen and her Korean girlfriend was about the same age.

"Oh, is that the name of the guy doing the funny dance?"

They both laughed and the American girl put her arm around Rusty. "Haven't you heard about the Gangnam Style?"

He looked blankly back at them. "The what style?"

They were really laughing now. "It's really a big dance craze everywhere. Especially here."

"It was certainly unusual," Rusty said.

"You're pretty cute," the Korean girl said. "You need to hang out with us. We could show you a good time."

Rusty looked closely at the Korean girl. She was wearing very high cut shiny shorts with a low cut top that had a plunging neckline. The view was great, he thought. The American girl had bleached blond hair and was wearing a short mini skirt that showed a lot of leg and he was sure a lot more. They were both still dancing and now started grinding against him while one girl still had her arm around his waist. She ran her fingers across his chest and look into his eyes. She repeated her statement.

"We could have a real good time together. Why don't you buy us a drink?"

This was very tempting and he knew the two girls were working the crowd. He first reached around to make sure his wallet was still in his back pocket.

The Lugar that he took from the Russian was tucked into his belt and his long shirt tails covered the handle.

"Sounds great, but I need to make a call first." Rusty reached into his pocket and looked back at the blond. "Shit, where is my phone? I have to make a call."

"Do you want to borrow mine?"

"Thanks."

She handed him her phone and he dialed Josh's number.

Josh looked at the incoming call and didn't recognize the number. He clicked the answer button and waited for the person to speak. At first all he heard was loud music.

"Hey honey, sorry I must have gotten lost. I can't find my cell phone but will head back to our place as soon as possible." Rusty hung up. He went back to the girl's phone call log and erased the number. He turned and handed the phone back to her.

"So how about you buying a drink for the two of us?" she asked.

"That is the best offer I've had in a long time." He smiled at the blond and then felt a small hand reach into his pants. At first he thought the girls were trying to pick his pocket but then he felt the fingers caressing him.

The Korean girl had her hand in the front of his slacks and Rusty got a big grin on his face. "You wouldn't be sorry. I can really show you a great time."

Rusty's face was flushed and the two girls smiled at him.

He turned to the Korean girl. "I'll give you ten minutes to quit that."

All three were now laughing.

"I'd love to hang out with you but I just can't. My wife is waiting for me and I know she will be pissed if I don't show up soon. She kind of has me on a short leash."

"It doesn't feel too short to me," she answered. Then the two girls laughed out loud.

"Thanks, but maybe some other time." They both looked disappointed. "You don't know how sorry I am to say that," He said.

"Okay." The Korean girl handed him a business card. Rusty took a deep breath, thanked them and turned away. He made his way back out of the crowd. It was clear, there wasn't anyone paying attention to him and the dancers on the runway had most everyone's attention. Rusty moved toward the cab stand and waited to catch a ride back to his hotel. Once he was in the back seat and headed back to his place he reached into his pocket and looked at the card the girl had given him. It was from a local night spot that employed exotic dancers. "Perhaps I'll hold on to this. Never know when it might come in handy." He let out a laugh in the back seat as the driver headed to his apartment.

Josh contacted all the men that were searching for Rusty to inform them that he heard from him and he would be returning back to the hotel. He also told them that he was following two Russians that appeared to be searching for Rusty in the market place. He planned to see exactly where the men were headed to before meeting everyone back at Rusty's place.

The two men seemed agitated as they pushed their way back through the shoppers in the market place and down the narrow walkway toward the line of warehouses. Josh kept back about fifty feet while watching them along the path. He knew the market area well and during his time in Korea spent much time working in an undercover assignment with vendors and exporters.

When they passed a large building with a tin roof the two men turned back to see if anyone was following. It was just then that Josh had seen a man he had used a few months ago in a raid on counterfeit goods.

"Hello my friend," Josh said in Korean. The man smiled back at him and they exchanged hearty handshakes. The man bowed and smiling as Josh continued to talk to him in Korean. Josh kept an eye on the Russians.

The two men watched Josh for a few more seconds and decided that there was nothing to be concerned with. They walked a few more feet down the path that widened out and turned into their warehouse.

Josh had noted what building they had gone into and had the location pin-pointed for future reference. He would make sure that his team of agents ran surveillance on the building and that they would strike when the men were inside.

The men re-entered the warehouse and the man that Rusty had rammed into the beam was still being attended to. He had a major gash across his forehead and it would take stitches to close it properly. One of them yelled at him, "How could you be so stupid?" He didn't want to tell them that the man took his gun.

They still had the packet that the old man in the Palace courtyard had given to Rusty. It detailed their location and one of their names as possible suspects in the bombing. It was all in Korean and they had to hope that their captive didn't get a chance to translate it. It was agreed that they would move their place of operation as soon as possible. It didn't make sense to take any chances.

Josh called in the location to headquarters and waited in the market place for instructions on how to proceed. It was clear that the men were still there and it was wise to strike now.

A helicopter was dispatched to run surveillance over the warehouse area and two teams of agents were headed to the spot that Josh had staked out. They would convene and make their final plans to attack. Josh hoped that the material that Rusty had from the old man in the Palace was still in the hands of Rusty's captives. They needed the material to help solve their case.

Fifteen

Steve Orrison waited at the special terminal in LAX. The Director would be arriving in the next few minutes. He wanted to meet him personally to go over progress on the case. The Director had felt relief leaving Washington and getting away from the constant conflict with the CIA and interference from other officials. Washington was a fish bowl and you were always under inspection. At least in Los Angeles he could throw himself into the case and get some real work done.

The LA Bureau had completed its forensic inspection of the bomb fragments brought in from the Seal team. The conclusion was as expected. The bomb was indeed of Russian origin and the same type that had been used in the conflict in Kosovo in 1998. The bomb was mass produced during the 1990's and many had been shipped to countries and groups that were supported by the Russian government. The final analysis only made this tougher. The bomb could have come from any source. The CIA had their contacts around the globe checking with every possible group that may have been responsible. The task was daunting but the need for a clearer path to the source of the bomb was critical. The findings were added to the crime board in the investigation room so all the agents were aware of current progress on the case.

Unfortunately the fragments offered no further evidence of its source.

Fitzgerald had the LA team send their findings to the CIA Director. He made sure they copied the Homeland Security Director. It was important to him that he showed that he was being a team player and complying with the directive he was given.

Blair and Kathy headed from the hospital to the office on Wilshire. They were meeting with the group of agents assigned to the case. Steve had wanted Blair to go home and get some rest. After all she had been banged around in the crash and he felt she needed to settle down. She wanted no part of it. They had the information from Manny Ramos at the hospital with the composite drawing that he helped put together on the man that maybe caused the crash.

Tony Kim had limped into the small clinic that was located along an alley way just off of Venice Beach. The small Asian girl at the desk jumped up as soon as he came in. "Tony what happened?" She immediately put her arm around his waist and helped support him. His pant leg was blood soaked and torn. Tony collapsed in a chair that she pulled out from the wall. He was the only person in the clinic. It would open to the public in an hour.

She called out for help to the nurse in the back and a lady rushed out to help. Both women were doting over him and trying to see how they could help. Sandy Kim had run the clinic in Venice Beach for the past four years and she was Tony's younger sister. Sandy had run the clinic on weekends only at first. She found solace in helping the homeless that hung out on the beach. Her niece started to work as the receptionist last year and was still attending school at Santa Monica College. Sandy Kim ripped the pant leg as her niece locked the front door to the clinic. She could see that the gash ran about five inches along his thigh and was jagged along the edges. "How did this happen?"

Tony grimaced when she ripped open the pant leg. Blood had dried and caked onto the pants and when they opened them it caused the wound to start bleeding again. He looked at his sister and said, "Don't ask."

It was clear that he wasn't going to tell her what had happened. She knew that he was a government agent and was always very secretive.
He never talked about his job and often was gone for long periods of time.

"Let me clean this out. I need to know something about how you got this so I can take care of you." She continued. "You know it is important to know the circumstances so I know how to treat this."

"Okay sis." He knew she was right. "It was in a car accident and I cut it while trying to climb out of my car. Guess the door panel was damaged and that's how it happened." He just looked at her after the confession of sort. Sandy knew it wasn't the whole story. "You're sure it was on a car part."

"Yes, why would I lie?"

She just shook her head. "You're going to need a tetanus shot." Sandy headed back into the rear of the clinic to grab the needed medical equipment. Her niece continued to work on Tony's wound. There was a knock on the clinic door. "Just one minute," the young girl said as she looked to Tony for guidance.

"Help me up. I'll go in the back so you can see who it is." She put her arm under his left shoulder and helped him hop to the back room. The knock came again but this time a person was calling out. It wasn't clear what they were saying but she pulled the curtain to the back room and headed to the front door.

"Yes what is it?"

A young man was holding a small child in his arms. "She fell on the rings and is unconscious. Please help us."

She brought him into the room and said she would get the nurse. Once she entered the back room she told Sandy what was happening.

"I'll come out there." Sandy pushed a gurney on wheels from the back room and grabbed a blanket. She motioned to Tony to move to the small X-Ray room off to the right side of the back room.

Both women were now helping the man put the little girl on the gurney. "Tell me exactly what happened," Sandy said.

"We were playing on the rings down by the beach and she flipped off and hit her head. She was out cold."

"What is your relationship to her?" Sandy was placing a cold compress on the little girl's head as she continued to question the man.

"I'm her dad. A policeman directed us here. He said that someone was here most of the time."

"Okay." Sandy asked her niece to go in the back and grab some saline solution. "You need to put it on some gauze and give it to Mr. Smith for his leg." Her niece nodded and headed to the back room. She looked around but didn't see Tony. There wasn't a back door so where was he? She peeked into the X-Ray room and saw him in the corner. "You need to put this on your cut while she is helping the man out there."

"Did I hear him say the police brought them here?"

"Yes but they just dropped them off. Once he came in I guess they left."

Tony was concerned. He didn't need any local cops hanging around. "Okay, but let me know if they are still out there."

Sandy's niece made her way back into the front room where the little girl was now sitting up. The dad had his arm around her back and Sandy was checking her eyes out.

"How many fingers do you see?" She was holding two fingers in front of the little girl.

"Two!"

Her dad smiled.

Sandy continued to look into the little girl's eyes with an instrument that had a light on the end. "Can you move your head up and down?" The little girl did. "Good, now side to side." She followed Sandy's request. Sandy then looked into her ears and leaned the little girl back down on the gurney. "She should be fine. She's going to have a nasty bump on the back of her head, dad. I suggest that you take her home and make an appointment to see your family doctor. Don't let her fall asleep for a while in case she has a concussion. I can't tell that right now. She may need further testing."

The man was very appreciative. "Thanks doc."

"I'm not a doctor just a nurse practitioner. You're going to have to fill out a few forms for my assistant before I let you leave. I want to continue to check your daughter out while you do that."

The man again thanked Sandy and moved over to the desk to get the forms. Sandy took her stethoscope out and checked the little girl again. She looked into her eyes and talked to her.

"How did you fall sweetie?"

"I was on the swings then my dad helped me climb up into rings. I guess I fell off of them."

"How do you feel now?"

"A lot better but my head hurts."

"It will hurt for a little while but you will be okay. I told your Dad what to do when he gets you home. Where is your Mom?"

"I have two brothers. I guess she's with them."

Sandy was being sure that the man's story checked out. In this day and age so many weird things went on and on Venice Beach you often saw the weirdest of the weird.
Once the man had finished filling out forms he thanked Sandy and headed out of the clinic. It was now time for the clinic to be opened so Sandy instructed her niece to try to keep anyone in the waiting area for as long as possible.

Tony pressed the pad with saline solution against his leg. "You're going to need stitches," Sandy said.

"Can't you just use some of the tape to hold it together?"

"Not unless you want to bleed to death." Sandy just looked at her brother. "Listen Macho man, I'm going to do it right, now sit down."

Blair and Kathy talked to the head of the team that was searching the data base for any link to the man that fled the scene. They had circulated the drawing that Manny had helped them make at the hospital. There was an APB out and all the local authorities would be on the lookout for the escaped man.

Police departments today all had on-board computers and it would be on every screen in a matter of seconds. Maybe they would get lucky and someone will spot him. Officials were sure he would need some medical care and all hospitals and clinics were also notified to inform them if he came in.

Sandy Kim now had three people in the outer office waiting for care when her niece waved frantically to her. She moved to the desk when she saw it. There it was a picture of her brother with the words," possibly dangerous. Do not approach but contact the police or FBI immediately." The two women looked at each other.

Tony had been gone only a few minutes. Sandy just hoped that he knew that he had been identified. Although the picture was her brother, the name was not. She was sure that it was an alias that he used, but still hoped he had a way of staying out of the limelight. She sent him a text to his cell with the hope that he would answer.

Robert Chiarini was in his office when his assistant came in. "You need to see this, sir." She proceeded to hit some key strokes on his computer and there it was - Tony Kim's picture with the warning under it, dangerous and wanted for questioning. It was being forwarded to every office across the country. He quickly got on the phone. The two numbers he had did not answer. He didn't leave a message. Robert called to another of his deep cover agents and gave him special orders. "We need to find our man. He has been compromised and we need to clean this up." The message was clear. Tony Kim would have to be erased from the CIA files and eradicated as soon as possible. Chiarini wasn't going to go down for this. He headed to Falls Church to make sure his plan was put into motion. The bunker would be able to track events on the other side of the world via the specialized satellite hook-up that it employed. Chiarini felt things starting to unravel and he planned to get his fail safe plan into action quickly.

Sixteen

Frank Fitzgerald and Steve Orrison were studying the composite drawing of the suspect on Steve's computer. "At least we have an identification to go on." Frank agreed. The investigation into the accident as well as the one into the bombing had every agent in the field working 24/7 to solve them. The Phoenix and Vegas Bureaus sent extra personnel to Los Angeles to help with the cases, especially now that Booth would be laid up for a while. Steve hoped to put Blair on a desk coordinating the search for the man that was responsible for the crash on the 405.

Kathy O'Connor knocked on Steve's office door. "Come in." He could see that she was holding a message. "Sir, a man matching the description of our suspect was spotted a few minutes ago in Venice Beach. A police cruiser along Windward Circle saw a man limping along in front of the Bank of America. They stopped to question him and he took off down the street between the Bank and restaurant. They are searching the area now and have three other units involved."

Steve was pleased that it might appear that they would be successful and capture their suspect. "Kathy I would like you and Chris to head out to Venice Beach. If he is captured I want him brought in here, not to a police station."

"We'll head out now." Kathy grabbed her keys and told Chris to follow her. They didn't want to tell Blair where they were headed off to.

Steve headed out into the office and saw Blair looking at the composite of the man that they had sent out. "Any ideas," He asked.

"No I've never seen him before. I still can't figure why someone would want to take the bomb fragments from us. Who could have known what we had?"

It was clear to Steve that the people responsible for the bombing or a Washington insider were trying to derail their investigation. The most likely scenario was that it was someone related to the actual bombing.

Tony Kim checked his cell phone and saw that he had six missed calls. Most of them were from Chiarini. He knew his boss was ruthless and had to get away as quickly as possible. Once he was in the clear he would return the calls and assure him that he was in the clear. Kim just had run across the school playground off of Main Street and now headed between the large apartment units behind the school. His leg was hurting but he had to get out of the area as soon as possible. Sirens were all around him. His best bet was to make it through the courtyard ahead and try to disappear into the maze of buildings. He knew the area and felt that he had an advantage if he could get to his sister's place. She always hid a key in the small statue in the flower bed along the right side of her entrance. Once he was there he could plan his escape.

Three police officers were running through the building that lie ahead and they split up to cover all possible exits to the street in front of them. He was last seen in the large garden of the Amber Ridge Apartment complex off of Windward Circle.

A lady said he was running through the palm trees that lined the walkway. Two officers radioed that they were in position at the exit at the rear of the garden and another group was at the front entrance.

The garden was now covered on both sides.
Two cars pulled up off of Grand Avenue and another unit parked on Windward Avenue. The area was now surrounded.

His sister's place was on the third floor and he had to lose the men chasing him. He saw a trellis that was placed against the side of an apartment on the ground floor and scaled it to the second level. From there he ran crouched down covered by the large palm leaves to the stairway that led up to the third floor. His sister's place faced the courtyard and he could see men down there searching the bushes and through the huge rock garden. The key was right where it had always been. He was bent down and opened the door slowly. Closing it behind him softly he made his way to the large picture window. Men were now standing in the courtyard looking up and others were still searching through the gardens. It looked like one group was doing a door to door search. He needed to contact his sister now.
Sandy Kim saw the number on her cell phone and excused herself from a patient in the office. "Sorry, I need to take this." Sandy motioned to her niece that she was walking outside for a minute. She hit call back and waited hoping to hear that her brother was safe. She waited for him to say something once it was connected.

Tony answered in Korean just in case his sister had been compromised. She was glad to hear his voice. "I hope to be gone in a little. So sorry to get you involved." He hated that he might have brought her into his problem.
Sandy told him about the photo that was being flashed across the television news. "It has the name listed as Choi Chung but it was definitely your picture."

"It's an alias that I have used and it will not lead back to you. No one knows me here, sis. You will be okay, I promise. I plan to be gone as soon as I see a clearing."

"There is a stairway that leads to the roof level just past my place. Maybe you can check it out. It might be your best bet to escape."

"They're doing a door to door search right now. If they come up to the third floor will any of your neighbors be home?"

"No, the people across from me are out of town and the apartment on the other side of me is empty."

That was great news. "Don't come home tonight. I'll call you as soon as I can."

Sandy hung up and went back into the clinic. She had just walked back in when a police officer followed her into the clinic. She turned around and almost jumped.

"Sorry I didn't mean to startle you," he said. "We are searching for an escaped man that may be seeking medical help. He was last seen in the area and I want to leave this poster with you."

Sandy looked at the picture.

"If you see him or he comes in, be careful. He is dangerous. Call us as soon as you can. Any chance that you recognize him?" he asked.

"No he doesn't look familiar. We haven't seen him."

"Okay but call in case you do." He left her his card and circled his phone number.

"Sure, no problem."

The officer thanked her and walked back out. Sandy turned and looked at her niece. She had a panicked look on her face.

"It's okay I told him we will help if we see who they are looking for." Sandy winked at her niece and headed back into the examination room.

The police scanners were being monitored by the FBI agents that were in on the search. They arrived at the apartment complex that the Venice Beach police had staked out. They sought out the officer in charge. "Any sign of the suspect?" Chris asked.

"No, we have the complex surrounded and are doing a door to door search in case he is holed up in one of the apartments."

"Could he have made it out of the area?"

"Anything is possible," he said.

Chris suggested that some of the men check the surrounding area and that they widen the search area out. The Venice officer just nodded. He knew the FBI would want to take over once they arrived. "I think we have a handle of this," he took a deep breath. "Why don't the two of you cover the area around the back of the complex?"

Kathy smiled at Chris. "Sure, no problem. Thanks for all your help." The two agents moved back out of the courtyard and headed to their car. "What an asshole. I'll call it in to the boss and see how he wants us to proceed." Steve knew his team would get some resistance and wasn't surprised at Kathy's information. "I suggest you cover the area past the complex, the guy probably eluded them. Maybe someone in the area saw something." Kathy agreed and they decided to drive around the streets that circled the complex. When they saw a group walking they questioned them. Maybe someone saw a man limping along.

Tony Kim had been in his sister's apartment for three hours now and could see that the group of officers had thinned out. There were two men still in the courtyard but it seemed that the door to door search netted nothing and had been discontinued. It was close to five o'clock and would soon be dusk. He changed the gauze pad on his leg in the bathroom. His sister had medical supplies in the cabinet over the sink.

He planned to wait a little longer before making his way out of the apartment and try the roof escape that his sister told him about.

Police scanners kept officials and the FBI aware of where the man was last seen. It was the information that the CIA needed. The man that Chiarini sent got a message back through his sources to the Director. "I'm on the scent and will take care of our problem."

Chiarini had to make sure that Kim wouldn't make it out alive.

Seventeen

Blair wanted to head back to the hospital to check on Booth. Steve told one of the agents in the office to take her. "Jim, I want you to stay with her the whole time. We don't know if the crash was more than someone trying to get the bomb fragments or her too." The agent understood.

Booth was now awake and pressed the nurse call button.

"What do you need Mr. Booth?" the young nurse asked as she entered the room.

"You got to remove this strap that is around my chest."

"Sorry I can't. The doctor doesn't want you to sit up for at least twenty-four hours."

"Well can you loosen it a little?"

"I guess, but you have to promise not to lift your head." She reached under the right side of the bed and pulled the buckle loose about two inches. "How's that?"

"Better, thanks." Booth hated being like this. He wanted to get up but guessed that this was for the best. He closed his eyes and tried to think about the details from the accident. Who rammed them and why filled his mind. Just then he heard Blair's voice coming from the hallway.

"How is he doing?" She was standing in the doorway talking to the nurse.

"Hey, I'm doing fine," he yelled.

She laughed. "Guess you're still alive and as grumpy as ever."

The nurse looked at Blair, "Good luck with that one."

She moved into his room and saw the monitor over his head. The numbers were changing from 119/79 now to 126/85. "What do those numbers mean?" she asked.

"They are his blood pressure readings." The nurse was checking his pulse and Booth rolled his eyes at Blair. "Mr. Booth you have to relax. Getting excited isn't good for you."

"Yeah, sure."

She looked at Blair. "You can stay for about ten minutes only. He needs his rest."

Once she left Blair said, "Jim came with me and he's in the waiting room. I'll let him come in later." Blair turned toward the door to make sure no one was there. She leaned down and kissed Booth. "I was so worried and scared. I didn't know what had happened when they had me in an ambulance and you weren't there. Booth, you were just lying in the car and not moving. I should have been able to help you but I couldn't."

Tears welled in his eyes and he smiled at her. "I love you Blair."

They kissed again, but this time it was a long lingering kiss and she held his face in her hands and looked tenderly into his eyes. "You're gonna get better baby. They said you'll have to lie flat for a while to make sure the breast bone heals okay."

"I'm going to be fine. Just get the asshole who hit us."

She laughed for the first time after the accident. "He's all mine." They looked into each other's eyes and Blair pressed her hand against his head. She ran her right finger through his hair and kissed his forehead. "You'll be better in no time."

It became obvious that the two agents had fallen in love.

They had never let on in the office and knew that they couldn't work together in the same Bureau office if anyone found out. But now that didn't matter. Blair held Booth's hands and whispered in his ear.

"I'll get the guy responsible for this." She was determined to succeed.

The nurse reappeared in the doorway. "He really needs his rest miss. We need to give him an hour or more of sleep. I'm going to give him something to help him relax."

"Thanks, I understand. If it's okay I'd like to wait around and see him one more time before I have to go."

The nurse looked at the young couple holding hands. "Sure, I'll come get you in a little after he gets some rest."

Blair ran her fingers along Booth's chin and smiled down at him. "I'll be back in a little. Get some sleep." She headed back to the waiting room.

"How is he doing?" Jim asked.

"They said he is better, still breathing hard but guess that is to be expected. They will come get us when we can go back in."

The two agents sat together in the small Intensive Care waiting room. Blair took out the composite of the person that Manny had described to the sketch artist. She studied the face and wondered about the name. She had lived in California for ten years before joining the Bureau and the name didn't seem right. Something was odd about it. Choi Chung was the name they had come up with. Choi was definitely a Korean name but Chung was a Chinese surname.

"What kind of cell phone do you have?"

Jim looked at her. "I have an Android 4G, why?"

"We need to do some research on the name and find out everything we can about this man. I'm wondering if he has any relatives in the area. You use your phone and I'll check with mine. Maybe one of us will get a hit."

The two agents moved to a small table in the corner of the room and started doing their checking. They followed the information that the guys in the office came up with. The California DMV records had the address of person with the surname Choi in Manhattan Beach.
The Bureau had already sent a team to the apartment in case he returned there. Blair called back to the office. She asked the agent who answered, "Did anyone check Internal Revenue records? What is his Social Security number? Where did he work? Did he have any returns and if so, for how many years?"

The agent wrote down her questions and said that he would check and call her back.

An orderly was walking through and stopped. "I'm sorry miss but you can't be on a cell phone in this area." Before he was almost done talking Blair flashed her badge. "FBI, were conducting a manhunt and it is of national security."

The young orderly stepped back. "Sorry, I didn't know." He quickly walked away.

Jim sitting across from Blair chuckled. "You scared the shit out of him."

"Good."

They both continued searching the data on their phones. Blair's cell rang.

"Hello. Oh that's great. I know the place well. My friend used to work at the bar and I'll call her. If I find anything out I'll call back."

Jim watched as she finished talking. "Well did they come up with anything?"

"The office said his last tax return showed that he worked in Venice Beach at the Sidewalk Café. My friend worked there a few years and she would have known him. I'm going to call her."

Blair dialed Amy hoping to find her home. Maybe they finally had a lead.

Eighteen

The search by the Venice police at the apartments netted nothing so far. The Police Captain was now on the scene ordered his men back out of the courtyard. He left two teams at the front and rear entrance to the apartment complex. If their suspect was still there it only made sense that he would have to use one of those exits.

"Let's cover the neighborhood in a mile-and-a-half radius." The Chief was disappointed in the results of the search. He mapped out the surrounding area for each search team.

His team of officers started their search, grid by grid, through Venice. They planned to search from Pacific Avenue to Venice Boulevard. The area was close to a mile-and-a-half square and it would take hours to cover. It was getting dark and the streets were becoming crowded with tourists and people leaving the beach.

Tony Kim watched from the roof as the men were moving out of the complex. It was now dusk and nightfall was on his side. He wiped off all the areas that he had touched in his sister's apartment and put the gauze pads and wash cloth he used in his pocket. In case he was captured he didn't want any evidence linking him to her.

Once he was out of the apartment he headed back up the stairway that led to the roof top. From there he could check on the action below. Tony was able to see a police car stationed off of Windward Circle.

From his viewing spot he could check Grand Avenue and Venice Boulevard East. They all ran off of Windward Circle like spokes in a wheel. The apartment complex was in the center of the action below. It made sense to him that they would be covering all sides of the building. Tony crawled along the ledge that was maybe three feet high. He followed the roof top to the opposite corner from where the local police car was sitting. He peered over the edge and spotted a drain pipe that looked pretty stable. The sun had set over the Pacific on the west side of the building. He was now on the south east corner and the dark would help shield him from those in pursuit. Just then from the corner of his eye he caught a glimpse of a shadow. He thought that it could be someone moving toward him. Tony pressed his body against the short wall and waited. What was it?

The man sent to erase the CIA's problem was an expert in hand-to-hand combat. He joined the agency after an illustrious career as a Navy Seal. Robert Chiarini kept the covert operation running although he had been ordered to disband the unit. He was running the action from his secret headquarters in Falls Church. This agent's deep cover identification was known only to a few and he reported directly to the Director. Chiarini had given his orders. Tony Kim was not to escape. Make it look like an accident. He had spotted Tony when he was looking out toward the courtyard. If he surprised Tony, he could toss him off the roof. The local cops would think it was an accident. The man moved quickly and with a leap caught Tony with a thunderous kick on the back of his head. Tony's body went crashing into the metal air conditioning unit on the roof. Blood flowed from his right cheek and he rolled to his side before the man landed another blow.

Tony Kim sprung to his feet and landed a kick to the assailant sending him skidding on the roof top. The hand-to-hand action was out of a Bruce Lee movie.

The jagged edges of the roofs tar cut into his skin and ripped his pants. Both men were bleeding and on their feet. Fists flew and each man landed blows to the other. The battle raged on for a few minutes with each man causing damage to the other.

Tony spun and was able to bring the man down with a kick to the side of his head. When the attacker went down this time, something slid out of his pocket. Tony leaped on top of him twisting his neck with a swift snap and dropped the lifeless body to the roof top. Blood puddled in the corner of the man's mouth and his eyes glared as if he was still alive. There was noise coming from below and a voice was heard yelling.

"Help, we need help. There is someone on the roof."

The fight now caught the attention of residents below. Tony had to get out of there fast. He spotted the item that came out of the man's pocket in the scuffle and picked it up. It was a cell phone. He put it in his pocket and lifted the body to the side of the rooftop. He did a quick search of the man's pockets but there wasn't any identification. He needed to create a diversion.

One of the officer's below said he heard a crash in the bushes to his right. He radioed it in and drew his weapon. He cautiously made his way to the side of the apartment building and flashed his light along the spot where he heard the sound. There it was. A body of a man had landed head first and was impaled on the metal fence. He moved closer and saw the lifeless bleeding body. The man was dead. The officer called in to the Venice Police office. "We got our man. He must have tried to get away by jumping off the roof."

"Bring him in before the feds get a hold of him." The local guys wanted to take the credit for this.

"Sorry, he's dead. We're going to need the coroner out here. He's impaled on an steel fence."

It was pretty quiet for a few minutes on the other end of the line. "Shit! Are you sure it's him? Can you get a good look at him?"

"I'll move closer." The officer was now joined by the other three men that were still guarding the exits to the apartments. They flashed their lights on the body and were giving the description to the office as best as possible.

"He looks Asian, maybe Korean or Chinese. It's hard to tell how tall he is because his body is almost folded in half. There's a lot of blood from his right leg and face."

They searched his pockets but there wasn't anything in either of them. "He must be our guy. He fits the description." The police were pleased if they had been successful. A call went out to the Los Angeles County Coroner's office. When the information came into the FBI office they were doubtful that the dead man was Kim. "That was too easy," Steve said. He contacted Kathy and Chris to follow-up and see if the dead man resembled the picture they were working from. When they arrived back at the apartments, the local police had the scene closed off. Kathy flashed her badge and they were reluctantly let in.

"Do you think it's him," she asked.

It's going take some time because his face looks shredded on one side, probably when he fell from the roof. The body is the same size as the description and he appeared to be Asian.

She called it into the Bureau Chief. "Not sure boss. He's pretty cut up and the County guys will have to cut him off of the iron rods."

"The iron rods?"

"Yes, he must have tried to scale down the gutter and fell onto the six foot high metal fence that surrounds the apartment building."

Steve was thinking. "Okay, the two of you need to search around the area. Our guy could still be around and maybe this guy was a burglar or something."
It was clear that the Bureau was at a standstill until positive identification could be made.

Chris had moved around the right side of the apartments and Kathy went around the left side. A large crowd had gathered in front and a television crew from Channel 6, LA Live had arrived. The County guys were pulling up and the residents had filled the courtyard and almost every light in the building was on. The scene had become a circus. Kathy asked a group of obvious residents if they had seen anyone that didn't belong.

"No," one of the men said. "Kind of hard to tell who belongs. So many people have more than one family member staying here all the time. People are always coming and going. The place has become kind of transient spot since the new owners took over."

She thanked him and continued to check the area. When the local guys found the body on the steel fence they all converged to that spot. Tony had watched them and saw his opportunity to head back down the stairwell to the third level. His face was bleeding and the right leg patch that his sister had put on was now soaked in blood. He had to get away and couldn't take time to take care of his wounds. Once he was safe he could contact his sister for additional medical assistance. All the commotion gave him the opportunity he needed. Tony made his way down the stairway on the opposite side of the apartments without anyone paying attention to him, although he was limping badly. He took his shirt off and tossed it over his shoulder to help cover his face. He put his hand over the gash on the right side of his face and continued down the next two levels and out of the area. He was running out of options and needed to get back to his boat in the Marina. His sister could meet him there if necessary.

He found that the rear of the apartments were almost clear of anyone around because of all the commotion in the front.

He limped along the alley way behind Windward Avenue to Main Street and stopped in front of the bicycle shop on the corner of Main. He looked into the picture window using it as a mirror to assess the cut on his face. It seemed to have stopped bleeding and was more superficial than he thought. He was just a block off of Windward Circle and there was a cab stand in front of the Bank of America. He headed back into the alley way behind the shops and searched through the trash for something to put over the blood stains on his shirt.

The County guys were using blow torches to cut the metal bars that the body was hanging on. The apartment manager was now yelling at them.

"Who's going to pay for this?"

"Don't get your panties in a wad." One of the officers told him. "Come to the office tomorrow and fill out the forms to get reimbursed."

"Hell that will take forever. This is bullshit!"

They handed him their card with the main address and phone number on it. "This is the best we can do right now. You'll have to move back while we finish."

Kathy and Chris had circled the apartments and there was no sight of their suspect or anyone that had seen a suspicious man limping away. They decided to head back into the apartment complex and headed up to the top of the roof. There was a Venice officer in the stairwell heading from the third floor to the roof.

"We need to check it out," Chris said to the officer. "Not now, our forensic team is heading here to take samples and see if there are fingerprints up there."

Chris wanted to push the local guy out of the way but thought better of it. The tug of war between local officials and the Bureau's people was evident in the officer's attitude. "Okay but we go up with them when they get here."

It was agreed that they would be allowed on the roof top with the local team. Kathy and Chris waited for them to arrive.

Tony Kim was now on the loose and looking for a way to get out of the area. Police presence was all around and he stayed in the alley ways and moved along deep shaded streets. He was now just off of Windward Circle behind some of the stores and restaurants. Tony had been searching through the trash behind the bike shop off of Main Street for something to help him escape. His clothes were torn and he had blood stains that would single him out from others on the street. He heard police cars heading up from Pacific Avenue through Windward Circle. At least the action was now a few blocks from his position. He now had two guns, one was his Glock and the other was a Russian made Sig-Sauer that he took off the man that attacked him at his sister's apartment. He would use them if necessary. Tony found a box behind the bike shop with some rags and two stained T-shirts. He tied one of the rags around his thigh to help slow the bleeding from his right leg and pulled the other T- shirts over the top of his. It had the logo of the Pacific Beach Bike shop and he was happy that it could serve as a cover if needed. He could always say that he worked at the shop repairing bikes. Tony moved out of the alley way closer to the street light so he could read the phone numbers on the phone he took from the assailant. He reached into his pocket and pulled the cell phone that he found on the roof top during the fight with the man that attacked him. He looked at the recent call list and froze. "What the hell!" The last three calls were all to Robert Chiarini's private number. It's the same number that Tony used when contacting the Director.

He was puzzled. Who was the man that attacked him? And why?

_____Nineteen

The cab driver looked back as his fare climbed in the back seat. The guy seemed to duck down when he got in. He didn't look like a normal cab ride at this time of night but he had shoved two twenties into the side window. His clothes were dirty and the driver first thought that he was probably homeless. Most of his passengers in this area were tourists. As he turned to look at his passenger he saw the T-shirt of the Bike shop down the street. It made him feel better that at least it was a local guy.

"Where to mister?

"Bora Bora Way."

The cab driver started driving and went through the round-about at Windward Circle. The second right turn took them to Venice Boulevard East and that would lead to Bora Bora Way. The area the man expressed to be taken to was pretty high class. The driver knew it would be busy along that stretch and he would pick up a good fare headed back once he dropped off the man in the back seat. Apartments, condos and three large marinas, along with a bevy of fine restaurants, filled the streets ahead.

"Do you have an address you want me to take you to?"

"I'll let you know when we get there."

At the end of Bora Bora Street led to a large Marina and three popular restaurants.

The cab headed down Venice Boulevard East and over to Ocean Avenue. The driver peeked back at his passenger and thought he resembled someone he had recently seen, but where?

There was no conversation as they headed through the homes that lined Ocean Boulevard.

Once they crossed Washington Boulevard the cab headed down Via Marina. Admiralty Way merged into Via Marina and Bora Bora was the second street past the merger. Boats that lined the slips on the right were all very large and there were expensive apartments and homes on both sides of the road.

"Okay pal let me know where to stop."

"Drop me off just past the side of the Cheesecake Factory."

The area was crowded with dinner guests and Tony instructed him to pull down the street a little further than the restaurant.

"Here's an extra twenty for getting me here so quickly."

"Sure mister."

Tony got out of the cab and watched the driver make a u-turn on Via Marina and head back down the street. The cab got in the line-up of vehicles hoping to catch guests needing a ride from one of the many restaurants. Tony headed back down the walkway that led past the restaurants to Via Marina. The boat slip where he had his boat docked was about a mile down the street. He did this just in case the cab driver eventually recognized him and told someone where he dropped his ride.

Questions filled Tony's mind. Who was the man that attacked him on the roof top? Who sent him? It was becoming clear to him that not only was the FBI after him but now his own organization found him to be a liability.

Tony Kim wasn't going to be easy to get rid of. His boat was fueled and he planned to move it to another location before contacting his sister. He needed to let her know that he was okay.

Sandy Kim was at her cousin's place and they were watching the news coverage that was consuming Channel 6 programming.

They were filming in front of her apartment complex and the reporter was telling viewers that a man had been captured trying to flee from authorities. There weren't any more details and the news team didn't know that the man was dead.

"It can't be Tony. He has to be gone." Sandy Kim paced the room. Her cousin was consoling her and both women hugged. The cell phone that was sitting on the kitchen table went off. Both women jumped. Sandy grabbed it and looked for the caller's number. It flashed unknown.

"Hello?"

The voice was clear. He spoke in Korean and the message was short. "I'm fine."

The two women grabbed each other and cried. "Thank God!"

"I cleaned off everything in your apartment and will be out of the area soon."

"What can I do for you?"

"Nothing, I just need to see who that was on your roof that attacked me. I'll call you once I'm safely out to sea."

Sandy Kim was thrilled that her brother was safe. What did he mean, the man that attacked him on the roof? The phone he used to call his sister was one of the many pre-paid burner cell phones that he had purchased. Tony tossed the cell phone in the deep channel water along his boat and sat on the Sea Ray contemplating his next move.

He needed to trust someone, but whom?

He had eluded the local police and was sure that the FBI was also on the scene. Maybe he needed to try to contact one of the agents that he was trying to abort their mission. He looked again at the cell phone that he found on the roof top. Had his Director planned to eliminate him? He needed to escape but didn't want to be on the run the rest of his life. Tony had only one person he thought could help. It would be very ironic but he decided to take that chance. He might turn to the FBI agent he almost killed. Could it be his last chance to not only get away but not have his own agency hunting him down? Tony had searched Blair's apartment twice before. Once when the CIA wanted to know more about this Blair Adams and again when he tried to get the bomb fragments from the FBI team on the 405. Although he failed in that aspect maybe she would be willing to help him for information that would be valuable to the Bureau.

He had to take that chance.

Twenty

The Market place in Seoul was teaming with people purchasing goods and groceries. It was well known for fresh seafood and meat. Beef was a prime delicacy in Korea. Most of it came from America and Argentina. The price for a good Kobe beef cut was often over $100.00 per pound. Josh had waited across from the warehouse for the strike team that he had called in. The surveillance of the warehouse had shown that the two Russians that Josh had followed were still in there. The Apache Helicopter had been dispatched to do aerial search in case they needed it.

Rusty had called in with critical information on the location of the building that he had been held as a captive. With this information Josh and the team of agents were able to put together a plan to infiltrate the place. They now had it surrounded and planned their move. Josh was leading the team of men with him toward the front entrance. "I'll knock and use the pretext of looking for a shop that I have an appointment for."

Two men were in position at each side of the doorway out of sight. Once Josh had a man occupied at the front of the building another team could enter the rear and make their way into the building and capture whoever was still inside. Rusty's information was that there was no more than three men at the location.

Josh knocked and waited for someone to come to the large sliding door.

One of the other agents had positioned a small truck in front of the door so that no one could escape by driving a vehicle past them.

A large man with full beard and wearing a trench coat appeared in the doorway. "What?" He stood with his arms to his side and his right hand was in his coat pocket.

"I'm here to pick-up the order of cameras."

"Not here! You got wrong place." The big Russian spoke broken English and was waving Josh away.

"This is the address." Josh was holding a piece of paper and thrust it toward the man. "I'm here for my goods that I purchased." Josh was yelling in Korean and the Russian was flustered.

The big man took his hand out from his pocket and grabbed the papers from Josh. When he looked down to read the note, Josh struck the side of his head with a pipe he had hidden and sent the man crashing to the ground. Agents rushed through the back of the warehouse and overtook another man who was in the office area rather quickly. A large man was now running toward the front of the building. Josh was busy cuffing the guy on the ground at the front of the building when the big man came running at him. Two shots rang out and the rushing man crumbled to the ground. The agents behind Josh shot the charging Russian twice and brought him down like a run-away bull. The siege was over in minutes. Two men captured, one dead.

They pulled the dead man from the front doorway into the warehouse. The large man who Josh cuffed was yelling in Russian. Josh looked down at him and spoke the only Russian he knew. "Вы находитесь под арестом." It meant that you are under arrest. The two other agents laughed at that. They now pulled their two captives into the office of the large empty warehouse. Both men kept answering every question in Russian. Neither was being very cooperative and the agents were getting tired of the process.

"Just shoot one of them and I'm sure the other guy will start talking." Josh pulled his weapon out and before he could cock it, they were both speaking good English.

"Okay, that's better. Now who are you working for?"

"Don't know their name."

"Bullshit, someone is paying you and you don't work for free. Again, who are you working for?"

The two men sat silently. One of the agents dragged the dead man's body into the office. "We can bury all three of them in here." He stepped over the body now at his feet.

One of the captives looked at the body of his Comrade.

"Make sure he's dead," Josh said.

The two men jumped when the other agent took his gun out and shot the dead body in the head. "I think he's dead now. Who's next?"

That's all it took. They were singing like humming birds. Every question was answered and the agents had written all the details down. They now also found the packet that Rusty had gotten from the old Korean at the Castle. Josh studied it. It was written in Korean. He could read and write Korean and he stood in the corner of the office scanning the information.

It gave the location of the warehouse where the bombs were stored near the airport. There was a map with directions to the building that was located just inside the Seoul Airport storage fence. The men were still answering questions when Rusty arrived with the agents that met him at his place.

Josh turned to see him coming in the building. "Happy that you're okay. We got everything we need here."

Rusty saw the packet that Josh held and was happy they got the information back. "Okay but I still have a score to settle." Rusty took out the gun that he got from the now dead Russian. "I need my phone and gun back, now!"

The two men looked at each other. Rusty stood over them waiting for an answer. He looked down at the man to his right.

"What's your name?"

"Dimitri."

"Okay Dimitri, where the hell is my gun and cell phone?" He was pointing the gun at the man's crotch.

"Don't know."

Okay asshole," Rusty shot Dimitri in the right leg.

"Now again, where is my shit?"

Dimitri screamed in agony and the other captured man pointed toward the large desk in the corner of the office. Rusty moved over there and started to pull open drawers. There were papers and photos of planes in the top drawer. "Josh, take a look at these." As Josh came over to check out the documents, Rusty kept checking the desk. He found his gun, a pearl handled beauty. His dad had given him the pistol when he joined the Bureau. It was a classic Colt 45 that officers carried during the early 60's. It wasn't approved by the agency but Rusty always carried it with him. His dad was the Police Chief in Philadelphia and he was so proud of Rusty joining the FBI. He gave his son the gun that he had carried for years on the force. It meant a lot to Rusty and he was glad to get it back. He found his cell phone and identification in there too. He holstered the gun and put the cell phone in his pocket. Rusty turned toward the men. "I've got just one more thing, which one of you assholes hit me?"

Neither man answered.

"Okay, no sweat off my back." Rusty pulled out his gun and shot Dimitri again, this time in the left leg.

"Now let's try that again. Which one of you hit me?"

Dimitri cried out in pain. He was yelling in Russian but Rusty was now pointing his gun at his head.

"One more chance big guy."

"He was the one." He was pointing at the dead man on the ground.

Rusty walked back toward the dead body and kicked it. "Okay, I'm good now."

The other agents in the room looked at each other. They had heard that Rusty was pretty cold but none of them had seen him in action before. It was rumored that he was once involved in the chase for Saddam in Iraq. Rusty was a tough son-of-a-bitch.

The agents grabbed their two captives. Dimitri was crying for help after being shot in the legs. They dragged him along not paying attention to his cries for help. They put both of them in the truck.

Josh told them, "We better get the dead body out of here too." They tossed him into the back with the two captives and headed out of the market place.

"Let's clean the place in case some of their crew returns." Josh was running the show and everyone was following his orders.

"Thanks for letting me get even," Rusty appreciated what Josh did.

"Well now we have bigger fish to fry. If this information is correct there is another bomb planted on a plane. We have to try to stop it from going off." They were looking at the photos that Rusty found in the drawer. One picture was of Asian Air 792 that went down near Newport Beach. There were photos of many other planes. "Oh Shit!" Rusty had a worried look on his face. "Does it give us any details on the planes, or where they are headed?"

"No, but if I am reading this correctly the information is in that building by the airport. We need to send a warning to the Director. They have to make sure every plane carrying mostly Americans is searched before it leaves Seoul."

"Yes but what if it is already in the air?"

"We've got to hope we can find out which plane or we'll have another tragedy."

The success of his team in Seoul was little comfort to Robert Chiarini. He must tell the President and Head of Homeland Security that there may be another plane headed to the States with a bomb on it.

His team hadn't found out who is responsible yet but the news of a second plane possibly going down won't help matters. Chiarini's other problem was bigger for him personally. He hadn't heard from his man that was assigned to eliminate Tony Kim. He didn't plan to contact him yet but was getting anxious. Things were starting to unravel for the CIA Director. He needed answers and time was running out. He had spent more time in his Falls Church location in the past two days than in the entire last year.

The information that the CIA Director brought to the White House only caused greater concerns for President Morgan. The nation had been waiting for a response to the bombing of flight 792 for close to a day-and-half and the only information so far was that a Russian team in Seoul was involved. Now they are finding out that a second plane might be brought down with a similar bomb. Who was to blame? Was there a third party trying to bring the United States to declare war on either North Korea or Russia? The President needed answers not more questions.

The information was passed on to Frank Fitzgerald who was now in Los Angeles and on the scene helping his team. They didn't have any leads except that an Asian man may have been responsible for trying to impede their investigation.

President Morgan knew the opposition to his re-election wouldn't wait much longer to jump on the bandwagon of the administration's failed foreign policies. How many lives would it cost and why hadn't the most powerful nation on earth solved this? Politics was alive and thriving and there was enough blame to go around. The President had been filled in on the action in Seoul. The CIA team was embarking on the mission at the warehouse located at the Seoul Airport. He hoped that would bring some answers.

_Twenty One

The news of the manhunt in Venice Beach was relayed to Blair and Jim at the hospital. "We need to head there right now," she told him. "I know the area real well. My friend lives in those same apartments." She hadn't heard back from her friend that worked at the Sidewalk Café on the identification of the man that showed on his tax returns that he once worked there.

"Let's head back to my place for a minute then over to Venice Beach."

"Maybe we should call it in to the boss first."

"We aren't sure what, if there is anything we can do, so let's first try something then we'll call it in."

Jim knew that Booth always said Blair ran with her gut feelings and they were often right. "Okay, I'm with you." "I'm going in to tell Booth first." She walked back down the hall and was met by the duty nurse.

"It's too soon to go back in."

"I know but we have to head out for a little. I'll just say goodbye."

"I'm going with you."

"Don't think so. I have to tell him something critical about a case and you can't be there. I'll just be thirty seconds." She left the nurse standing there in the hall. Booth looked like he was sleeping. Blair leaned over him and looked back at the doorway. It was clear.

"I'll be back baby. Love you." She kissed Booth on the cheek and softly touched his face.

"Okay we're out of here!" She announced to Jim as she came back into the waiting area. She was almost running down the hall and he had to pick up the pace to stay with her. "My place is in the Marina and I need to grab some stuff first." Jim knew better than to argue with her. They headed to the car and she gave him directions.

"I haven't been to the Marina del Rey area in a long time," he said. "We used to go there for the 4th of July fireworks show every year."

Blair was punching in information to her cell phone and just nodded. A few minutes later her phone rang.

"Sorry I didn't return your call before but I had to work a double." Her friend was just getting off of work and saw the text from Blair.

"I need to know if you every worked with a guy named Choi Chung at the Café?"

"Never heard of anyone with that name, why?"

"He listed that he was employed last year as an employee of the Sidewalk Café. We need to find him."

"Are you still in the office working this late?"

Blair had told her close friends that she only did research for the government in her new assignment. "Yes, it's important."

"Hey Blair, I'm turning off of Windward Circle and there must be ten police cars all over the place. I wonder what's going on."

"I'm not sure. I'm just getting off the 90 at Lincoln Avenue. I was going to ask you if you were home. The news is running a story that said a fugitive was seen near your place."

"When did you see it?"

"When I was leaving the office I saw the breaking news in the lobby. Maybe you better not go home yet."

"I'm going to stop and ask a cop what is going on. I'll call you back. Are you done working for the night?"

"Kind of, I need to check something out first. Call and tell me what you find out."

Jim listened and waited for Blair to let him know what was going on.

"Okay my friend never heard of Choi at the Café and she's been there a long time. She said there are Venice Police cars all over the area by her apartment. She lives just off of Windward Circle. Something is not right. If they caught the guy why are they still searching the area?"

That made sense to Jim. "Why are we stopping by your place?"

"I've been in these same clothes for over twenty-four hours and just have to change real quickly." Blair's phone rang again. She answered as Jim continued following her directions to her place. They turned off of Lincoln in front of the Toyota dealership and onto Admiralty Way. The right lane was closed so Jim merged left and at the end of the road turned left on Via Marina. They passed the Cheesecake Factory on the left and headed to the Mariners Village Apartments.

Blair was still talking to her friend from the Sidewalk Café.
"Blair there must be ten police cars all around the place. The cop I asked only said it might not be safe to go to my apartment and that they had the place blocked off."
"Okay, do you still have a key to my place?"
"Yes."
"Go there and spend the night. I'm just on my way and we will figure this out."
"Thanks."
Just as she hung up Blair's phone rang again.

_____Twenty Two

Tony Kim decided to take the chance. He was running out of options and he needed to trust someone. Maybe Blair Adams would be the one. When he had searched her apartment earlier he found her cell phone number listed on the inside of an address book. He had done some checking on her and found that she had baffled the FBI a few years ago after her husband had sent her a package that they were looking for. Maybe she could be trusted. He couldn't afford to get his sister involved and now that Chiarini had sent someone to clean up the mess and kill him he was desperate. If he could get her to help maybe he could disappear.

Blair was doing most of the listening on the phone when they passed Bora Bora Way, Blair hollered, "Stop!"

Jim hit the brakes, "What is it?"

"Turn left into the Marina." She held the phone in her right hand and pointed toward the line of boats off to the left of them.

Jim was happy no one rear ended him after the sudden stop. He pulled into the Marina and slowed down when Blair told him to.

"There, right over there." She was pointing to a man that was standing on the bow of a large Sea Ray in the third slip off the road. "You need to pull over and let me out."

"What the hell. Let you out here?"

"Don't ask me anything yet. Just trust me."

Jim pulled into a spot near the third slip and watched as she got out of the car. He was confused and wondered what the hell was going on. "Why don't you let me come with you?"

"Not yet, I've got to do this myself."

The call to her was a calculated risk. He told her that he had important information about the man that tried to kill her and her partner. "You need to come alone. I will only talk to you and you must not contact anyone. If you do, you will never find out why all this happened."

She agreed to the request and he gave her directions to where they could meet. Jim was watching her as her expression seemed to tell him the call was of grave importance.

When Tony called her he was stunned to find out she was right in front of the Marina. Tony didn't know what to think. Had she discovered his identity? Was she following him from the apartments in Venice Beach? If so maybe he didn't hold the upper hand. Tony wished he had more time to plan the meeting but he needed to solve his current situation.

Jim was beginning to wish he never went to the hospital with her. "If something happens to her the Boss will have my ass. "Why me," he said aloud while sitting alone in the car.

"That's far enough. You need to take your gun out and put it down on the bench along the side of the railing."

"You know I can't do that," she answered. "I'm a Federal Agent and it would be suicide to come any further without a weapon. How about we talk from here?" She could see that he was slight built and although it was dark he appeared to be Asian. He definitely resembled the sketch of the man they were searching for. He was leaning against the cabin of the Sea Ray and had a tourniquet around his leg. Was this their suspect? She had to be sure.

"This is a golden opportunity for both of us." Tony started the conversation.

"I'm listening."

"I also work for the Federal government and it appears that you and me are caught up in the middle of something bigger than both of us."

She was puzzled. How did he get her number? What did he mean he worked for the government too? "Who do you work for?"

"I report to only one person, the Director of the CIA. He is my boss and authorized this mission."

Blair took a deep breath and looked back at Jim in the car. "I need to make sure my partner doesn't get out of the car, can I call him?"

"How do I know you don't have a sniper trained on me right now?"

"I guess you have to believe me if you want me to believe you. You can listen to my call. I'll move closer if that's okay."

"Okay."

"Jim, this guy has important information for us and I need you to stay right there. Do not call anyone, understand?"

"Okay but this doesn't make any sense." Jim was concerned but followed her directions.

She moved closer and saw a bench along the side of the boat and sat down. "Okay, first tell me what happened to your leg?"

"That's not important right now. I'm finding it hard to trust someone because my boss just sent someone to take me out."

Blair leaned forward. "What!"

"I was trying to get out of the area and was attacked by a man who tried to kill me. I found out that he was sent by my boss and I need to get to someplace safe."

"So, I'm guessing that you're the son-of-a-bitch that tried to kill me and my partner on the freeway."

Tony Kim nodded.

"Why in the hell would I try to help you?"

"I have information that you and your boss will want. I'll give it to you in return for my safe passage out of the area. Once this is over you will have to promise that somehow I don't exist. I can't take a chance of the agency tracking me down."

"What is the CIA doing operating in California anyway?"

He didn't answer her.

"Okay, then why did you crash into us?"

"My orders were to get the bomb fragments from you before you got to your office. I tried to get them from the FAA guy but was too late. I didn't have any other options."

"Why try to kill us?"

"I was trying to complete my mission. If you were ordered to, wouldn't you take someone out?"

Blair knew he was right. In the name of patriotism both the CIA and FBI were responsible for terrible acts.

"Okay, what is this important information?"

"I have the cell phone from the assassin that was assigned to take me out. It has conversations from my boss Robert Chiarini on it confirming his involvement in all of this. I also have the details from his call to me that I will give you regarding trying to scuttle your investigation."

"How do you know that I won't just go ahead and use this without promising you anything?"

"I don't know for sure, but I have to trust someone and from what I've found out I think you can be trusted."

Jim continued watching from the car and felt better when he saw Blair sitting on the bench talking to the contact. He wondered how she found this guy and who was he? When did she have the time to do all of this?

"I'm not sure the phone conversation will be enough evidence without you coming in too. I need more proof."

"That can't happen. I'll never get out alive, and lady, I want to live a little longer. I have a lot of details that your people will want and can use to resolve the conflict between our agencies on this issue."

This all sounded too good to be true. "Okay, we've got to trust each other. I'll come aboard and check out your information. If it is as you say I'll do everything to help you accomplish your goal as long as I can accomplish mine."

"Come on up."

Twenty Three

It was almost daylight and the County Coroner was
ready to release his findings. The man that was found dead at
the apartments was not the suspect that the police and FBI
were chasing. Although his identity had not been verified
they were now using facial recognition techniques. His
features did not match that of the suspect. The LA Bureau
had sent a crime lab team to the county to assist in the
identification. Frank Fitzgerald had contacted the Los
Angeles County Chief and detailed the national implications
of the investigation. They also informed the California Bureau
of Investigation on their progress. The two men agreed on a
shared operation. Fitzgerald knew that once they had the
suspect in custody, either dead or alive, the case would revert
back to the feds.

Steve Orrison wasn't sure how this new dead body fit
into the equation and exactly who killed him but it all has to
be part of the puzzle. Because they were so busy with this
situation neither he nor anyone in the office thought about
Blair or Jim. The last they knew they were both at the hospital
checking on Booth. It was close to four a.m. and they must
have both gone home they figured.

Blair had been on the Sea Ray with Tony for over an
hour and once she had a good look at his information she
motioned Jim to come aboard. She filled him in on what the
agreement was and the last part would be how to get Tony
out of the area without revealing his whereabouts.

The Marina was pretty quiet at that time of night and their conversation had lasted until the wee hours of the morning. Blair looked at Jim. "I've got an idea but you're not going to like it."

"So far I don't like any of this, so try me."

Tony intently listened to the conversation. Blair had looked at his leg earlier and changed his bandage. In doing so they put the blood soaked bandages in a bag. She also checked the gash on his face and used some of the medical supplies from the cabin to clean it up as best as she could. "We agree that the information and this cell phone will give the boss and our Director all the ammunition they will need to take care of your boss and the CIA."

"Agreed."

"The goal is to find out who bombed the plane and why we were crashed into on the freeway."

Jim moved to the edge of the padded seat in the cabin. "Okay, continue."

Blair nodded, "Tony will be hunted down by whoever is left in charge of the CIA. Our last thing will be to make sure that doesn't happen."

"I won't agree to anything that doesn't protect me," Tony was adamant about that.

"I'm getting to my idea. We kill Tony here in the Marina."

"Wait a damn minute!" Tony stood up waving his hands.

"Hold on, I'm getting to the good part."

Both men were now both standing and looking at Blair like she lost her mind.

"We're going to say that we stumbled on you when Jim was driving me home and before we could call it in, we got in a shoot out. We will take some of the bloody bandages and put them on the rocks.

If you're not opposed to shedding a little more blood we'll put it on the pier where I supposedly shot you. You fall into the ocean and they will never find your body. The CIA figures your dead. We'll have two FBI agents swearing that we shot you and have some blood to match to your DNA."

"One big problem is that my DNA has never been cataloged for a comparison."

"Maybe you're right. But the fallen CIA Director will be forced to release whatever data he has on you. Chiarini will be done for. They must have taken some samples somewhere down the line."

Tony stopped to think about her proposal.

"Let's say you're right but it still depends on Chiarini giving up the data. The group is a black ops operation and he will never admit that he had such a clandestine team in the States. A few years ago when it was rumored that there was such a group he testified at a Senate hearing that it had been disbanded before he was appointed."

"What was this group's name back then?"

"Code name was Silverstone."

"If we can link him to the continued operation of this Silverstone group and produce this evidence he'll have no choice."

That's when Tony told her about the Falls Church bunker. It almost sounded like a Hollywood movie version. There couldn't be a place like that, could there? She had all the material to bring the CIA Director down. Blair continued to detail her plans to Jim and Tony.

Jim shook his head. "Do you stay up all night thinking of this crap?"

"Shit I hate to say this but it makes sense to me," Tony said. "I can still use my boat to escape and we might even use a spot that some tourist will witness the killing."

"I've got it!" Blair jumped up. "The south side of the channel runs close to LAX.

We can say we spotted you and chased you to the point by the rock ledge. It feeds right out to the Pacific. Everyone around here knows that the current is very strong and by the time they get a team to drag the water your body will have floated far out to sea."

Jim leaned back, "Shit now this is starting to make sense to me. I must have been hanging out with you way too much."

They all agreed. The plan was for Blair and Tony to take the boat to that spot. Jim will travel there by car and park just east of the apartments on the far side of the channel. Tony will dock his boat along the other side and once they have the shoot out and he falls into the water he can swim back to his boat. They will call it all in and wait for a team from the Bureau. Blair wanted to stay with Tony in case he changed his mind.

They still didn't have the answer to the bombing of the plane but at least Blair and Jim would have solved one problem and would have the goods on the CIA. They knew that Fitzgerald would love that aspect.

The sky looked weird with dark clouds hovering low to the ocean in front of them. They put their plan into motion. It would be light soon and everything had to go perfect. The Marina would be quiet except for a few fishing boats filled with day fishers. The charters usually left around seven in the morning so they had an hour before any of them would cast off.

The Sea Ray bobbed in the water as Tony headed through the Marina and out to the channel. The sun was just rising in the east and the sky was starting to lighten up when he pulled the boat to the designated spot along the south side of the channel. He waited until Blair confirmed that Jim was ready.

Jim called with some details. "I found a perfect spot at the far end of the rock ledge that is about fifty feet past the end of the bike path."

They agreed that it would fit their needs.

"I'm sorry that I caused you and your partner any harm. How is he doing?"

"He'll be okay in a while but he's pretty banged up. You should have asked about him earlier, he's a great guy."

"You're pretty cool to Blair Adams."

"I'm going to enjoy killing you Tony Kim."

Tony had some blanks in the cabin that he had used on another operation and gave both Jim and Blair a few. They decided that they would each use two blanks first and aim at each another. Tony would fall into the water after the second shots and then the pair of agents would use live rounds. We'll get rid of the blank shells before anyone gets here. Jim knew a shooting would mean an internal investigation.

It was all set and Tony headed to the rendezvous spot first. Blair followed a few minutes later and met Jim along the bike path. There were a few men just returning from the end of the path on their bikes and Tony passed them. He purposely limped badly and made sure they noticed him. It was now close to six forty five and the light from the rising sun was bringing the beach to life. Tony kept looking back as if he was being chased. The bike riders turned twice to watch this stranger.

Blair took out her cell phone and called the action in. "This is Agent Adams, this is an emergency I need to talk to the boss right away."

The call was patched through to Steve's cell phone. He was at Shutters Hotel in Santa Monica picking up Frank Fitzgerald.

"Boss, Jim and I think we've spotted our guy. He's running along the south side of the marina at the end of Admiralty Way."

"Great proceed with caution. I'll call it into our guys and you two continue to track him."

"I got it Sir."

"Why are you both out at this time on the Marina?"

"Jim had dropped me off last night after the hospital and he was picking me up when we spotted him. I'm sure he's the guy."

"We are in Santa Monica and should be there shortly. Try to hang back and not spook him."

She turned to Jim and said, "Everything is in place. Once Tony was in place they put the plan into action. Jim yelled, "There he is!" He and Blair were running and passed the two bikers. "Stop, FBI."

Now the two men on the bikes stopped and turned to watch the action. Shots rang out from the suspect who was limping along toward the edge of the channel as the two agents chased him. Both men on bikes hit the ground as more shots came from the direction of the two that were chasing the suspect. Must have been two or three shots in all when one of the bikers looked up to see the suspect grab his chest and fall backward into the foaming water. The two agents that were chasing the man shot another round as they continued charging to the ledge. The bikers turned around and started to head to the action. They watched the two people who were chasing the man now climb on the rock ledge and into the wash of water over the large rocks. One of them appeared to look like he was trying to climb down into the water. Waves crashed against the rocks getting both of them soaked. People were pointing from the other side of the channel. The morning had brought out walkers and people taking their dog to the beach. It was hard to make out clear details from that side but they saw some arms pointing their way.

Sirens surrounded the area and within minutes a patrol car was seen but on the wrong side of the channel.

The two men that had been on bikes had dropped their bikes in the sand about ten feet from where the two agents were fighting the raging tide.

"Do you need help?" One of them yelled.

Blair looked up and hollered, "You better stay back, we think we got him but have to make sure."
Jim was now drenched and climbing back up the rocks. He could be heard telling Blair, "The tide pulled him away from me. I had grabbed his jacket but the waves pulled him loose and all I got was the jacket. He went right under. The current dragged him below and I couldn't do anything else. He's got to be dead."

There were more people now coming out of the apartments and you could see a few more pointing from the marina. Tony Kim went under as planned and came up a few hundred yards from the action. Like many Silverstone agents he had tremendous training underwater and could swim ten times further than most men. He was able to tread water and make his way back to the Sea Ray that was moored a hundred yards from all the action. Everyone was looking at the end of the channel and no one was paying attention to the man getting out of the water and onto the boat. A rowing crew was just coming into view as Tony pulled into the main channel and headed out to sea.

Three men were now running along the bike path and headed to the spot where all the action took place. A black Suburban was flying down the beach from the south and two more vehicles were right behind it. The area was now surrounded by FBI agents and two California Patrol units joined them.

Blair sat along the rocks holding the jacket that Jim had given her. She placed the cell phones that Tony had given them in the pocket.

Although the jacket was wet, the phone would not soak up enough water to compromise its data.

She wanted it all to look good for both the news coverage and the cover story for the CIA. After all she gave Tony her word and planned on keeping it. Now she had to explain all this to the Bureau Chief.

Jim had placed the blood soaked bandages onto the top ledge of rocks. He also made sure some of the blood samples ended up in the sand where Tony had grabbed his chest. How this would all play out would be anyone's guess.

Twenty Four

The shoot-out in Marina del Rey filled the morning news. Television stations were rushing to the scene. Steve Orrison stood along the rock ledge with the Director looking into the water. White foam washed up on the boulders as the two men seemed puzzled by all that had happened. Forensic teams had been summoned and Blair handed Steve the jacket from the man that disappeared into the swift current. Two other agents were searching the scene and bagging shells found along the path. They followed the track that Jim had shown them where they chased the suspect. The evidence was verifying the story the agents gave and the blood along the ledge was being preserved by the team that would try to get DNA evidence. Following protocol the two agents handed their weapons to the investigative team that arrived. They would be questioned separately to make sure their stories matched up. Agents were taking details from two men who said they witnessed the whole thing.

"We were riding our bikes back from the end of the trail when a man, probably Asian, ran limping past us. All of a sudden two people were chasing him and they called out that they were FBI."

The second man jumped in. "I knew the guy looked familiar."

They nodded when shown the picture of the suspect
from the drawing the FBI had circulated. It was all coming
together just as they were being told.

The witness continued telling their story. "The guy that was
being chased shot first, maybe a couple of rounds. We hit the
ground and the two FBI guys started shooting back."

"When did you know that the two people chasing him
were FBI?"

"I guess it was right away. They hollered to stop and
then called out that they were Federal Agents."

"Were any shots fired before they called out that they
were with the FBI?"

"No, the man being chased started shooting right after
that."

The witness statements helped clear the agents of any
wrong doing. It was always a concern especially when a
suspect was killed in the action. The investigation continued
with witness statements being taken and forensic material
gathered. The entire area was roped off and Steve Orrison
made sure his team was putting all the evidence and data
together.

Blair and Jim were sitting on the back of the Suburban
being attended to by a medic. Jim had cuts on his right arm
and hand where he fought the tide trying to grab the suspect.
Blair just sat there quietly. Steve walked over and checked on
his two agents.

"How are you two?"

Jim looked up. "Good boss, just surface cuts."
Blair hadn't said anything.

"I thought you would go home after leaving the
hospital, not get into a shoot out." Steve was concerned about
his agent and just couldn't figure out how she got involved in
this chase.

"I was going home and Jim was taking me there. Then I got this call. There is more to this story Boss but we've got to do this somewhere else."

Steve Orrison had a puzzled look on his face. "Okay, where do you have in mind?"

"Maybe we should go back to the office." Steve knew something was wrong. Blair was too subdued after such an exciting event and the killing of the key suspect from the accident on the 405. "Do you want to tell me anything else first?"

"No, Jim and I will lay it all out for you but don't blame Jim for any of this. It was all my idea."

Steve didn't know what to think now. "Just answer one question. Was the man that you shot the suspect we were seeking?"

"Yes Sir."

Steve wasn't sure what was going on. All the information was adding up. Blair and Jim found the suspect, chased him and shot him in a gun fight. Everything made sense until now. What was Blair meaning?

"Frank we need to let the team do their work here and we'll head back to the office. Blair and Jim want to fill us in about the shooting. She said there is more to the story."

"Is everything okay?"

"I'm not sure. They said there is more information that we need to know but will only share it with us."

"Okay, let's do it."

Word spread that the FBI had caught their suspect and all the local police along with the California Bureau of Investigation were given a stand down order. The FBI would have their forensic guys do the DNA investigation and finalize the report with a courtesy copy to the head of the California Bureau. One part of the case had been solved.

Steve and Frank headed back to Wilshire Avenue and the FBI building and Frank called the Director of Homeland Security. "Orrison's team captured and killed their suspect in the crash on the 405. I'll have more details once we interview the two agents involved."

Blair and Jim sat quietly in the back seat.

Frank was updated on the CIA action in Seoul and that their agents were searching the Seoul airport for possible links to the second bomb.

It wasn't confirmed if the second bomb was already planted on a plane that left or was in progress. Every plane leaving Seoul that day had been re-routed to the closest airport for inspection. There had been three that took off earlier and were all routed to Hawaii's International airport in Honolulu.

The ride back to the office was quiet except for the occasional question from the Director. Jim had given his car keys to another agent that would bring his vehicle into the office. Blair finally spoke.

"Director I have to tell you and Mr. Orrison the full details of the shooting today. Everything I tell you is of my doing; Jim didn't have anything to do with this."

"Oh no," Jim interrupted. "We were in this together." Blair patted his hand, "Thanks Jim."

Fitzgerald turned in the passenger seat and looked back at her. "You can't surprise me. I've heard some dandy's in my time."

"Well there is one big surprise in this one."

"I'm guessing you didn't kill the suspect."

Blair looked stunned that the Director figured that out. "No we didn't, but more important we got a lot of critical information for you from him."

"So where did you stash him?"

"That is one part I'm afraid you're not going to like."

"Try me."

"I let him go."

Steve swerved the vehicle and jerked his head around. "You What!" The veins in his neck protruded and his face was flushed.

"Hold on Steve," Fitzgerald said. "She must have a good explanation. At least she better."
Blair told them the whole story. She started with Tony Kim calling her and that they met in the marina near her apartment. When she told them about Silverstone and its operation the Director yelled. "I knew it! That son-of-a-bitch is double dealing again."

"We have proof for you sir." She handed Fitzgerald the cell phones that Tony had given her. They had messages from Chiarini detailing that his agent should take-out Tony Kim and report back to him when it was done. She also had a second cell phone that belonged to Tony. It had messages from Chiarini giving him orders to thwart the FBI's investigation into the bomb fragments. "I have dates and times written down that Tony gave us and more details on Silverstone and the operational headquarters."

Frank Fitzgerald was thrilled with the information. He finally had what he needed to get rid of his nemesis. "This is great! Why didn't you bring him? We could have had him testify to all this?"

"He figured if it was reported that he was killed and we had proof of his death that no one would be looking for him in the future. He said regardless if Chiarini was removed or not, someone would always be looking for him. He would never be safe."

They both knew she was right.

"I'm sure he has family or someone he cares about, so he wanted to protect them too." Blair had slumped down in the back seat after explaining all the details to her boss and the Director. "I hope you're not going to fire me for this."

Jim put his arm around her. "Blair did a hell of a job convincing Tony that he needed to trust us. She got him to tell her all the information you would need, and with the two cell phones you have proof to back it up. She was just great."

"You're right," Fitzgerald answered. "You both did great. I still have a few questions."

Steve got off of highway 10 at the La Brea exit and headed north to Wilshire Avenue.
He let the Director handle the rest of the conversation. The two agents continued to answer his questions as Steve drove to the office. Fitzgerald said, "The official report will show that Tony Kim was shot twice by the FBI agents and died at the scene."

The two agents nodded.

_____Twenty Five

Josh Smith led his team of agents to the warehouse at the Seoul airport. The information that they got from the Russians gave them the exact location of the storage area that was used in the bombings. The top men that operated out of the unit were said to be of Russian and Korean mixed ancestry. The unit did not appear to be guarded from the outside but that could be a decoy so as not to attract attention. Intel said that there was a high degree of weapons and men stationed inside the unit. Josh's team still did not have an answer on what country was responsible for the tragedy. The main concern now was to stop another plane from being blown out of the sky.

The Seal strike team was amassed outside the row of buildings. Josh and his group were to handle the second wave in the attack. Teams of agents and South Korean police were searching two planes that had been scheduled to depart to Los Angles within the next few hours. One plane had taken off for San Francisco two hours earlier. The FAA was contacting that plane and advising it to land in Hawaii. All the passengers would be deplaned and the aircraft would be inspected.

There were three other planes that left for various destinations earlier in the day.

Messages went to those pilots to divert their routes to the nearest airport possible. Every plane would be searched before allowing it to return to the air.

The CIA didn't want the news of the search or the planes being grounded to get out until they uncovered more information.

The building they now targeted was on the airport outer rim past the runways. There were four similar buildings in the same rows that were used by companies that had large shipments being sent airfreight to North America. Korean goods were in high demand due to the cost and the quality being very good. Much better than the Chinese knock-offs. They shipped mostly leather goods including shoes, purses and coats. Most bore names of fashion designers and found their way into high end department stores like Macy's, Neiman-Marcus and Bloomingdales.

The building the CIA was interested in was at the end of the row and closest to the high fence that surrounded the airport grounds. Agents were clearing everyone from the first three buildings as Josh and his team moved into place. It was critical to take everyone alive. They needed to gather all the information on where bombs may have been planted. Once they accomplished this they may be able to track who was responsible for the bombing of flight 792.

President Morgan and his National Security team were in the White House Situation Room watching a feed from the action taking place live. This was the first time since former President Obama watched the killing of Osama Bin Laden from the same spot that a live feed was employed. Robert Chiarini was describing the action of his team as the President leaned in closer to the monitor. The results of this event could affect what action the President's administration would take.

The investigation of the bombing of flight 792 was in the third day and unless something broke soon the President would face a loss of confidence from the American people.

Maybe this was the break he hoped for.

The CIA along with Seal team six were amassed along the outer walls of the small building.

It was dusk and all the men involved had night vision equipment. Chiarini was telling the group, "My team will solve this and get us the answers we need. We will handle this for you Sir."

The element of surprise was in favor of the strike team. General Armstrong of the United States Navy looked back at Chiarini. "Your people are there to back-up the action, my team is in charge. We will take these men and get your answers Mr. President."

Morgan waved both men off as he moved to the seat to the right of the monitor. The room became very quiet as they watched the team move closer to the front of the building. Men had surrounded the small warehouse and had their weapons aimed and ready for action. Two men rammed the front door as three more team members dashed inside the building. Shots rang out from inside and the Seals responded with gun fire. The first of Seal team six rolled onto the ground and came up behind two large crates off to the right side of the unit. He barked out orders to hold their fire as he used his night vision to locate where the shots were coming from. They wanted to take the men alive but needed to defend their position.

Josh and Rusty were now outside the building with their vehicle in position making sure no one escaped. The Navy Seals had pinned the gun fire down and could see that it was all coming from men that were in the back corner of the building. Their view was obstructed by the large crates stacked up in front of them.

Shots continued to come from that same area but now they were staggered.

Maybe the men didn't have a lot of ammo.

The warehouse was about sixty feet wide and a hundred feet long. Whoever had been shooting at the Seal team had to be in a spot higher then ground level. The Seal team now had all three of their men inside and in position. They called out a warning to the men that they were surrounded and needed to surrender. They did not get a response.

Just then a vehicle came crashing out of the back wall of the building sending men jumping to get out of the way. It was a large black military Humvee that left a large gaping hole in the side of the warehouse. Just as it crashed out of the side gunfire sprayed across the front entrance keeping the Seals down.

The men inside were responding to the gunfire coming from the back corner of the warehouse. Josh kept his vehicle in position just outside the building in case he would be needed. The Seal team in the back of the warehouse broke through the barrier that held the back door closed. Once they were inside they could see a man exposed on a ledge firing toward the front of the building. They now had him cornered and were able to subdue him. He had run out of bullets and held his hands up as two Seals grabbed him. They had him on the ground and called to their team members that the building was secured.

Seal team six had one man in custody inside the warehouse. The action had everyone in the Situation Room jumping in their seats as the noise of rapid gun fire erupted and then the sound of a vehicle crashing through the walls. President Morgan and General Armstrong were now standing and listening to the chatter as Josh and the Seal teams chased the escaped Humvee.

Rusty radioed back to the head of the Seal team that he was in pursuit of a black military truck that was headed toward the gated area east of the airport. The Humvee was going close to seventy miles-an-hour and picking up speed fast.

Rusty pointed his gun out of the passenger window hoping to get a shot at the tires but because they were throwing up so much dust he couldn't get a clean shot off. The black Humvee swerved to the right and made a move toward the eight foot tall barbed wire fence that engulfed the airport. It went crashing through the fence bringing down the two metal poles that held it in place. Josh continued in pursuit as two other vehicles joined the action.

The White House Situation Room is a 5,000 square foot conference style room and intelligence center in the West Wing basement of the White House. It is run by the National Security Council and they stand watch on a 24-hours basis, constantly monitoring world events and keeping senior White House staff and the President appraised of significant events. This was one of those events that had close to 30 senior officers and key members of the President's staff involved. The last time it had this much attention was in 2011 when President Obama and Vice-President Biden received live updates on a mission to capture Osama bin Laden. It was a scene of chaos when the Humvee crashed through the walls of the building surrounded by the Special Forces. The President was standing as he and General Armstrong watched the chase of the escaped suspects from the building at the Seoul airport. Morgan was pressed up against Armstrong's side as the two men peered at the large monitor. Chiarini tried to push his way next to the President but John Martin and General Armstrong had him flanked on both sides. The Secretary of State was holding her head in her hands almost afraid to watch as other members of the staff clutched their fists in front of themselves. It was very tense and the action had everyone on the edge of their seats.

Morgan turned to Armstrong. "Shouldn't they have blocked the area so the men couldn't have tried to drive away?"

"Yes but remember they drove through the side of the building, not an entrance. We had vehicles stationed at both ends of the unit."

President Morgan nodded.

They watched as the black Humvee bounced over the downed chain-linked fence and three vehicles continued their pursuit. The two Seal teams joining the chase had live radio contact that was being fed back to the Situation Room and command staff.

An order went out for air reconnaissance to join the action. A Sikorsky UH 60 Blackhawk and an AH 64 Apache Helicopter took off from the east end of the airport where the U.S. had a station. Army Special Forces used the Blackhawks and they were substantially armed with guns and missiles.

The Seal team radioed that the Humvee was equipped with a hood mounted machine gun. It was probably an older U.S. vehicle that may have been stolen or bought from a third party. Josh wasn't as experienced in this sort of chase and gave way to the Seal teams but followed them. The Blackhawk started to sweep down on the run-away vehicle and was now just ten feet over the rear hatch. The helicopter called out on a loud speaker.

"This is your one warning. You must stop or we will blow you off the road!"

The Humvee quickly turned right to avoid the potential attack and when it did so the vehicle came up on two wheels and almost tipped over. The Seal team following gained ground after that maneuver and was now just fifty feet behind the suspects.

The Blackhawk again swept down like a bird of prey about to pick its target up. A flash came out of the side gun of the attack helicopter and blew a hole in the pavement just in front of the Humvee. It was too close and too late for the vehicle to adjust and they hit the hole with maximum force sending the vehicle end-over-end.

It rolled three or four times before coming to a halt just in front of the chase units. The Navy Seal team jumped into action running out of their vehicle and encircled the Hummer that lay on its side. Guns were drawn as five Seals along with Josh and Rusty stood over the carcass of the wrecked Humvee.

"Get out with your hands up." They approached knowing that the inhabitants must have been thrown around and couldn't have time to aim weapons after the fierce tumbling they took.

One of the members of Seal team six pulled the passenger door opened and grabbed a man who was unconscious and pulled him from the vehicle. The driver's door was thrust open and the man behind the wheel was bloodied and dead. His neck was broken and he did not have a seat belt on so the rolling took its toll. They were surprised to find a third man lying in the back of the vehicle also unconscious. He appeared to have some head wounds and cuts and scrapes but was very much alive.

Cheers went up in the room as President Morgan and General Armstrong high-fived each other. Now that they had captured two men in the Humvee and another in the warehouse they should be able to get information on the bombings.

Morgan hoped that he soon could tell the world that they found and captured the people responsible for this tragedy. Time was slipping away and he needed something soon.

_____Twenty Six

Frank Fitzgerald sat in Steve's office in a quandary.
This would be the second time in recent history that
information from the FBI would lead to the resignation of the
Director of the CIA. Blair had given him all the material and
evidence that Frank's team would need to put the final pieces
together. He couldn't make the same mistakes of a few years
ago in the General David Petraeus case. This was bigger than
an extramarital affair. If all the evidence Fitzgerald had
panned out, then Robert Chiarini defied direct orders. The
President and the Congressional investigation had called for
dismantling of Silverstone. A call to the White House and the
Chiefs of Staff was the next move. The question in his mind
was until they had the responsible party for the bombing
should he wait to tell the President.

Blair and Jim sat with Steve in the conference room
going over the details yet another time. Fitzgerald had sat
with them the first time they went through the explanation
and covered the evidence. Although both men heard the story
on the ride back to the Wilshire office there was too much to
comprehend.

Steve mumbled aloud, "How could the Director of the
CIA attempt such acts? Not only did he continue the
Silverstone operation but he used those men against FBI
personnel."

"Boss, don't forget he also used another Silverstone
agent against Tony Kim, one of his own."

Blair was right. Steve knew all of this was above his pay grade. Fitzgerald would have to decide their next move.

"I'm so sorry that I didn't bring you into the loop sooner," Blair had tears in her eyes. She figured her career was over.

"Hey, I was in it too," Jim responded.

"Don't worry you both did the right thing. You had to make a decision and make it quick. I'm sure Tony Kim would have taken off from the Marina and never been heard of. None of this would have come out and we needed to know." Steve was proud of his team.

The door to the conference room opened and Fitzgerald came in. "I'm going to wrap all this material together in a neat little package. The White House will be brought up to speed but I'm not sure we need to do it now."

Blair and Jim looked at each other. "What do you need us to do Sir?"

"I want you to leave out the part about making a deal with Kim. It only complicates the issue at hand. If we say you shot him and his body was washed away at sea it allows us to concentrate on the facts not the decision to let him go."

"What if he re-surfaces?"

"That's always a possibility but you have his version of what happened and the cell phone conversations to use in case there is a trial. We can always say we were sure he was dead."

"Understood."

"Steve, I need you to have Blair and Jim put all their evidence and details together. I want you to make sure we are protected so let's make a copy of everything including recording the phone messages. I don't want anything to disappear."

"We have been going over it all again," Steve said. "I will transcribe the material myself and have duplicates made for you."

"Keep the second copy in your safe here."

"Yes Sir."

Frank started to leave the room and turned around. "This should go without saying but I'll say it anyway. There is never, and I mean never to be any discussion with anyone about this. Am I clear on that?"

Blair and Jim nodded that they understood.

"When this comes out, and it will be big news, I plan to leave everyone here out of the equation if possible. It won't do any of us any good to have you in the news too. Of course I'll have to tell the President that members of the LA Bureau were involved and that is all I hope to have to tell him."

Steve stood up, "We will iron all of this out today and have it for you. My only question is, when asked, how will you say that the evidence came your way."

"That's a good question. My benefit is that I was on the scene and can say that I was personally involved in the chase for the deep cover agent. I hope the evidence will more than answer everyone's questions. I cannot tell you how proud I am of this team. You did the right things for the best interest of the Country."

"Thank you." Blair and Jim smiled for probably the first time since this all started.

Frank shut the door to the conference room and Steve walked around the table. He put his hand on Blair's shoulder. "I know you feel responsible for making the decision but like Jim said, you are a team. Booth would be proud of what you did."

She nodded. "Once we are done I need to go back to check on him." She felt guilty because she hadn't thought about Booth since she left the hospital.

"Sure."

Fitzgerald walked back into Steve's office and dialed the White House. He knew the important thing was still to find out who bombed flight 792 so he would wait to update President Morgan of who tried to stop the FBI investigation.

When he called he was informed that the President was in the Situation Room with the Chiefs' of Staff. "Patch me through."

Morgan had been standing with General Armstrong and John Martin when the call came in. "I'll take it here," he said.

"Sorry to break in Sir," Fitzgerald knew if Morgan couldn't talk he would tell him.

"Go ahead Frank, what have you got?"

"We captured or should I say we got the man that tried to thwart our investigation here. He's dead but I have material for your eyes only that I need to give you on my return."

"Do you have any lead on who's involved in the bombing?"

"Only that the bombs are Russian made and at least ten years old. They could easily have been on the black market and who perpetrated this is still unknown. I plan to return to Washington this evening."

"Good. We have just captured two men in Seoul that may be able to lead us to who was responsible for bombing flight 792 and now we are concerned about another bomb planted on a flight out of Seoul."

"Is there anything we can do here Sir?"

"No, but I hope soon go on the air to announce that we have in custody the men that planted the bomb on flight 792 and that we should soon have the persons responsible. I need to tell the World that we are making progress and put those responsible in a position of concern. I'll call you if we have any other news."

The President knew he needed more details before making any announcements. At least some progress had been made.

The two men hung up and Morgan told the Chiefs' that Fitzgerald had secured the man who tried to kill his agents and steal the bomb fragments. Everyone was pleased in the room.

No one noticed the concerned look on Robert Chiarini's face. He wondered what Morgan meant when he said Fitzgerald secured the man. Did the FBI capture Tony Kim? Will he detail what Chiarini was doing? How could all of this have happen?

_____Twenty Seven

The men they captured from the vehicle chase were patched up and taken back to the scene where it all started. The second unit held the man that was captured there. While the second Seal team searched the building they discovered three more Russian made C4 bombs that had the same markings that the dive team found in the wreckage of flight 792. They knew that they had the source of the bombs or at least where they were stored. Now to find out who was responsible?

Josh and Rusty were handling the interrogation of the suspects. The Seal team handled security and staked off the building so that no one would interrupt them. One of the men pulled from the Humvee had a broken left arm and multiple cuts and bruises. The man who had been found in the back of the vehicle seemed to have only a bad bruise on his forehead and a few cuts on his arm but surprisingly seemed okay. He had been unconscious and the Seal team was able to bring him to as well as the man in the passenger seat. The body of the driver had been put in the back of one of their chase vehicles and would be fingerprinted for possible identification. All three men appeared to be of Russian decent. This followed the information that Josh had gotten during the raid on the building in the Market place.

The three Russian made bombs were secured and taken to the Seal headquarters for further examination.
The markings will be sent back to the Situation Room for comparison to the fragments found at sea. The interrogation of the three men had to be handled as quickly as possible. President Morgan was scheduled to go on air to detail the capture of these men and maybe with luck they could get him the person or persons responsible for this.

Josh knew that the possibility of another bomb planted was the first concern. If he could find that out he would then proceed further. The Seal team had tried to get information from the man captured in the warehouse but he did not cooperate. Rusty wanted to handle the questioning but Josh knew that he would resort to tough tactics first and he would rather save Rusty for later.

"Your choices aren't great," Josh stated. "You will be tried as terrorists and enemies of The United States of America and hung. The only way you can avoid this is by telling us what we need to know."

None of the three looked up at him. The man that was in the passenger seat decided to speak.

"I got broken arm. You need to fix me up."
Josh turned to Rusty and said, "This man is right. You can help him?"

"I'd be glad to." Rusty brought over a chair and pulled the man off the floor. "Let me see your arm."

The man smiled at his comrades and said something to them in Russian. One of the local agents leaned over to Rusty and related what the man said. "He told his friends that Americans were weak and pushovers."

Rusty nodded and winked back at him. "Watch him. I have to get my bag to fix him up." He returned with a little black bag. As Rusty went through the bag he looked over at the man. "Do you understand English?"

The man had a puzzled look.

"I have to give you an injection in case you get an infection." The man raised his eyebrows and Rusty knew he understood. The needle came out of the bag and Rusty stood in front of the man and filled the syringe with fluid from a vial. He motioned to the man to raise his sleeve and then proceeded to inject him.

"This will take a few minutes to start working." Rusty went back to the black bag and pulled out some gauze and tape.

The man again smiled at his friends and sat up straight in the seat. He was feeling confident that he would show the American up. It was just a few minutes after that he slumped in the seat and started to weave in the chair.

"Not feeling too good?" Rusty asked.

The man leaned forward and vomited. He turned red in the face and fell out of the chair face first into the vomit.

"Who's next?"

The other two men had a panicked look on their faces. The one from the warehouse siege started talking in English. "We are only workers. We know nothing about these things." They saw their comrade lying in front of them foaming at the mouth and his body quivering as he lay on the dirt.

Rusty shouted, "I have two more injections, whose next?"

Now both men were speaking very good English. "We just work here and don't know what you want."

"Bullshit!" Rusty yelled. "I'd just as soon kill all three of you but will gladly do it one at a time if you want." Rusty kicked the man who was lying on the floor in front of the chair over to the side. "I need to make room for the next one."

"No, we will tell you what we know."

"Okay, who's paying you for your work here?"

"Don't know his name."

At that Rusty pulled another syringe out of the black bag and started to fill it with another vial of fluid. Panic took over and the two were now willing to tell everything they knew.

They were just stooges. They operated the warehouse but the real men in charge were located elsewhere.

Josh hauled one of them to the chair as Rusty held the syringe in his right hand. He shot a line of fluid in the air to make sure the needle was filled. The man in the chair squirmed and ducked down. "Tell me what I want to know now!" Josh looked deep into the man's face. He grabbed the man's shirt and held him a few inches off the seat. "Who do you work for?"

Josh held the man down as Rusty pulled his sleeve up and started to insert the needle in the man's right arm.

"Stop! Stop! I will tell you want you want to know."

"You've got ten seconds to spit out a name."

"Viktor Kevchef. We work for Viktor."

"Okay, where do you meet this Viktor?"

"He comes here to tell us what to do."

"Did you plant the bomb on the plane headed for Los Angeles that crashed?"

"Yes."

"Did you plant any other bombs on airplane's earlier today?"

The man turned toward the other Russian. "He's yours Rusty." Josh backed away and the man cried.

"No don't, I will tell you."

Josh again asked, "Did you plant a bomb on a plane today?"

"Yes."

"Where is it headed?"

"One to Paris the other one to London."

This information stunned them. They hadn't figured that a plane headed west would be a target. Now they knew that there were two more planes as targets. "When did they leave here?"

"This morning, maybe five hours ago."

There was panic in Josh's face." He spun around and asked. "How long is a flight to Paris from here?"

One of the agents grabbed his Smart Phone. "Flights from Seoul's Incheon Airport to Charles De Gaulle in Paris take nine hours, if it was a direct flight."

"Oh shit, that's no good."

"How about to London?"

"Incheon Airport to Heathrow in London was just a little longer, close to ten hours."

"Someone get on the phone right away. We've got to warn them."

Rusty called to Robert Chiarini who was now headed back to Langley. "Boss, we know that these men planted more bombs this morning. One is aboard flight 1801 headed to Charles De Gaulle in Paris. Another one is on British Airways 362 to London. They both left here close to five hours ago."

Chiarini jumped at this new information. He was glad to be back in the driver's seat with these details. "I'll call it in. How much time do they have once we radio them?"

"Both flights are nine to ten hours. They have maybe four hours before they land and get the passengers off the plane."

"Do we know where the bombs are planted?"

"We are still working on that."

"I'm headed back to the White House and will call the President right now. Anything else?"

"No but we are still questioning them right. They said their boss is a man named Viktor Kevchef."

"We'll check that out. Great job! Tell Josh to call as soon as you have who this Kevchef works for." Robert called the Presidents direct line. "My guys have critical information from the men captured. They planted two more bombs this morning on flights headed to Paris and London." He gave the President all the information. "I'm headed back there now Sir."

Morgan was glad that they had some time to warn the British and French. He turned to the Secretary of State. "Whoever is behind this is involving our allies now. I'll call the President of France and the Prime Minister and let them know. I better hold off before going on air telling people what we have. Chiarini's guys may have solved this for us."

Robert Chiarini was now feeling like the man back on top. He again will be the person the President will look to for information. He called his office with the name Viktor Kevchef. "Get a search on this man. We need to gather everything we can." He forgot all about the news he heard in the Situation Room earlier. Who will remember any of that once his team solves the mystery?

Twenty Eight

President Morgan was holding a briefing with key members of his Cabinet in the Oval Office. He went over the events that the Director of the CIA had given him and told them that they should re-convene in the Situation Room in fifteen minutes. He had already talked to both the Prime Minister and President of France regarding the potential of a bomb on planes headed to their countries. "Chiarini will be here in a few minutes. Have him join us downstairs."

The Secretary of State turned to the Under Secretary. "Meet him at the door to the West Wing and bring him to the Situation Room."

The wall of television screens and monitors captured the events world wide as President Morgan and his staff watched. The flight from Seoul's Incheon Airport to Paris was the first one to secure landing instructions. They were cleared to land in Athens, Greece at the International Airport in Spata. It was a state-of-the-art facility that had many upgrades due to the large tourist traffic. The plane would land and passengers would debark. Authorities would move the plane to a remote location to inspect it for the bomb or bombs aboard.

The plane headed to London was flying a more northern route and the current flight plan took them directly over Moscow. Due to poor International relations with the Russians they were routing it to Stockholm.

It would only take thirty minutes longer but if the calculations were correct they had time. The staff in the Situation Room had satellites picking up the action in both Athens and Stockholm.

There were pockets of people gathered in the Situation room watching various monitors and talking in low voices. Morgan was glad to see Chiarini when he arrived. Waving to him, "Robert over here."

Chiarini smiled as he was high fived from everyone as he passed. "Sir I'm glad my team got that information for you."

"Great job. I know we were all excited watching the assault on the warehouse and then the chase. The information your team gathered will help avert a further worldwide disaster."

Robert Chiarini was the toast of the town. Everyone would know that President Morgan personally congratulated him. "I'm always at your service Sir."

Just then the Secretary of State called attention to the team of explosive experts exiting flight 1801 that was headed to Paris. The men coming out of the plane were wearing special protective suits and held two black containers. There was a truck standing to the side of the plane waiting for this cargo. The men were signaling that both boxes held explosives of some type to the team waiting at the steps of the plane. A CIA operative stationed in Athens was on site and he radioed that one bomb was found in the baggage area and the second one was attached to the landing gear.
A cheer went up in the room. The information that the CIA agents gathered was correct. That was critical to the investigation. A call came into the room from the President of France.

"Mr. President, the people of France thank you and your team for saving the lives of so many French citizens. We will be indebted to you."

"We are friends and allies Mr. President," Morgan said. "We still have to find out who is responsible but along with your teams we are closer to that discovery."

The French President said, "I have given orders to our agents to cooperate with your people in every way possible." "Thank you," President Morgan knew relations with France had been strained recently but this could make all of that go away.

Attention now turned to the action in Stockholm. Flight 362 was landing and would be handled just like the flight to Paris. All the passengers would be taken off the plane and then the plane would taxi to the far end of an unused runway where bomb experts were waiting to search it. Hopefully this would go as well as the Paris flight.

Chiarini leaned over to President Morgan. "One down Sir and one to go."

The people in the room watched with anticipation as the bomb techs scoured the plane for the explosive devises. Everyone's attention turned to the large screen in the room as three men wearing elaborate bomb safety suits exited the plane. One of them was carrying a metal box that was labeled explosives, danger.

"They got it!" Chiarini called out.

Information was coming into the room from Stockholm.

"We found two detonation units that have time triggered mechanisms geared to go off in one hour and ten minutes from now."

Chiarini was quick to ask, "Can you tell us what type of bombs they are?"

"Yes, we found two separate packages. Each contained a bomb consisting of 300 to 400 grams, eleven – fourteen ounces of plastic explosives and a detonating mechanism. One was in the luggage compartment and the other was in the right wing."

This was similar to the findings that were found on the Paris flight.

Again congratulations were heard around the room as the President picked up the phone to talk to the Prime Minister. Disasters were quelled and now the question as to who was responsible still had President Morgan's attention.

Twenty Nine

While the action was being beamed to the Situation Room Josh and Rusty were now continuing to question the men captured in Seoul. Josh had Rusty bring Dimitri into the room. The men from the warehouse were stunned to see that he had also been caught. He was severely injured and tied to a chair with his arms strapped behind him.

The other men were taken into separate rooms and cuffed to a table in the center of the room. There was a large wooden apparatus in the corner of that room with chains along the side. It was rough wood and had dark stains all along the sides. Anyone with historical knowledge recognized it as a rack from medieval times. In the other corner was another table that seemed to be tilted. At the bottom of one end wash a large tub. The two men starred at both the rack and the water board units, just as Rusty hoped they would.

Rusty was taking charge of the interrogation and that was bad news for the prisoners. He went back into the first room and looked at Dimitri.

The two agents felt they needed to get the men they just captured together with the ones they found at the Market Place. Although Dimitri was nursing gunshot wounds they had patched him up. Maybe once they had him together with the men from the warehouse they would make more progress on who was heading up the operation.

Rusty looked down at his captive. "Where is Viktor Kevchef?"

Dimitri seemed surprised at the mention of that name but looked away from him.

"We found the bombs that were placed on the two flights and if you want any chance to live you need to cooperate. Now where can we find Viktor?"

Dimitri lifted his head and sneered at him.

"I'm going to give you a minute to think about that." Rusty turned away then spun back around and punched Dimitri knocking the chair over.

Dimitri now was lying on the floor still cuffed and blood flowed from the side of his face.

"Leave him there, I'll be back." Rusty said.

The agents watching just nodded.

When Rusty entered the other room Josh was on the phone. He signaled that critical information was coming in. "Okay I've got it Sir. We'll use it when interrogating the prisoners." He hung up and checked the encrypted message that was coming through. He filled Rusty and the other agents in. "It seems that Viktor Kevchef is a former KGB operative and well known in the spy world. Seems he has been freelancing the past few years to the highest bidders. They are sending the last known location that he was heard from. Not sure if this will help but they are also sending an old photo of him. It's close to twenty years old but at least we have something to go on. I'll print it."

Both Josh and Rusty looked at the picture being transmitted from Washington. Viktor had to be close to sixty years old now. He was six foot tall and on the heavy side with a goatee. Neither man had ever seen him. "I can use this with Dimitri. I left him with a little something else to think about." Josh laughed. "You mean he's still alive?"

"For now, but if he doesn't give us something soon we will go back to the two comrades in the storage room."

With that Rusty took one copy of the picture and headed back into the room guarded by the other two CIA agents.

"Well my friend Dimitri looks like we won't need you much longer. Viktor is being rounded up as we speak." Maybe he could bluff Dimitri into thinking they had Viktor. Rusty held the picture to his side so that Dimitri could see it. He motioned to the other two agents to pick up the chair with Dimitri up. "Tell you what. If you give us some helpful information I'll get you some real medical attention."

Dimitri was still defiant. "I tell you nothing more. The Geneva Convention says you have to get me medical help."

"Maybe you hadn't noticed this but there isn't anyone around to say what happened to you. Once I kill you we'll drop your body in the ocean. You don't think anyone will come searching for you, do you?"

Dimitri was quiet. Rusty grabbed the back of his chair and dragged him into the storage room where they were holding the other men captured from the Humvee. "Look what we here, a little reunion. I got all of you now."

The men just looked at each other. Dimitri was bleeding from both legs and his face was cut up and puffy. One of the men cuffed to the table had a broken arm and lacerations all over his face. The third guy was the least injured. He was the man found in the back of the Hummer and had acted strange the whole time. That was the guy Rusty turned his attention to.

"We got the two planes that were headed to London and Paris down safely and removed the bombs. Viktor is being brought in and you're all done. I don't think Dimitri is going to make it. I'm not sure what will happen to him, but it isn't going to be pretty." Rusty turned and looked in the direction of the ancient rack. "I hope I remember how to use that thing."

The men looked back at Dimitri. He certainly wasn't looking good. Bleeding, dirty and slumped in the chair.

Rusty had his pearl handle pistol in his right hand and smiling. "I think you need to close the loop for us or you will be joining Dimitri."

Just then one of the men captured from the Humvee yelled out.

"I had nothing to do with this. They forced me to help."

"What do you mean they forced you?"

"My family, they have my family and said they will kill my wife and daughter if I didn't help."

"What did they need you to do?"

"I used to be demolition expert for KGB. They wanted me to make bombs."

Just then Josh came into the storage room. "Rusty I need to see you."

"Okay one minute."

"I will tell you everything I know."

Rusty nodded and turned to the other agents in the room. "I'll be back." He turned back to the man that admitted being the bomb maker. "Get him a glass of water." Josh stood at the doorway as Rusty headed toward him. He let out an evil shrill sound that caused even the agents guarding the men to jump.

As the two agents stood outside the storage room Josh had a fearful look on his face. "We have another problem. The team analyzing the chemicals in the warehouse discovered three compounds that aren't in the bombs we found on the planes. There is also trace of radiological C4 material and the makings of a device that can trigger the explosion. If their assessment is correct the amount of material found put together in a dirty bomb could kill thousands of people if it is in the right place."

Both men looked at each other for a minute. "We got to find out more and if they did make another bomb where is it?"

"This changes everything," Josh added.

"We need to make them think we knew about that the whole time," Rusty answered. "Let's go at them together."

Rusty pushed through the door to the storage room and it opened with a thud. "Well boys we got all the stuff from your warehouse. They concentrated their remarks on the man that said he was the bomb maker. We handled the bombs on those planes and know all about the dirty bomb you've planted."

The man claiming that he was forced to help spoke first. "I told you, they made me do it. I didn't want to do any of this but they said they would kill my wife and daughter if I didn't help."

"Okay tell us more, if we believe you I promise we will get your wife and daughter to safety."

The man was maybe in his late 70's and had withered hands. "I worked with KGB years ago as a chemist. I have been teaching in University for past few years. Two weeks ago they came into my lab and told me they had Anna, my wife and daughter. I had to help or they will kill them."

"Who took you?"

"The man you called Viktor along with another man."

"What is the other man's name?"

"Ivan Shankoff."

"How did you get to Seoul?"

"They took chemicals from my lab and we flew on a plane from Moscow."

"Give us your home address and we will send men to rescue your family. As long as you cooperate we will do everything to help get your family back safely."

The man appeared relieved. Dimitri called out in a disgusting tone back to the man.

Rusty motioned to one of the other agents and they dragged Dimitri still strapped to the chair out of the room.

"We need to know more about this so called dirty bomb." Rusty knew the agency referred to them as RDD's or Dirty Bombs.

Radiological Dispersal Devices (RDD's) or Dirty Bombs are often used as psychological rather than physical devises however given the chemicals found in the storage area along with C4 said this was a massive ordinance and would cause great destruction. Around the World there are many sources of radioactive material that are not secure or accounted for. Rogue nations and/or terrorist groups can obtain these materials easily. Because the man was a professor in Russia he would have access to all the materials without anyone asking questions.

The man was now hoping that he might be okay and the American's will help save his family.

Rusty filled the others in on the findings. "We found major compounds of ammonium nitrate, nitro methane and radioactive material along with C4l. When detonated it could blow a mile wide. It would cause uncontrolled mass evacuation and havoc that would result in many more deaths from the panic."

He turned to the professor. "Where is it now?"

"I don't know where they sent it to but it was loaded on a cargo plane yesterday."

Everyone in the room was stunned.

"Shit, Shit, yesterday?" Josh ran from the room. We have to find this device and stop it from reaching its destination. Rusty turned back to the man that had just given them the bad news. "When yesterday did it leave?"

"Just before they put the bombs on the other two flights."

"Do you know where it is headed?"

"No, I had to help put it in a large crate and did not see them put it on the plane or where it is headed."

It was now just past one and it could have gone almost anywhere. "We need to put an alert out for any cargo plane arriving from Seoul to be checked. We don't have much time."

Josh and another agent checked their watches. It was past noon and they scrambled to see the flight times from Seoul to destinations around the world. It would be a problem if it was headed to anywhere in Europe or the Middle East. It could have arrived hours ago anywhere in Europe. If it was headed to Hawaii it would have also already made it there. Los Angeles was the closest destination in the continental U.S. It would take a little more than twelve hours to get to LA. If the plane carrying the bomb left at midnight it would have arrived in Los Angeles an hour ago.

Calls went to the White House, Robert Chiarini and every agency worldwide to be on the lookout for any cargo plane arriving from Seoul.

When the call came into the Wilshire office of the FBI Frank Fitzgerald and Steve Orrison were finalizing the information from Blair and Jim regarding the details Tony Kim had given them. Steve listened as Fitzgerald got the information and relayed it to him.

"I'll get every agent out to the airport now." Steve ran out of his office and was giving details to everyone in the outer room.

"We want to be involved too!" Blair and Jim said.

"We'll need everyone. Grab your gear and head to LAX." Frank was on the phone talking to security at LAX. "Has any plane arrived from Seoul Korea in the past few hours?"

The person that was checking came back with the answer they didn't want to hear. "We had only one cargo plane but it arrived close to an hour ago."

"Has it started to unload?"

"I'm not sure, let me check." It seemed like a lifetime passed when the TSA security agent finally came back on the line. "They started unloading right away and a few crates were taken off. They are still unloading the plane now."

"Do not let them take anything away from that plane. Stop everyone and everything. Do not let any vehicle leave the area. Do not let any other cargo plane unload until all our agents are on the scene."

The TSA agent looked at his monitor as Frank was shouting into the phone.

"We are on the way to set up a perimeter around that plane and if necessary shoot anyone that is trying to get away."

Agents were rushing to their vehicles and Frank was talking to the White House to advise them that they had a possible situation at LAX with a cargo plane landing in the last few minutes and unloading.

President Morgan turned to his National Security Chief. "Call out the National Guard to secure the area around LAX." The National Guard had a location at the southern end of the airport and could be in position in minutes.

Lincoln Avenue would soon be the site of a massive military deployment at the entrance to the airport. Arriving and departing flight would be diverted to other airports. United States military men had weapons drawn at all gates and no vehicles were being allowed to exit.

They couldn't let this information get out to the public or it would result in worldwide panic.

Thirty

The FBI mobilized their personnel. Blair and Jim were flying down highway 10 headed to the 405 close to ninety miles-an-hour. Five other units were in close pursuit and headed to LAX. The National Guard had sent three Sikorsky helicopters that had just landed on the tarmac at the freight terminal and another helicopter landed in the middle of the entrance to the airport just west of Lincoln Avenue. Traffic that tried to exit was at a standstill. The National Guard had opened a lane into the airport for the FBI personnel to enter. All vehicles would have to show credentials to get past the two blockades.

Radio reports were coming in to all the agents that traffic could make it difficult to get to LAX. Agents were advised to use their emergency lights to bypass the clogged roadway. Frank and Steve had already called and ordered a police chopper to the roof of the FBI building. They would be in route to the scene to handle the action. The chopper would get them there fast.

The National Guard had set a perimeter around the Korean National cargo plane and held the crew and the men that were unloading it. Information was coming in to Steve that three trucks were next to the plane as it started to unload. Only two trucks were still there.

"Where is the other truck?"

There was silence on the other end of the line.

"Son-of-a-bitch, where in the hell is the other truck?"

"Sir we're checking the cameras to make sure there were three trucks."

"Damn TSA security can't get anything right." Steve and Frank were just about to land at LAX when the TSA agent came back on the line.

"We've confirmed that there were three trucks at the unloading site and the one that is missing has been identified."

"Okay, what are we looking for?"

"The missing truck is a white, Chevrolet high cube van no identification on the sides."

"Did you get a plate number?"

"Yes, it is California plate 2PC8776. We are sending the information down to the Guard members right now."

Steve radioed an APB to all agents and local authorities to be on the lookout for the van. He and Frank made their way to the TSA tower. "With the blockade there is no way it got out of the airport grounds." Steve was steaming that a truck got away from the scene.

"You know we have them cornered on the airport grounds. It's just a matter of time." It was obvious that Frank was trying to make him feel better.

The National Guard Captain started walking across the tarmac toward Steve and Frank. He extended his hand toward them. "Captain Justin Brooks, National Guard unit Fox787. My men have circled the outer rim of the airport and are now starting a search of all the grounds for the missing Chevrolet van."

"Thank you Captain. My name is Frank Fitzgerald and this is Steve Orrison head of the Los Angeles Bureau." Steve was surprised that Frank only gave his rank to the Captain.

"We have FBI Agents en route to LAX and I would appreciate it if your team lets them through as quickly as possible."

"Roger that Sir."

The three men walked toward the cargo plane and saw that the Guardsmen had five men cuffed and on the ground behind the rear hatch.

"Nice job Captain." Frank moved to the first man and motioned for him to get up. "Do you have a shipping manifest?"

The man nodded and pointed to the front of the plane. "It is in the cockpit."

"What was unloaded first?"

"I'm just the pilot. I have no idea what was on the plane other than what the manifest said."

"So what does your manifest say?"

"The shipment is crates of Kia car parts destined for the warehouse in Glendale."

"Okay, why such a hurry to unload the first crate and where is it?"

"That's not my assignment. I'm just the pilot."

"You were a pilot. After this you'll be lucky to fly paper airplanes."

Frank turned to Steve. "Let's get these men in overalls that unloaded the crate into the TSA office. They unloaded the shipment. They may have information for us."

Steve agreed and saw that three of his agents had just arrived. "Get up!" He grabbed one of the men off the ground. "Take them into the TSA office. I'll follow in a few minutes. Keep an eye on these two."

The information Frank had from Seoul was the material of the bomb was the same material used in the Oklahoma City bombing in 1995. That bomb took out the Federal Building and killed hundreds of people.

Steve knew that the National Guard had already started a search of the airport grounds and felt their best plan of attack is the men they had from the cargo plane.

He and Frank confirmed their approach to questioning the men both on the tarmac and the two that they were taking to the TSA office.

Blair and Jim pulled up next to the cargo plane and jumped out of their vehicle. One of the Guard members said that he hadn't seen that many black GMC Suburban's in one spot except at a dealership lot. They chuckled to each other and then they caught a glimpse of the agents who just arrived. "Wow, check out the blond." The two guys smiled and one of them decided to walk over to Blair.

"Hey babe, what can I do for you?" He turned and smiled back at his friends.

Blair extended her hand and he leaned in closer. The Guard member smiled and turned back to his friends. She whispered in his ear, "Listen little man, first thing you can expect me to do is yank your balls out through your ass if you don't get the hell out of my way." She pushed past him and Jim let out a loud laugh.

"You're way out of your league son." Jim said.

The Guard member's buddies watching busted out laughing at their friend as his face turned beet red and he lowered his head.

Blair spotted the Captain ahead and moved toward him. Holding out their badges, she announced, "Special Agents Blair Adams and Agent Jim Canfield. We're looking for our Director and Bureau Chief."

"Glad to meet you Special Agents. The Director and Chief headed into the TSA office over there." He pointed to the small building ahead. "They were going to question the men that were unloading the plane."

"Thank you Sir." The two agents walked into the building on the right and went in the door on the ground level. They showed their credentials to the guard stationed at the door. He motioned them upstairs. One of the agents from the office was at the door on the second floor.

When he saw them he motioned them over. "Traffic was almost impossible. We just got here and Steve asked us to guard the door."

"Yeah we had a hell-of-a-time getting down Lincoln but the Guard had a clear lane once we passed Sepulveda Boulevard. How many guys they got in there?"

"They got the two guys that were unloading the plane. We're not sure either of them knows what was being unloaded but they have details on what came off and maybe where it went. The pilot is being held in another area."

"Guess all we can do is wait for instructions."

Just then Steve came bouncing out of the room. "The National Guard chopper spotted the van outside of the Delta International cargo building. We need to get over there now." Blair and Jim followed Steve as the man guarding the room stayed to keep a watch. Frank Fitzgerald continued questioning the men and waited for confirmation that the van had been captured.

Two black GMC Suburbans came charging toward the west end of the Los Angeles Airport where all the storage terminals were located. Steve had an agent with him and Jim drove his vehicle with Blair riding shotgun. There it was a lone white Chevrolet high cube van. The plate number matched their information. It sat about fifteen feet from the front of the building. There wasn't anyone that could be seen around the vehicle and Steve motioned to the agents to proceed with caution. It was the right the vehicle they were searching for. If the van held the explosive it might be rigged to go off.

Steve and the agent with him moved to the back of their vehicle and Blair and Jim joined them. "The information from Seoul is that there is an IED, possible high grade uranium that is powerful enough to level a city block in there. We must move in carefully and make sure nothing goes wrong."

They moved from behind Steve's vehicle and flared out so that they continued to have the van covered. Blair and Jim went wide around the right side of their vehicle as Steve and the other agent went around to the left.

They now were only about fifteen feet away when machine gun fire came from the back of the van. Jim rolled on the ground and Blair hit the tarmac face first. The gunfire sprayed across the front of Jim's vehicle and sent a stream of coolant spraying from the grill. More shots rang out overhead.

"You okay," Jim yelled.

Blair rolled over toward their vehicle and hollered back, "I'm fine."

The gunman now wielded around and turned his attention toward Steve and the agent coming from the other way. He moved closer to the right side of the white van and kept firing across the landscape. All four agents were now on the ground.

Blair returned fire while lying on the ground. The gunman moved fast and stopped at the side of the white van as the driver pushed the door open for him. He sent another volley of bullets at his targets.

Steve was now crouched down and saw where the gun fire was coming from. "He's getting in the van."

Another round of bullets from the gunman found its target and the front of Steve's vehicle was it. The front tires went down and the windshield shattered into thousands of round pieces.

Steve yelled back to his team. "The marksman isn't shooting at us he's trying to disable the vehicles. They're going to make a run for it."

Just then the van speed off squealing tires and leaving a streak of black tire marks on the ground.

Thirty One

The National Guard chopper hovered over the storage unit continuing to follow the van making its get-a-way from the Delta warehouse. As long as they had a bead on the van the FBI and other authorities could continue the chase. Just then the van made a sharp right turn into another storage building that was close to the last runway on the west side of LAX. The building had four logos on the metal roof. This was an international storage unit for four foreign air transportation companies. The men radioed the information back to the Bureau Chief who was at the National Guard headquarters. "We lost sight of the van. It headed into the multi-national storage building just past runway twelve."

Steve listened to the report as he and his special agents jumped aboard the Suburban that picked them up at the Delta warehouse. "Good job. Keep an eye on them. We are on our way." He made sure that the chopper knew that he was still in the chase and running the show.

Suddenly the van came charging back out of the rear of the storage building and was headed toward the wired fence area along Lincoln Boulevard. "They are on the move but there isn't an exit in the direction they are going."
Steve appreciated the information. "Keep me informed."

"Sir they stopped at the end of the pavement. One man got out of the van. They're back on the move," the message came from the chopper to Steve and the Guard.
"They just crossed two runways and are heading toward the fence that leads to Lincoln Boulevard."

Steve was quick to answer the message. "Whatever you do, do not fire on them. We don't know what's on board and it could be the mother of all explosives. I'll have a unit try to pick up the man that got out."

"Roger that."

A call went out to the Guard unit that was stationed at the entrance to LAX on Lincoln to head west under the runway bridge away from the airport. Another call went back to the El Segundo, Manhattan Beach and other local police to inform them that a white van, plate number 2PC8776, was possibly headed out of the airport toward their area. Another chase unit followed and caught a glimpse of a man running along the outer runway. They drove toward him and when they were close he stopped and started shooting back at them. The agents spun to the left and took cover along the side of their vehicle. The man was in the open and had no cover but kept shooting at the agents. They called it in to Steve and requested orders.

"Try to take him alive. He's probably a diversion hoping to help the van get away."

It wasn't a fair fight. The agents took cover along their vehicle and now were joined by a National Guard unit from the other side. The man was trapped between the two vehicles and he was now lying on the ground shooting back sporadically. "He's probably almost out of ammo. Let's close in on him."

The agents got back in their vehicle and ducked down as they pulled to within a few feet of the suspect. One of them called out on their loud speakers. "Surrender now!"

The man got up and started to run and the two agents looked at each other. "He's got to be kidding." They gunned the engine and tracked him down in seconds.

The Guard members watched in disbelief. "What the hell!"

The agents were now along side of the man and one of them leaned out of the passenger door. He jumped out onto the man and wrestled him to the ground. They rolled over a few times as the driver spun around and watched his partner pin the man on the ground. They handcuffed him and tossed him into the back of the Suburban.

They called it in to Steve. "Hold him with the other guys back at the terminal." Steve told them.

All air traffic had been diverted from LAX with the chopper hovering over the runway and the National Guard and FBI driving across the western three miles of the airport. The chopper was now joined by another helicopter from the Los Angeles Drug Traffic Task force. The LA Police Chief called it into the action when the information came into his office.

The white van was close to the wired fence and picking up speed when it hit the barbed wire at close to eighty miles an hour. The van went airborne hitting the pavement sending sparks across the highway and spinning as the driver tried to regain control. They were now headed through the intersection of South Sepulveda Boulevard and Highway One. Once the driver regained control he continued down Highway One through El Segundo south to Manhattan Beach. Steve and his team of agents were closing in when the van leaped through the wire fence. The Suburban slowed and all four passengers watched as the van made its get-a-way down the highway. "We still have the chopper following. No sense killing everyone in this vehicle." Steve knew the move would be dangerous and he had others chasing the van.

Blair and Jim agreed but wished they were still in the chase. "We can head down the gated area along the west side of the fence Sir," said Blair.

Steve turned toward the back seat, "Why would we do that?"

"There is an old gate before they extended the airport to the west. It leads to Imperial Highway and the 405."

"How do you know that?"

Blair cleared her throat. "Well when Hunter was home one time he took me through that gate with one of his friends that worked at the airport. It isn't used anymore but I know how to get there."

Steve turned toward the agent driving. "Head wherever she tells you to."

The chopper radioed back to all units that the van was heading down Highway One at high speeds and that two cars from El Segundo were close in pursuit.

"Tell them to follow but not to apprehend." Steve was concerned about the possible explosive contents of the van and needed to get a bomb extraction team involved as soon as they could.

The Suburban traveled along the fenced area and then they saw the entrance Blair told them about. "You're going to have to ram the gate but the road is level and once we're out turn left. It will lead right back to Highway One and we'll be west of El Segundo closer to Manhattan Beach."

The chopper following the van reported its location and Steve and his agents were just a few minutes to the west of them. The short cut through the airport put them in position to cut the van's progress off. "Okay now we need to get aggressive," Steve said.

He radioed the chopper. "I want you to descend to the lowest safe level over the top of the van. Spook them so that they pay more attention to you then us coming from the other way."

The chopper dipped down and now was twenty feet over the roof of the van. The driver tried to maneuver across Highway One to get away from the helicopter without getting into on-coming traffic. The chopper went back up and continued to play cat and mouse with the men in the get-a-way vehicle.

Steve asked out loud, "After all this crap why are they staying on the main road. It doesn't make sense for them to drive down a major highway. They're sitting ducks on Highway One."

The Suburban was now headed north in the direction of the van. They would meet at Sepulveda and East Grand Avenue. The driver of the van continued south on Highway One knowing that the chopper was just overhead and that local police were joining the pursuit. They never saw the Suburban until it was too late. Everyone in the vehicle braced for the collision. The agent driving planned to side-swipe the van with the purpose of derailing its progress and immobilizing it. They had to be careful not to hit it head on. They van didn't see it coming.

The Suburban side-swiped the van on the driver's side, sending it into the grassy field on the right side of the road where it came to a sudden stop. Blair and Jim jumped out of the back seat, guns drawn and rushed toward the disabled vehicle. They surrounded the van and Steve and the other agent positioned themselves at the rear of the vehicle.

"You're surrounded. Come out with your hands up." The passenger door slowly opened and one man raised his hands out of the door. "Don't shoot!" As he made his way out of the van Steve continued covering the rear doors and the other agent made his way to the driver's door. Blair pulled the passenger to the ground, cuffed him and pointed her weapon at the opened door.

Jim moved in pulled the van's door all the way open and saw the driver slumped over the steering wheel. He climbed in and had the driver pulled back from the steering wheel. "He's unconscious." Jim cuffed him to the steering wheel.

All clear boss, no one else inside. Jim found two sub-machine guns on the floor and a pistol was jammed into the driver's seat. They had the right van captured and the two men that were attempting to get away.

Steve moved around the back of the van and pulled the rear panel doors open. To his surprise the van was empty.

Thirty Two

The agents stood with their Bureau Chief shaking their head at the empty van. Why did the van try to get away if it was empty? It must have been a diversion? They found the machine gun that was used to hold them off at the Delta warehouse.

The man that they captured running away at the airport from the van was probably also a diversion. Where was the damn bomb?

"The Delta warehouse," Blair said.

"What?" Jim answered.

"The Delta airfreight warehouse! It was a ruse. They had to either unload their cargo or switched vehicles at the Delta warehouse and led us on a wild goose chase. They needed to give it time to get out of the airport or hide it." Steve nodded and said, "Yeah, but they also went into the large International warehouse. They could have switched vehicles or cargo there too!"

Steve was right. He grabbed his phone. He got his agents and the head of the Guard on the line. "Make sure no one gets out of LAX with any cargo. Send a search team to the Delta warehouse and another to the International warehouse." Because the FBI was chasing the white van the National Guard figured they had their vehicle with the bomb and relaxed the blockade at the entrance to the airport.

Now who knows what vehicle the crate could be in? Whatever they used they might have gotten the dangerous cargo out of the airport. Steve knew this was a major setback and now the entire population of Los Angeles and maybe all of Southern California was in danger. Steve and his team of agents headed back to the airport and the National Guard was securing the two buildings so that nothing else went in or out. The call went back to the Director who was still questioning the men that unloaded the plane.

"Sir we captured the van but it was empty. We're thinking they may have switched vehicles or dumped their cargo at one of two warehouses. I've got the National Guard securing them and we should be there in a few minutes."

"Okay Steve, I'm going to go with one of your agent and will meet you. I'll get someone to hold our baggage guys here."

Traffic was still a mess around the airport, "Let's head back through the gate we came out of," Steve said. They were speeding back down Highway One to Imperial Highway.   It would take them less than thirty minutes to get back on the scene.

The Delta warehouse was now surrounded by teams of FBI and National Guard personnel. A second group covered the International warehouse. All entrances and exits were blocked off and the National Guard had a chopper circling overhead on both places. Air traffic was again diverted from LAX to John Wayne Airport to the south and Ontario Airport to the east. Frank Fitzgerald headed the units while Steve and his team headed back.

"We need to proceed and check every vehicle's cargo. Do not leave anything unchecked without inspecting the contents." The Director now knew that the explosive could be hidden in any type of large container.

The bomb squad was on the scene and had mobilized its mechanical detection device along with bomb sniffing dogs. There must have been close to fifty armed men now scouring the warehouses for the bomb.

There was another group of local authorities and National Guardsmen combing the airport in the event that the device was still on the LAX grounds. More units had been dispatched to blockade the roadways around the airport and stop and search every vehicle.

Steve had left the captured men in the custody of the Manhattan Beach Police Chief. He was going to bring them back to LAX to be interrogated along with the baggage handlers. Someone knew the information they needed. It was imperative that the FBI find out soon.

Two local news helicopters had followed the action along Pacific Coast Highway One and had broadcasted the chase and apprehension of the white van. Although they only speculated as to what exactly was going on, never-the-less they had millions of viewers now tuned into the action. Request for details were rejected under the terms of National Security. It was a little past two in the afternoon and Steve was glad this all didn't happen at rush hour. Frank Fitzgerald had been in touch with every local law enforcement team and given them enough information to satisfy the need to be selective with details. After all National Security was the umbrella that the FBI and CIA could always hide under.

_____Thirty Three

Teams were now searching every possible storage area at LAX but were coming up empty. Hours had passed and they had not found the missing contents of the Korean Cargo plane. Their hopes picked up when a few of the dogs started scratching at a crate on the floor about half way through the Delta warehouse. The agents on the scene radioed it in and Steve said he would be there as quick as possible. The crate was about ten feet long and six feet wide. It seemed much too tall to be what they were looking for. It had Air France shipping tags with a manifest attached to the right side. The Guard Commander pulled the manifest from the plastic sleeve located along the left side of the crate. It read that the shipment was coffee beans from Morocco. It stated that the crate arrived yesterday. None of that fit their information however the dogs continued to react to the contents whatever they were.

The crate was stationed on a large dolly that had metal wheels. "Let's carefully roll this out into the aisle," the Commander instructed his men. The dogs hovered around the crate and were clawing at the edges and sniffing. This was a sign to the handlers that there was something of concern in the crate. The dogs were giving their trained alert signal, continuing to sniff and scratch at the bottom of the crate.

There were now close to six dogs all exhibiting the same actions.

The Commander ordered his other men to continue their search through the warehouse as he awaited Steve's arrival. "Glad your team was on top of this," Steve was saying as he approached the Guard Commander.

"We didn't want to proceed without your direction, Sir."

"That's appreciated. I'll call it in to the bomb squad. I know they are stationed just outside and have the materials needed to check this out."

As Steve talked on the phone he was given directions. The Bomb squad would be on the way. "They want us to open the crate from the top and we can inspect the contents."

"My men will be glad to do it Sir."

"Steve nodded in agreement. First let's get all the other personnel as far back as possible until we know what is in it and that it is safe."

The warehouse was evacuated and the search teams left markers where they ended up. Steve and the Commander gave the order to pry open the crate slowly. "We need to be careful and not disturb the contents."

The crate had eight wooden slats with quarter inch gaps between each one. Two men started the work by removing the slats one by one from each end. Once they had the top completely opened Steve climbed on the stools they were using. The crate was packed with cardboard liners about three-quarter of an inch thick. He and the Commander of the Guard unit started to remove the outer liners and leaned across the crate slowly handing the liners to the men at the base of the crate. They were now down about six inches into the crate when the Commander said, "I feel a plastic liner, like a thick bag or something."

"Okay," Steve said. "Can you see anything under the plastic?"

"It's pretty thick but looks kind of brown or dark colored stuff under there."

"That would fit the manifest of coffee beans. Maybe we need to get a bomb expert here in case we need to disarm the thing."

They stopped at that point and waited for the bomb squad's arrival. Everyone watched as the squad's men dressed in their protective gear and pulled the contents of metal bins from the truck.

Other FBI personnel along with airport security was still busy emptying the entire cargo plane only to find cases of auto parts and knock off clothing still on board. This fit what the men earlier said that they were carrying Kia car parts. A thorough search of every truck and car in and around Los Angeles International Airport was also coming up empty. Was the bomb on the plane or was this too some sort of misdirection?

Interrogation of the two men from the white van along with the men that had unloaded the cargo continued. Fitzgerald reported back to the White House that if there was a bomb on that plane it had not been found. President Morgan asked Chiarini to contact his agents to get as much information from the bomb maker as possible. "We have to know what we are dealing with and how to resolve it." Warnings went out to every Federal and State location to double their buildings protection. Specifics were that a creditable bomb threat was uncovered by the Bureau. After the Oklahoma City Federal Building bombing special equipment had been installed in every location across the country. That event destroyed close to 324 buildings across a sixteen block radius. Another 258 buildings had all their windows blown out. If this device was anything similar it would be a major disaster.

President Morgan contacted South Korea's President Lee Myung-Bak to co-ordinate efforts with the CIA agents operating in his country. He wanted to make sure that our allies had total knowledge of what action was taking place and avoid possible repercussions.

The relationship between the two men had been good and Morgan didn't want to damage that.

Rusty and Josh continued their work with the bomb maker. The information he had furnished was sent to Washington with the chemical composition that was used in the device. The ammonium nitrate and nitro methane were fairly common chemicals used in so called dirty bombs. However the addition of radioactive materials set this off from the run of the mill terrorist explosives.

There was a worldwide search for Viktor Kevchef and Ivan Shankoff. They would be the key in solving what country or group was responsible for all of this. The CIA sent information to Interpol and the Office of Strategic Services. The OSS was the French version of the British and American agencies. Agents from countries in Europe, Asia and the United States leaned on every contact to find the two men. The British Prime Minister said his contacts in the old Soviet Union were working with underground groups to see if either man was still in Russia. President Morgan had also contacted the Israelis President to get help. Their undercover agents had men stationed across the region and could use contacts to help in the search. The blame prospects were narrowing but proof was needed.

The area around the Los Angeles International Airport was still blockaded. Traffic on Lincoln Boulevard in Marina del Rey was at a standstill. The area south to Manhattan Beach Boulevard and north along the Pacific Coast Highway was covered by massive State Police and National Guard road blocks.

There was no avenue for the men to escape west

with the airport on the coast so the only other escape route was east.

Road blocks were set up along every highway and thorough-fare going east. Vehicles were searched, trunks opened and packages inspected. Until the agents in Seoul furnished more details it was like looking for a needle in a haystack.

An alert was given to news media that an international incident had the police and FBI conducting a search. It was important not to cause mass panic with the general population. The Bureau did not want people to know that a bomb was causing all the action.

Back in Seoul, Josh had separated the bomb maker from the other men and he was giving the agents a full account of the materials, timing device and description of the bomb. He again confirmed that it was larger than most explosives and weighed close to fifty five pounds. The bomb had two triggers and that news was even more devastating for the searchers. The fear was, if captured, the men could remotely detonate it. At least now they knew that it was three feet long and resembled a large square package. It won't be easy to hide and could not be made any smaller.

The search plan continued to close the ring area in as they continued to check every vehicle. By narrowing the area there was a better chance of catching the suspects. For the first time in this endeavor all agencies were working together. The FBI was heading up the search and the National Guard and all local police officers were working with one goal in mind, find the bomb.

Steve and the Guard Commander were filling the Chief of the bomb squad in on the possible contents of the crate. His men were all wearing bomb protecting suits and they wanted everyone out of the warehouse.

Steve hesitated but the bomb squad chief made it clear.

"It's our ballgame now, once we have the contents inspected and disarmed we'll call you back in."

There was nothing he could do. He knew they were right. They moved the rest of the guard unit and agents out of the area as the bomb squad went to work. Steve called it back in to Frank Fitzgerald. "We have something here but not sure if it's what we're looking for."

Steve stood about fifty yards from the Delta warehouse and watched a dozen men that all looked like the Pillsbury Dough man but in brown. They had a large steel cart that they were pulling into position along with two robots following. One team was unrolling a curtain of padding that was being pulled into position at the opening of the warehouse.

The Commander of the Guard stood next to Steve and shook his head. "Guess all we can do is wait."

Steve looked back at the Commander and said, "I hate waiting!"

Thirty Four

The South Korean Military had arrived at the location that the CIA was holding the Russians that were captured. President Lee Myung-Bak had sent orders to cooperate with the Americans and assist in any way necessary. The agents detailed the extent of their investigation but Rusty wasn't too happy to have to work with the South Koreans. Josh made sure that the South Koreans were being used to hold the captured men and he and Rusty would work with the professor. He held the key to the bomb's components. Josh also got confirmation that a tactical force raided the home of the professor and freed his wife and daughter. It was just as he had told them. Two men were holding his family at gun point and the wife said she saw her husband dragged off by two other men a few days ago.

Josh had the Professor standing next to him and took his phone out and held it so the professor could see his wife and daughter. Having Skype on his phone proved very valuable. The man cried out in relief and hugged Josh. "Я благодарен Вам." Josh smiled back at the man not quite sure what he just said. "I am grateful to you. You saved my family." The man kept hugging him. "Okay we fulfilled our promise but we still need your help. Our people haven't found the bomb yet. We think it was sent to California. Los Angeles, California had a Korean cargo plane land and has been searched but no bomb found. Can you tell us anything else that might help?"

The man was still overcome with joy and sat down. He asked for water. "I told you the bomb is big, maybe three feet long and in a square crate."

"Yes, we sent that information along but with no results. Can the bomb be moved around without disturbing its contents?"

"Oh yes, it is packed very carefully and will only detonate when the device is activated. I made sure it was safe for them to move it around. My only hope was to help them so my wife and daughter would be released."

"That was understandable."

"But now you have saved them and I will be forever grateful."

"Our people will get your family out of Russia and we will protect all of you."

"Did you pack the bomb in the crate?"

"Yes, I put it in the crate but not in the plane. They took the crate from me. I never saw it again. I don't know what they did after."

Josh didn't have anything new to help with the search.

John Martin was glad that his FBI and CIA teams were finally working together. President Morgan sat along the bank of televisions that were now focused on the search of the Los Angeles airport and the warehouse. The Situation Room had been crowded for close to half a day with action from Seoul to Los Angeles beamed into the room and no one had left. Food and beverages were replenished and the Secret Service was at full force working the hallways of the White House. Morgan instructed his press secretary to inform the news media that he would be holding a press briefing later. Hopefully he would have more details and his coverage would be on every prime time news show. The news of a questionable crate in the Delta warehouse gave them hope. Maybe the end to this terrible ordeal was close to an end.

President Morgan certainly couldn't tell the world that the bombings were South Korean, Russian or any other Nation or group until he had more information. If he had to, he could at least show that his team had discovered the source of the bombs and tracked down two other bombs planted on a British and French plane. He would tell the world that they had the bomber in custody and would soon know who was to blame. With the cooperation of the English, French and South Koreans he would have positive information and show his team was making solid progress.

The nation had waited for some answers and the President knew he had to tell them something, and do it soon.

Morgan turned to his press secretary. "Tell the press core that I will be giving an update at ten this evening. I need to let them know what success we have had. Maybe in the next hour we'll have more details that I can add."

"Yes sir."

"Get Armstrong in here so we can go over the speech."

The press secretary headed out of the room and would make sure a message went out to all White House reporters as well as national television networks that there will be a press briefing at ten o'clock in the White House.

The nation had been waiting and the President's opposition was starting to make accusations that he was weak on foreign policy and this was a result. The leader of the other party had recently given the New York Times a quote that President Morgan was too soft on dissents and did not have good relationships with other foreign heads of state. The press secretary was glad that most European and Asian countries had applauded the United States efforts in thwarting bombs that were meant for both London and Paris. The administration would make this a key point in the upcoming speech. Politics would play as much a part of this as informing the people. Morgan would be able to show the American public that not only was he more than capable of handling International situations but he would be successful doing so.

Thirty Five

Teams of agents and National Guardsmen covered the two warehouses along the row of LAX storage buildings. Although they had a suspected crate in the Delta warehouse the search continued through the International warehouse. The California Joint Terrorism Task Force was now involved with the Bureau's people on the search. The task force often becomes involved when learning about a creditable threat but in this case they were informed from the LA Bureau office and working with the local agents on the case. Frank Fitzgerald was using all the resources available to resolve the problem.

Blair had known two of the men that were assigned from the task force from an earlier case. One of them was asking about the crate and contents. "From the information we're getting there is a three foot bomb that resembles the make-up of the one used in the Oklahoma City bombing. Guess the CIA team in Seoul found the bomber and he is working with them."

One guy nodded but had a frown on his face. "What is it?" She asked.

"This whole wild goose chase is based on the word of a known bomb maker. What if he's lying?"

"I thought about that, however his wife and daughter were being held captive unless he helped. They were able to free them and confirm his story. I think they're pretty sure he's telling them the truth."

This would be the third search of the two warehouses. Some members thought it was a waste of time. There were men in every aisle of the International warehouse and other teams unloading the semi trucks.

"This is crap, we've been through this twice," one guy was overheard saying.

The Guard Commander heard the comment. "If we have to do this a thousand times we'll do it."

The guardsman jumped when he heard his Chief. "Yes Sir. I'm sorry Sir."

Tensions were riding high and many of the searchers had been at it for hours without any sign of success. A refreshment station with food and beverage had been set up for all the men. Reserves were being sent in. The sky had darkened and it was only natural that fatigue set in on the men and women searching. Boxes were measured and anything smaller than three feet was not inspected. The information from the Professor was clear. The bomb itself was three feet long. There was no way to make it smaller. The International warehouse was close to three football fields wide and had five drive lanes through it. Semi tractor trailer trucks and other trucks often carted boxes and crates to their final destination. There were three large semis still in one of the drive lanes and a team had just started to go through the first one.

Steve and the Guard Commander stood outside the Delta warehouse pacing as the bomb squad continued to inspect the discovered crate. It had been over an hour when the lead officer was seen walking out of the building. Steve rushed over to him. "What did you find?"

The officer had taken off his helmet and his face was dripping with sweat. "There has to be the largest stash of hash I've ever seen in one place in that crate."

"Marijuana?"

"Yes, we unloaded the top of the crate close to three feet down and they have the hash packed in five pound bags stacked up like bricks in there. I sent a probe down a few more feet and nothing spiked. I think you may have uncovered a huge drug ring. Do you want us to unload the whole thing?"

"No, guess that is why the dogs went crazy. We need to let the Joint Drug Task Force know what we found and have them take control of the contents." Disappointment shown over Steve's face. He turned to the Guard Commander. "We'll need to continue the search."

The two men had been waiting together and conjecture was that they found the bomb.

The Commander shook his head, "We'll find it."

Steve appreciated the remark. They got their teams back in the Delta warehouse going through the stacks of boxes and crates. Blair and Jim were standing close to Steve and shook their head when they heard the news. "Guess this is your baby now," she told the guy from the task force.

"We'll get the crate out of your way and let you all get back to the search." He was calling his Captain to inform him what they had. The orders were simple. Get the marijuana loaded back in the crate and transport it to their warehouse. The California drug team had a large warehouse downtown Los Angeles on Pico. It was just blocks from their headquarters. California was the State with the largest captured amount of drugs because of Mexican cartel activities along with ships coming into the many harbors the Drug Task Force was always busy. Once they had the drugs hauled off their inspectors would trace the shipping manifest and their investigation would begin. The men from the task force got together with Steve and the Commander and arranged to move the crate out of the warehouse. The Guard Commander said, "I'll have my men load it on a transport if you want."

"That would be great. We can haul it out of here and out of your way."

The Guard got to work with the drug task force on completing the task and then getting back to the search.
Teams descended back into the Delta warehouse. Many of the replacement searchers were new to the investigation. Steve and the Commander gave them a rundown of the details they would need to perform their task. It was good that there were fresh people involved in the project. Everyone knew that the pressure was running high and having a relief team available was important.

Frank Fitzgerald updated the White House and knew that the President planned to go on air with a special report to the American people. He wished he had better news for him.

_____**Thirty Six**

President Morgan looked over the speech that his team
had put together. He knew that he needed to be positive and put to
rest the rumors that his team had failed to find out who was
responsible for the bombing of flight 792. Tomorrow would be the
funeral for Senator Harding and it was important that he could tell
the nation they captured the men responsible. He held out hope that
the team searching in Los Angeles or the CIA team in Seoul came up
with a last minute answer to what country or group was behind the
attack. Right now he had to portray the capture of the bomber and
conspirators as a terrorists group operating out of the Korean
Peninsula. He didn't want to tell the world that they were still
searching for Viktor Kevchef and Ivan Shankoff. He knew they held
the key to the final answer.

The news stations came on every channel with the flash of
breaking news. The screen showed the White House press room
with the flag of the United States in the foreground. The
podium had the press secretary telling the group of assembled
reporters the details for the funeral tomorrow for Senator
Harding. President Morgan stepped up behind his secretary
and thanked him for giving the details to the country.
Morgan was wearing a dark blue sweater and red and white
striped tie. His informal attire was designed to show
everyone that he had been hard at work and not concerned on
his clothes. It also gave him a more relaxed look.

"My fellow Americans, it has been three days of sorrow for the family of Senator Harding, our great Olympic team and everyone that was lost on flight 792. Over three hundred lives were stolen due to the work of a terrorist organization operating out of the Korean Peninsula. Our agencies have been diligently working to resolve whom the person or persons were responsible. I am pleased to announce that we have captured the men that planted the bombs on not only flight 792 but also planned to blow up planes headed to London and Paris. The French and British were warned in time and together our three countries thwarted the impending disaster. I am grateful to both our FBI and CIA agents that have worked tirelessly on this investigation. I also appreciate the cooperation of the other countries organizations that have been involved in the joint action. My team has continued to investigate this incident and will not rest until we have everyone involved under arrest."

The room erupted with hands flying in the air waiting to ask follow up questions. Morgan looked around the room and acknowledged Diane Sawyer.

"Thank you Mr. President. Do you know where this terrorist organization is headquartered or what country they represent?"

"Our International team is continuing to work with other world organizations and will have that answer soon. As you know it would be in our best National Security to wait until we have the final details before releasing that information."

Hands again flew up and Morgan held up his right hand. "Ladies and Gentlemen of the Press. I wanted to give you and the American people key details of our action but again National security issues along with the on-going work with other world agencies preclude me from saying more." The room grew quieter. A few more hands jolted up and Morgan turned to David Gregory. "David?"

"Thank you Mr. President. Can you tell us when your teams discovered the bombs planted on the flights to London and Paris and what is the plan for the captured terrorists."

"Once our investigation began we had agents along the Pacific Rim that were quick to uncover an organization that had gathered materials that matched those of the bomb on flight 792. They followed leads and uncovered the plot. I was able to convey the information to both the French and British and the planes were diverted and landed. The bombs were the same as the one found on the flight headed to Los Angeles."

"Where will the captured men be taken Sir?"

"Yes, David. That falls under the Terrorists Task Force and the information is covered under my National Security Administration. Obviously they will continue to be questioned and any further information will be passed along to the American people. Thank you all for your prayers for the families that lost loved ones and God Bless America." Morgan moved from the podium as cameras showed him patting his press secretary on the back. The news conference was a success. The President was able to make it a positive announcement and he hoped that would be how the newspapers around the country and world would play it. He headed back down the hallway of the West Wing and was talking to his National Security Director.

Everyone in the Cabinet was pleased with the information that Morgan had given the Press and how he wove the story of involvement with both the French and British. International relations had been at an all time low and this would boost it greatly. Like anything, perception was the key and how the press and public perceived the information would be critical. Morgan, if anything, was a great speaker and his ability to come off as sincere and involved would help sell that.

Back in Los Angeles Steve and Frank Fitzgerald had watched the press conference on their phones.
Both men smiled at the news and were happy that their ongoing search wasn't compromised. Without any results except uncovering one of the largest drug bust in history they felt less than successful. The search of the Los Angeles airport grounds would continue through the night with teams of agents and National Guardsmen combing every possible storage area where the bomb could have been hidden.

The Drug Task Force had removed the crate with the stash of hash from the airport grounds with the help of the National Guard. It would be gone through at their downtown Pico warehouse location later once they completed the research on where in Morocco the shipment originated and how it got through customs. The stickers on the side of the crate showed that the crate was supposedly checked at both Moroccan and French airports. As with all international shipments it would have been checked at LAX before being released. Most International cargo is held for at least a short period and checked. That had not been done yet.

The search continued at LAX through the two warehouses. Steve sent some of his team home to get some rest as others arrived. Blair and Jim wanted to stay but he insisted that they go get some rest. "Blair you need to check on Booth anyway." He knew that would convince her to leave.

She felt guilty because she had been so consumed with the events including Tony Kim's capture and now the search for the bomb that she forgot about him. "Okay, you're right Boss. Jim, could you drop me off at the Memorial Hospital on your way home?"

"Sure, I'd like to stop in and say hi to him too. I don't mind staying with you."

"My car is still in the hospital parking lot and I might just hang out there for a while."

"Sure," the two agents got in Jim's car and headed out of the airport. Blair was pretty quiet. "You okay," Jim asked. "I feel like I should have been more worried about Booth. I'm not a very good partner."

He could see that she was struggling with it. "Hey, wait a minute. We found the guy who crashed into you both. Discovered the CIA involvement with trying to scrub our investigation and have been searching for a mother of all bombs. It's not like you've been on vacation."

She smiled back at him. "You're right. Beside Booth had probably been sleeping the whole time."

"Yeah and he might have some hot chick nurse giving him a sponge bath." Jim laughed.

Blair laughed too, but thought to herself he better not.

Thirty Seven

The search of LAX airport storage areas turned up empty. Steve and Frank were exhausted as were all the men and women involved. The National Guard left a skeleton crew at the airport reporting to the FBI personnel still checking the grounds. It was almost eight in the morning and Frank called it in to the White House. Once they had his information they planned to get back to Josh and the CIA team in Seoul. They must have missed something. Maybe the bomb didn't go to Los Angeles. Maybe it left later in the day after the planes were heading to London and Paris. The White House made sure that the National Security Chief would convey to every country that they need to check every air cargo plane that landed at any of their airports. Where was this mother of all bombs that the Professor told them about? Was it all a ruse? Nothing was sure except that the Professor stated that he did make a huge bomb and the materials found in the Seoul warehouse confirmed that it was possible.

Blair had been sleeping in a chair along the side of Booth's bed when she was awoken by an orderly. "I need to go over his vitals and complete some blood work," he told her.

"It's okay, I'm an FBI agent assigned as a protective detail until he is better," she answered.

That took the young man by surprise. "Wow, he must be pretty important."

"You bet," and she smiled at him.

The man took Booth's blood pressure and the pressure of the cuff compressing on his right arm woke him. "Mr. Booth, I'm just taking your vitals. I'll be done in a minute." Booth rubbed the sleep from his eyes and caught a glimpse of Blair in the corner with her legs over the arm of the large chair. "How long have you been there?"

"Not too long, they said that you had a rough day so they gave you something to help you sleep. I didn't want to wake you."

He watched the instrument record his blood pressure readings and then the young man said he needed to take some blood samples.

"You'll have to prick him pretty good because there's not much blood in that tough one." Blair laughed as she said that.

Booth smiled at her and turned to the orderly. "At least you'll find some in me. Don't try to get blood from her. She'll kill you." Blair was happy that he was starting to joke around. He still had his head on the pillow and was being good about the doctor's orders not to sit up or lift his head. When the young man completed his task he smiled at Blair as he left the room. "Oh, you have a secret admirer."

"At least someone appreciates me." She was now sitting up in the chair and looked back at the door. The hallway was clear and she moved closer to the bed. Blair leaned over Booth and put her right hand on his face and stroked it softly. She was facing the door so if needed to she could back up. Her lips pressed against his and the two exchanged a long lingering kiss. "I love you baby."

"Me too," Booth said as tears welled in his eyes.

"Jim came with me last night but we didn't want to wake you.

Steve and all the guys asked about you and said to pass along their get well wishes."

"When I woke up last night the room was full of flowers. Shit, I thought I had died or something."

They both laughed. "Not on my watch," Blair said. She was holding his hand and pushing his hair back off his face. "What can I do for you?"

"How did you get back in here without Nurse Ratchet kicking you out?"

"I told her that the Bureau wanted to put a guard 24/7 on you and I had been assigned." That got a big smile from her partner.

"Damn nice body guard. I approve."

Blair saw the nurse walking by the front of the room and stood up next to the bed. The nurse turned and walked in. "Well Mr. Booth I hope you got a good night's rest."

"Yes I feel a lot better."

"The doctor said he would be in early. We arranged to send you down for more x-rays to see how your breast bone is doing. Someone will be here in a little to take you downstairs." She turned to leave and stopped at the doorway. "Will you be here all day Miss?"

"I'm not sure. My Chief will call to update my orders. He might have another agent on duty later on."

Once she left, both agents chuckled. "Well Miss, what's next," Booth asked.

Blair wanted to apologize for being away for so long but knew he would understand. She updated Booth on what had happened with Tony Kim then the action at LAX. He was disappointed that he couldn't be involved. The two of them talked for about fifteen minutes when a young blond pushing a gurney came into the room.

"Mr. Booth I'm here to take you downstairs to x-ray. I have to get you to slide off the bed and onto the gurney.

You need to stay as flat as possible." She pushed the cart next to his bed and locked the wheels. "Can you move okay or should I get someone to help us?"

"I can help if you need", Blair said.

"Thanks."

Booth slid his butt over slowly onto the cart as Blair and the young girl helped him. Blair pushed the sheet over his legs as he was sliding across the bed so that he wouldn't get cold. Once he was on the cart the young girl turned to Blair. "He'll be gone about an hour Miss."

"I have to get back to my office anyway. Booth, I'll be back as soon as possible." She wanted to kiss him but knew better.

He said, "I understand, tell everyone thanks for the flowers." They winked at each other as Booth was being pushed down the hallway. When Blair passed the nurse's station she told the head nurse that either she or another agent would be back soon. She grabbed her phone and dialed the office.

Kathy O'Connor answered. "How's Booth," she said.

"Better I think. He's going back down for x-rays and I was coming in unless I'm needed somewhere in the field."

"I think Steve wanted to talk to you. Hold on."

Blair was worried. What did I do wrong now? She waited for about a minute when Steve came on. "How's our patient?"

"Mean as ever. They took him down for more tests."

"I really think you should go home and get some rest."

"I slept all night. I'm fine and ready to go."

"Okay, head in to the office. We need to finalize the information you and Jim have on the Tony Kim issue for the Director before he leaves for D.C."

"I'm on my way Sir."

The press conference that Morgan held last night had been widely applauded and most newspapers headlines read, *'Bomber Captured!'* Comment from news anchors ranged from outstanding news to positive developments. President Morgan's decision to appear in a sweater came off just as he and his press secretary hoped. One British Tabloid read, *'Confident President Captures Fugitive!'* Washington politicians were now gathering for the funeral of Senator Harding. The First Lady and Press Secretary had gone over all the details with Mrs. Harding and made sure all her wishes would be incorporated into the funeral. The President made an overture to the Majority Leader of the Senate who represented the other party to speak along with him at the funeral. Morgan's star was again on the rise and the key members of the other party knew it. A special carriage was set to take the Senator's body across the Arlington Bridge to the cemetery and a twenty one gun salute was planned. The Senator would be laid to rest alongside that of his great Grandfather former President Harding.

No one spoke of the political fallout from the events of the past twelve hours but everyone knew that the President and his party were stronger than ever with the election around the corner. The funeral for Harding would be the chance for him again to show the American people and the World that he was a compassionate man and led his country in victory and sorrow. The Vice-President and many Cabinet members had attended various funerals for those aboard flight 792 across the country and many newspapers hailed that their attendance showed unity and respect for all people regardless of position or stature.

Thirty Eight

The Meeting between Steve Orrison, Fitzgerald, Blair and Jim took about an hour. The two agents again apologized for making a decision without getting approval from their boss but as Blair said, "We didn't have too many options." Tony Kim had given them all the necessary documents and material they would need to prove the CIA's involvement in trying to scuttle their investigation. The news that Robert Chiarini still operated his special ops group, Silverstone, would be their ace in the hole. Frank Fitzgerald swore them to secrecy and that once the time was right, it would be used. "You may never read about any of this but you will know when certain things take place and why."

The two agents thanked him and as they got up to leave Blair told Jim. "Give me a minute then I'll meet you at your desk." Jim left the room and Steve and Frank wondered what she wanted. "Sirs, I'm the one responsible for getting Jim in this mess. If necessary I will give you my letter of resignation."

Steve was quick to answer. "Blair, you made the best decision given the circumstances you were presented with. I'm not sure many of our agents could have done any better. You've proven yourself many times over and are a key member of our team."

Frank seconded that opinion.

"Now you need to get with your team and help us figure out where in the hell that damn bomb is!"

"Yes, Sir, Thank you Sir." She turned and walked out of the office with her head up high.

"Steve you got a winner there."

"Yes I know it Sir,"

Everyone in the Bureau office was working on assignments that the Chief had given them. They were contacting airports around the world questioning if any cargo plane from South Korea had landed. One group was plotting the air patterns from Seoul to a variety of places and the time frame it would take for the plane to arrive. A new theory was that the plane may have stopped at an undisclosed destination only to be sent to its final destination later. It was like looking for the proverbial needle in a haystack. Somehow, somewhere that bomb was sitting someplace and the FBI was pulling out every stop to find it. Kathy O'Connor and Chris were working in another avenue. What if it was sent on a regular flight? Although security on passenger planes was much tighter, they had to work that angle too.

Blair and Jim made their way to Kathy's desk. "What are you working on?" Jim asked.

"We were thinking that the Professor said when the plane left or at least when he thought it left Seoul. What if they put it on a passenger flight versus a cargo plane?"

Jim was quick to answer, "I'm not sure given the dimensions of a three foot square crate that it would have been loaded unchecked. Especially after flight 792 went down."

"You're probably right but we are all scrambling for a clue."

Blair pulled a chair from her desk into Kathy's work area. "Jim, grab another chair and let's work together with them. Kathy and Chris might have something or at least four heads might be better than two."

Chris laughed as Jim pulled a chair up to the corner of the desk next to Blair. "So far our two heads have got nothing," he said.

"Okay," Blair started. "What do we know so far?" The team of agents reviewed all the facts that had led up to the failed search of LAX. They went over the details that Josh had sent from Seoul and the material that he got from the Professor. They were putting it all together on the board that Kathy had moved into her work area. It was starting to look like they were tracing a crime scene with suspects and lines drawn from one thing to another. "Maybe if we put this all together in one place we can get a better perspective. I think we should also figure out why would they send the bomb here or where else would be a likely target." They liked Blair's idea and all four were diligently plotting down details known so far in the investigation.

The funeral for Senator Harding at Arlington National Cemetery had just concluded and President Morgan was on his way back to the White House. Although Mrs. Harding was at first reluctant to hold his funeral in Washington she was happy that she agreed to do it. The event was carried live on every television station and Senator Harding's grave site was close enough to the tomb of the Unknown Soldier and President Kennedy's eternal flame that stations incorporated the two sites into their broadcast. Her two children would always remember that their father was treated with the highest honor and the country appreciated his service.

President Morgan had thanked both his wife and that of the Vice-President's for all their work and that it was well done. The line of black SUV's crossing the Arlington Bridge was something many of the local residents had become accustomed to.

The Vice-President's car was three behind the President's and the Secret Service had beefed up their protection details since the murder last year of the Chief Justice. Washington, like many other Nation Capitals, was on edge with heightened security.

Morgan wanted to fly to the funerals of the Olympic Team members but it was discouraged by his security team. His press secretary suggested that they hold a memorial service in Washington for all those lost on flight 792 and invite family members that could attend. This would honor both the Olympic Team and all those that were killed aboard the plane. It was a great idea and other members of the administration agreed. Show compassion for everyone and make sure no one person or group felt left out. Plans were being drawn up for the event to be held at the Kennedy Center for Performing Arts. The schedule was set to hold the event in two days. The President wanted to do it before his scheduled trip to Los Angeles. He was planning an event to honor many key political supporters at The Staple Center in downtown LA on Sunday. It would be nationally televised with Hollywood personalities and movie stars receiving special awards. One of the key persons being honored was Steven Spielberg for his film, Lincoln. The film had been hailed by everyone and the details of the last four months of the life of Lincoln and the fight to end slavery would play well in an election year.

With the press conference last night and the funeral today, along with the two upcoming events at the Kennedy Center and in Los Angeles at the Staple Center, President Morgan should comfortably increase his lead in the polls. What appeared to be an election too close to call, according to most polls, was now becoming a double digit lead for the President.

Some members of Congress were busy padding their own re-election campaigns by blaming the other party for dragging their feet in support of Morgan and his efforts with our allies.

Just a few days ago some Congressional leaders were hesitant to link their campaign with that of the President but now everyone was jumping on his bandwagon.

Robert Chiarini had been working with the Head of Homeland Security to get the Professor and his family brought to the United States for helping in the bombing plot. Although he made the bombs used in the flights and the one that had somehow mysteriously vanished he had cooperated with investigators. The Professor was forced to participate due to threats to his family. His wife and daughter had been flown to London and would be arriving tomorrow to an undisclosed location. The Professor would join them once the final bomb was found and he could assist in disarming it. Chiarini and his team continued to be critical in this case. Orders were given to Josh and Rusty who headed the action in Seoul to work with the South Koreans and see if they could get any other details from those captured at the warehouse in Seoul.

The investigation in Seoul had slowed to a snail's pace. The captured men weren't talking and the Professor had given Josh everything he knew. He agreed to help disarm the bomb when it was found and said that the main problem was that there were two radio control timing devices that could detonate the bomb from almost anywhere.

Rusty had reverted to utilizing CIA tactics from the Cold War era to accomplish the task of getting the information needed from the captured men at the Seoul warehouse. Water boarding had, of course, been outlawed however; Rusty didn't care. Along with three other CIA operatives he continued to try to break the key men in the case. Not too many people could hold out under this type of torture.

One of these men had to be involved in packing and placing the bomb on a plane and if he had to Rusty would continue until he killed them or he got the information needed.

Josh was the agent that would work with the South Koreans and the Professor. He was diplomatic and understood the aspects of working with members of another country's military. He knew they needed an answer and needed it soon. One of the men Rusty was interrogating had that answer. It would only be a matter of time until he broke them.

_____**Thirty Nine**

Frank Fitzgerald was scheduled to appear along with
Robert Chiarini at the White House later that afternoon.
Frank had been at his office in the J. Edgar Hoover building at
935 Pennsylvania Avenue. His teams were working along
with the agents across the country plotting the possible
destination that this massive device may have been sent to.
Steve Orrison had updated the Director on the progress his
agents had made and their only conclusion was that the bomb
had to be somewhere in Los Angeles. There had been agents
assigned to inspect all foreign cargo at LAX along with teams
from the Alcohol Tobacco and Firearms group. The ATF
always had a presence at LAX due to the number of
International flights and persons arriving daily but now they
were assigning a group to team with the FBI and inspect cargo
along with other airport security.

The Los Angeles Bureau was retracing the action from
the evening that they searched both the Delta and
International warehouse. "We had to miss something," Steve
told his agents. A new concern was developing with the
upcoming visit of President Morgan to Los Angeles and the
event at the Staple Center downtown. Steve knew that with
so many Hollywood events like the Oscars and Golden Globes
always in town that his team was more than capable of
handling a Presidential visit.

He just wished that the search for this bomb had been
solved.

He was organizing a detail that would be in charge of handling the Presidential motorcade and had coordinated plans with the Secret Service.

They still had close to a week before President Morgan was to arrive. At least he would be coming in on the day of the event and planned to fly out later that evening after the celebration. That was one of the greatest advantages Orrison had being in Los Angeles. With the three hour time difference east coast to west coast often dignitaries often arrived the day of an event and could leave later that day to get back. Hopefully the President's visit would just be a short distraction for his team.

The meeting in the White House with Chiarini, Fitzgerald, John Martin and the President focused on the handling of both agencies in the bombing of flight 792. The President was writing on a pad at his desk when they all came in and stood in front of him. Morgan put his pen down and looked up at all three men. "I wanted to congratulate all of you and your teams on how you worked together on this problem." Morgan turned toward John Martin. "You have shown great leadership and your people should be recognized and awarded for their performance."

"Thank you Sir," Martin said. "Robert and Frank will submit the names of their key personnel involved in this case for the awards."

President Morgan turned in his chair from behind the Resolute desk and gazed at the flags stationed behind him. "You all did our country proud," He said now standing up. He walked out from behind the desk and shook each man's hands. "Many men have stood in this office and other great Presidents have sat behind that desk. Kennedy handled the potential showdown with the Soviet Union during the Cuban Missile Crisis in 1961. Bill Clinton sat there during the first bombing of the World Trade Center in 1993 and

George W. had to deal with the events of September 11, 2001 when the World Trade Center collapsed after being attacked by two planes. Men, I hold this office and our responsibilities to the highest level and I expect everyone on our team to do the same."

All three men could see the determination in Morgan's eyes as he spoke. He did not take his position or that of theirs lightly. The meeting lasted just about fifteen minutes and the men walked out of the Oval Office. Each one seemed a little taller and walked with a strut of confidence and pride. John Martin reminded them that they still had a mission. We must find that bomb that the Professor said he built. We cannot let the President or our great nation down.

On the way out of the White House Frank turned to Chiarini. "I have my teams stationed at every possible airport and inspected all incoming cargo. If I find anything I'll let you know immediately."

Chiarini was surprised at the comment but appreciated Frank's information. "I'll do the same. If my men find out anything else from the guys we captured I will get that information to you right away."

This was the first time the two had a cordial conversation since Frank had been appointed to his position. Maybe things would be better. They parted at the driveway along the side of the White House and each got into their respective cars and were driven off.

The Drug Task Force along with members of the ATF was tracing the shipping manifest from the cargo confiscated at LAX. The amount of marijuana was thought to be one of the largest drug captures ever. They had been at it for the past two days looking into the flights that carried the product from Morocco in North Africa through French customers and then finally to Los Angeles. It would be weighed and check out once they had more details.

It was their hope to find out who originated the shipment and catch them too. The Task Force was working with Interpol and the General Direction for External Security in France trying to track down the information.

President Morgan had continued to keep an open conversation with the two leaders of Britain and France on the bombs planted on planes and the progress on the search for the one that had not been found. International relations with the two countries were at an all time high and Morgan hoped to capitalize on that with the election just weeks away. Back in Los Angeles Steve Orrison made sure that he had every airport along the California coast stationed with agents checking cargo coming into the country.

The small charted flight was making it final approach into the Burbank Airport and the captain radioed the tower for clearance. He had been given instructions to land on runway three and would soon be on the ground. The Cessna 560 Citation V was a midsized corporate jet and held up to twenty passengers. There were only five men on the flight today. It had originated from Phoenix and would be making a return flight after being serviced. The charter service was normally reserved for corporate clients and often would make flights to and from Los Angeles and San Francisco. Once they were on the ground the passengers headed into the terminal. One of them was a gentleman maybe sixty five to seventy years old and very distinguished looking. He carried a pearl handled cane and black attaché case. He held the case close to his side as he followed the other passengers. The man was tall with a tailored beard and wore a dark black beret. The other four passengers headed to the baggage area but he just walked out of the terminal and waited at the curb. He took out a cell phone and dialed someone. Soon a long black limo pulled up to the curb and another gentleman stepped out. They shook hands and got back into the limo.

"I trust you had no problem, Viktor," the man sitting in the back of the limo said.

"Everything went as we hoped. Is everything all set here?"

Ivan Shankoff smiled at his guest. "We have fooled everyone just as you planned. The bomb is just waiting for us. I have a team watching the warehouse and it will be ready for us when we want."

"The American's, they are stupid," Viktor said. "I know they think they have the correct information that we fed them. The Professor played his part well."

Both men laughed out loud at the statement as the limo pulled away from the curb and headed toward downtown Los Angeles.

Forty

It had been three days since the original search of the two warehouses at LAX and still no sign of the mysterious bomb. Something didn't add up but what was it? Frank Fitzgerald and John Martin wondered if there really was this mother of all bombs. Martin requested the CIA to do a thorough background search again on the Professor. "How do we know he's telling us the truth," He asked.

"Our only thing is his family was being held captive and our forces did take them by storm to free his wife and daughter." Chiarini was right. His agents did follow up after the rescue. They confirmed that the Professor was indeed teaching at Moscow University and CIA research showed him to be an ex-KGB operative from the nineties.

"We need to do a little more digging," Martin told them. Chiarini agreed and assigned one of his teams in Russia to do more follow-up.

Fitzgerald told the Director that his agents were still searching every International flight's cargo although it had been scaled back. "We will keep up on it Sir."

John Martin knew he was getting complaints from companies that their shipments were being held up due to extra searches but it was critical that they kept a presence at the airports due to the inter they had on the possible bomb.

President Morgan's press secretary had requested all department heads to be in attendance at the Kennedy Center tonight for the Performing Arts. Tonight was the night he would be honoring all those that lost their lives aboard flight 792 and wanted to make sure the country saw that all of Washington had pulled together on this. The Speaker of the House along with the Head of the Senate and both members of the other party were asked to sit on the stage with President and Mrs. Morgan. The Vice-President and Cabinet members would flank all of them. It was Friday in Washington and many members of both chambers often would head to their respective states; however, with the opportunity to be seen along side of the President at such an important function, most planned to attend. Election years make many people adjust their schedules on the fly. You never know what or how your constituents viewed you being at one of these things. One thing for sure, honoring men and women killed by a terrorist group could only mean good press.

As always with these types of events, security would be the highest priority. The Secret Service along with the FBI and other agencies had men and women running checks and background information on every attendee. Close to one thousand requests had come in from family members to attend the memorial and each one had to be checked out thoroughly. Frank Fitzgerald and the Washington Bureau Chief had every agent working this task. There were request from Canadians to attend who had loved ones aboard flight 792 and the Prime Minister of Canada had been invited once they saw how many Canadians wanted to be involved. The Secret Service thought this was turning into a nightmare.

The inclusion of Canadian citizens and the Prime Minister came as an afterthought. Organizers forgot that many lost in the bombing were from Canada. Many of the Canadians were coming from Toronto and Montreal.

Flight 792 was a connecting flight for many that were headed on from Los Angeles.

The President didn't want anyone denied attendance unless credible information was discovered. It was fruitless to argue this with him or his staff. Morgan made it clear. "Every person that lost someone on this flight should be here if they want to be."

In Los Angeles the search for the bomb that the CIA had said existed was futile. It almost seemed pointless to keep on searching and every location had cut back on the number of agents stationed at major airports checking international cargo. Steve Orrison was busy working on his security plans for Sunday's event at the Staple Center. Both the Los Angeles Lakers and LA Clippers shared the Arena for NBA games but the schedule had them both out of town. With the pre-season just starting it was much easier to schedule an event there. The Los Angeles Convention Center was adjacent to the Staple Center and had a home show scheduled for the next weekend. It was easier to handle traffic at the Staple Center because S. Figueroa Street was a one-way traffic street heading north. West Pico Boulevard bordered the Center to the south and Chuck Hearn was on the north side. Most guests would be arriving from either the Santa Monica Freeway south of the Center or the 110 freeway that was west of the building.

The Nokia Theatre was on Chuck Hearn Ct. just past the Staple Center and the LA Kings hockey team played across from the theatre. The Kings, along with the rest of the NHL, was involved in a season long lock out so there would be no hockey traffic to contend with. The Nokia Theatre hosted many events such as the American Music Awards, The EMMY's and the ESPN annual awards banquet now named the ESPY's. The Bureau was happy that there weren't any other events scheduled for that Sunday at any of the venues around the Staple Center.

If there was, it would only complicate everything.

The area along West Pico was a warehouse district. There were two large buildings that stretched all the way to S. Figueroa Street. The largest one was where many local clothing designers stored their products. American Apparel was the largest of them and all their clothing was made in downtown Los Angeles. It was one of their greatest appeals along with the trendy designs that were sold in their stores all over California. Three other clothing retailers had facilities in the same warehouse. The second building belonged to the Federal Government and was operated by the Drug Task Force and the ATF. The first two floors were the main offices of the two Federal agencies and the top two floors were storage areas. It was there that they stored confiscated materials that were found along the California coast and border. With the drug trade from Mexico so prevalent the building was always full of drugs. It was well guarded and had 24/7 protection. There were cameras at every entrance and exit and was one of the safest buildings in town. Due to its contents the LA Police department also cruised past on a regular basis.

Steve had two days to finalize his plans and he organized a meeting with the Los Angeles Police Chief who would be handling traffic and the parade route that the President's limo would be taking. Whenever the President was arriving in town the Police Chief dreaded the traffic back-ups it caused. They would have to shut the 405 down from LAX all the way to the Santa Monica Freeway. "Thank God," He said, "At least it is a Sunday."

The two men put their plans into work and agreed that each would keep the other informed of changes. When it involved a Presidential visit there was always changes.

Blair had been at the hospital with Booth and on the first day he was allowed to sit up.

They had a neck brace on him and suggested he wear it for at least a week until he returned for follow-up exam. "You will be able to go home Mr. Booth," the doctor was explaining.

"It is critical that you rest and keep the brace on unless you are lying flat in bed."

Booth was nodding but Blair knew he didn't plan to do any of that. "Doctor, don't you think he should stay here another day or two," Blair suggested. Booth gave her a dirty look.

"Oh no, as long as he follows orders I think he will be okay. We did x-ray's again this morning and everything is healing according to schedule. I will give you a prescription for pain Mr. Booth. Please, if you start hurting take them. They will help you relax and make you more comfortable."

"No problem doctor. I'll do everything you say."

When Booth said that, Blair laughed out loud. "Doctor I'm not kidding, he's worse than a child. He'll want to be out and about when we leave the hospital."

"Oh no, Mr. Booth, you must follow my orders or you could be paralyzed if something goes wrong."

Even with the doctors Indian accent Booth knew how serious he was. "I promise."

"Will you have someone there to take care of you, Mr. Booth?"

"I'm in charge of him, doctor," Blair said. "He isn't getting out of my control."

Booth knew she was determined to make him follow the doctor's orders.

"Mr. Booth I know you are probably feeling much better and that is good but don't think you're healed yet. You have a C-3 and C-4 vertebra that are pressed too close together because they are swollen. They are at the base of your neck and lead down to your spine. You must be very careful."

The doctor's warning about his spine and the prospect of being paralyzed got Booth's attention. Blair looked worried too. She asked again, "Would it be better for him to spend a few more days here?"

"We can't do any more for him here than he can do for himself at home. Just follow doctor's orders."

They thanked him for everything and waited for the nurse to bring his discharge papers.

"You have to promise me that you're going to do everything he said, Booth."

"I promise baby, I don't want to end up in a wheel chair for the rest of my life."

Blair moved to the side of his bed and sat down. She leaned in and kissed him softly on the forehead. The two sat there quietly holding hands and waited for the nurse to appear.

"I want you to stay at my place until you're feeling better."

"I can just stay at my home."

"No, if you're at my place I can check on you and beside I want you there at night with me." There was no denying it, the two were in love and she wanted to make sure she could keep a watch on Booth. Steve had ordered her to take a few days off and hoped that she would also get some rest while Booth recovered. He was starting to see that the two partners meant more to each other than just a working relationship.

Just then the nurse appeared. "Mr. Booth I have your release orders and two prescriptions from your doctor, one for pain and the other to help you sleep. I've requested a wheelchair to take you downstairs and your friend can pull her car up to the door in front. We'll bring you right down."

"I don't need a wheelchair."

"Sorry, hospital rules. When you are in here we are responsible for you. We've taken care of everything with your insurance and here are your papers. The doctor wants you to make an appointment for next week."

Booth just sighed.

Blair opened the closet and got his clothes out. She had brought some from his house a few days ago. "They had to cut your pants and shirt off in the trauma center so I picked these up for you."

She helped him put his pants on and he had the saddest look on his face. "What's wrong now?"

"Just what you need, a boyfriend that can't even put his own pants on."

"Hey don't complain. Maybe later I'll take them off too!"

That brought a smile to his face. "I love you babe!" She looked back up at him as she tied his shoes. "I love you too!"

An orderly came in with the wheelchair and Blair helped Booth out of the bed. He looked kind of sad with the neck brace and tried to sit up tall.

"You're going to be okay. I'll be downstairs to get you."

Blair headed out of the room and wiped away a tear as she entered the elevator.

_____Forty One

It was the night of the big event in Washington. The
John F. Kennedy Center for the Performing Arts was located
on F Street in northwest Washington. With so many people
from out of town attending, traffic would be at a standstill. It
was five o'clock and many government buildings were
closing. Workers would be on the roads headed home and
many lived in the outskirts of the Nation's Capital. The
Kennedy Center was just off the Potomac Parkway and the
two bridges that crossed back into Virginia were always
jammed at that time of day. Today was no different. The
event was to start at seven tonight and people had already
started to arrive at the Center. Constitutional Avenue merged
into the Rock Creek and Potomac Parkway and that was one
of the busiest streets.

The view of Theodore Roosevelt Island from the steps
of the Kennedy Center was a popular tourist site. It would
not be available today. The District of Columbia Police had
the route blocked off and every car that headed to the
Kennedy Center would have to show tickets for tonight's
event. The FBI conducted vehicle searches and reminded all
attendees that only small hand bags or purses were allowed
inside.

The Kennedy Center's Grand Foyer was lit up like a
Macy's Christmas window.

Press gathered along the entrance and snapped photos of arriving dignitaries.

The Secret Service task now had to protect the President, Vice-President and Canadian Prime Minister along with key members of the House and Senate gathered in one place.

It was not unusual for Washington to host such events but given the recent events extra precaution was put into place. Fitzgerald, along with his Washington Bureau Chief, Andrew Jackson, headed up the security detail. Andy was to escort the Vice-President and his wife to the event and Frank was to ride along with Mr. & Mrs. Morgan. The Secret Service would accompany both vehicles to the event. The Prime Minister, Stephen Harper, was being escorted to the event with his security team and three Secret Service agents.

The Secret Service performed their usual search and inspection of the Kennedy Center. That included a thorough search both the night before the event and the day of the event. Everyone involved in the protection detail had gone over every aspect of their assignment many times over. Mr. Harper became Prime Minister in 2006 after federal elections in Canada. He headed many programs including a stimulus to help spur the economy and pushed a plan to build a new bridge from Windsor to Detroit. He was very popular and well liked. His request to be included would also enhance Morgan's International cooperation initiative.

President Morgan's press secretary had informed the President that new election polls that the New York Times planned to release in Sunday's paper showed him with a twelve point lead and a sixty percent approval rating. This was his highest rating since his election four years ago. Everything was working to his advantage.

The schedule of events for the evening had Morgan opening the night and introducing special guest including the Prime Minister.

He then planned to introduce Diana Ross who would sing *Amazing Grace*. It was one of those events that needed to be somber but uplifting for all the families involved.

CBS planned to televise the show in its entirety live. Every news show planned special tributes that evening to the individuals lost on flight 792 and CNN would air Anderson Cooper's interviews with many of the family members that attended telling their stories. This would be the first time since the events of 9/11 that so much news coverage was dedicated to the families of victims. Other tragedies like Hurricane Sandy and the Newtown shooting concentrated on the actual victims not as much on their families. Tonight's event was all about those family members being recognized and telling the story of those that they lost.

The press secretary had talked to some family members about their loved ones and two agreed to tell their story on stage. One of them was Mr. Thomas. Not only did he lose his son Brandon, a decorated Olympic athlete, but his daughter Jenny and two grandchildren were also killed on flight 792. Mr. Thomas at first said he didn't want to do it however once he understood that he spoke not only for the Olympic team but for those parents and grandparents that lost someone he agreed. The press secretary offered to help him put together his remarks. That eased Mr. Thomas' mind and made it more comfortable for him.

CBS had cut a few promos for the upcoming event and showed clips of the Olympic team after its final victory in South Korea and pictures of the flight crew.

They also got a picture from Mr. Thomas of Brandon and Jenny at the airport along with the two grandchildren before they left for the games.

Mrs. Thomas didn't want to attend the event in Washington. She had been hospitalized after the funerals for her children and grandchildren and was on a suicide watch.

Her sister and brother were staying with her and they hoped that once this was over their sister might be able to pull herself together. No one understood she would say, "I lost all of them!"

It was now quarter to seven and the Kennedy Center was packed with distinguished guests, reporters, television cameras and families of flight 792. They were just waiting for the arrival of the President and Vice-President. Mr. and Mrs. Morgan were getting out of their vehicle on the north side of the Center and the Secret Service was escorting them to the stage. The Vice-President and his wife had just greeted the Canadian Prime Minister, Mr. Harper and his wife, backstage.

The Washington FBI Bureau and Secret Service were in full force and the District of Columbia Police Chief had the majority of his men in and around the Center. The National Park Service covered the route from Constitution Avenue all the way to the Potomac Parkway. People lined Constitution hoping to see the President's motorcade pass. There was a large crowd that made its way from the Arlington Memorial Bridge all the way past the Lincoln Memorial. They were cheering and waving banners. Flags draped the route of all the United Nations countries. It had turned into the second largest event dwarfed only by the President's Inauguration.

Security was at the highest level and there was always a fear of something going wrong. Outside there was an incident with a vehicle being detained due to the people not having their tickets for the event. The driver, a tall distinguished looking man that spoke broken English, demanded that they had been invited and had to be let into the Center.

Orders were clear; no one gets in without proper passes.

The man was becoming physical and his wife, a much younger looking woman than the man, swung an umbrella at one of the police officers.

Calls went out for assistance and one of the local FBI agents headed to the scene. The two people were put in the back of a patrol car and the local cops waited for direction.

"What have we got here?" the arriving agent inquired. "We got two people that said they forgot the tickets in their hotel room. When we told them they couldn't enter without tickets they got angry." The officer was flushed when he relayed his story to the agent and was speaking rapidly.

"Okay I'll handle it from here." The agent moved to the squad car and could see that the lady was crying and her husband was trying to console her. He looked at his attendee list and was glad that it was in alphabetical order. "Folks I'm sorry you are having trouble but due to the nature of who is involved at the event we must be sure only those invited are let in."

"But we got ticket to come."

"What is your name sir?"

The man still had his arm around his wife and was sobbing. "I am Vladimir Babikov and this is my wife Anna."

"Okay Mr. Babikov, I need to know why you think you should be let into the event."

"Our daughter Irene was killed on the plane that was bombed. We got tickets to come to Washington. We drove all the way from Toronto today and I forgot ticket in hotel."

"Give me a minute Mr. Babikov." The agent moved back toward the officer. "Shit, why now," he said to the officer. "I've got the Babikovs' name on my list of invited attendees. It does show that they would be coming from Canada and that their daughter Irene was on the flight. I'm going to have to call it in."

He called the information in to the lead agent and confirmed that they were on the list.

"Bring them to the side entrance and they would have to be searched and if everything checks out they would be let in.

You have to tell them that they are going to miss a big part if we can get them in at all."

The agent turned back toward the couple in the police cruiser.

"Mr. and Mrs. Babikov, I might be able to help you. First we need to head to the side door of the Kennedy Center and they will need to search both of you and ask you a few more questions."

"Good we will do what you tell us," Mr. Babikov said. He put them in his vehicle and said, "Someone will watch your car for you." How the agent wished they weren't Russian but guessed if they were sent to blow up the President the terrorists wouldn't use such an obvious couple. Beside where would they hide a bomb? It's supposed to be three feet square. He pulled up to the side entrance where he passed the Babikov's to another agent at the door.

President Morgan was making his opening remarks and flags of every country that had lost someone on flight 792 slowly descended from the rafters behind those on the stage. "I am humbled by the lost hopes and dreams of all your family members that have been lost." He continued to praise the people gathered to honor the lives of their loved ones. A hush was heard from the crowd as pictures of many of those from flight 792 were flashed on the large screen on the stage. The President now turned and introduced Diana Ross. She came out from the left side of the stage and had on a long flowing white dress. Music filled the auditorium as she moved on to the stage and a group of close to fifty singers gathered behind her. Ms. Ross opened with singing *Amazing Grace* and tears welled in the eyes of almost everyone in attendance. The music lasted about ten minutes and Ms. Ross held her arms out wide as she completed the last verse. There was a loud spontaneous applause as the audience stood clapping and crying at the same time.

The President and Mrs. Morgan moved to Ms. Ross's side and Morgan held out his hand inviting the Vice-President and Prime Minister to join them.

There was now a thunderous applause as the three couple along with Ms. Ross, stood on stage all holding hands and the music again played. They sang the first verses all over again and the standing crowd joined in. It was beautiful. It couldn't have been planned. Voices rang out. *Amazing Grace how sweet the song............*

It seemed that no one wanted to stop singing. The song went on for two full verses when President Morgan moved forward and motioned the crowd to be seated. Applause filled the Center and people were hugging each other in the audience. It took close to five minutes to regain control but everyone in attendance said it was one of the greatest moments they had ever seen.

Forty Two

Headlines of every newspaper captured the theme of the night. The New York Times often a critic of the President and his administration had nothing but praise for organizing the event. Canadian and European newspapers hailed the event and showed the view of all the flags from every nation flying at the Kennedy Center. It was a press bonanza for the President and his team. The press secretary was jumping up and down in his office with the review of every article that the team was reading. President Morgan and his team had invited Prime Minister Harper and his wife to the White House on Saturday morning for breakfast. It was almost unheard of to do that, especially, on such a short notice. The two men had a good relationship but last night they became bonded in resolve to improve things between their two countries. The U.S. often took Canada for granted and the President wanted to improve that.

Many papers highlighted the speech that Mr. Thomas had given. His tribute to his son, the captain of the Olympic swim team, and his daughter and her two children brought everyone to tears. His remarks hit home with so many that had lost a loved one on flight 792. It helped that the Thomas kids were part Korean. The press secretary was pleased and surprised on how solid his speech was delivered and glad that they had asked him to do it.

Mr. Thomas had to stop a few times during the speech and clear his throat and when he finished President Morgan and his wife hugged him on stage at the podium. There was a standing ovation that lasted for at least ten minutes. It would be shown over and over on every news channel across the world. The message he delivered was one of hope and love and stressed the value of every life.

President Morgan and the Prime Minister had discussed the prospects of a large bomb somewhere out there and Morgan filled Harper in on what his team had found so far. It was a very informal meeting with a lot of substance. The President told Harper that he was headed to Los Angeles on Sunday for an event and once their schedules allowed he would like to come to Ottawa to talk about common goals.

The election was just a few weeks away and already the new political polls were putting Morgan at close to a landslide victory. Just weeks ago the election was too close to call. CNN in the morning said they had conducted a poll in five states thought once be toss-ups but now had Morgan close to a double digit lead in each one. Colorado, Pennsylvania and North Carolina all reported a surge in support for the President and most people surveyed applauded how he was handling the events since the crash of flight 792. No one argued that the President always held a lead in foreign affairs, however, recent events and the Kennedy Center tribute showed him to be a great leader. The fact that it still wasn't clear what group or country was responsible for the bombing of the flight escaped the public's attention.

Josh arrived at the safe house where they had taken the Professor for protection. Chiarini had wanted him to go over the details of the bomb one more time. Too much time had passed without any success in finding any type of explosive. The CIA safe house was one they had used many times and sat in the outskirts of Suwon.

They were far enough from Seoul so as not to create a lot of attention and close enough to Josh's house so that he could keep tabs on it. Two agents were put in charge of guarding the Professor and his family had been put on a plane in Moscow to join him. They offered him, his wife and daughter asylum in the United States for his help.

"Something wrong?" one of the agents asked.

"The boss wants us to go over it all one more time with the Professor. Where is he?"

"He was pretty sick last night so Benny went out and got him some stuff. He's been sleeping all day."

Josh walked up the stairway to the second floor and knock on the door. There wasn't an answer. He knocked again and called out, "Professor, sorry to bother you but I need just a minute." About thirty seconds passed and he called out again. "Professor I'm coming in, just need a minute or two."

He opened the door and saw the bed with the covers pulled up over the Professor's head. The room was cool and the Professor had told the agents in charge that he felt sick to his stomach and freezing. Josh called out again and moved to the bed and grabbed the top cover and pulled it back. "Shit he's gone," he yelled out. The agents downstairs ran up to the bedroom and burst into the room. "He's not here, where the hell have you guys been?" Josh was yelling at the top of his lungs and the two men stared at each other stammering.

"What do you mean he's gone?"

"You two jackasses, he's not here what the hell do you think I mean."

The two agents searching the room and Josh could see that the lock on the tall window in the corner had been removed. "Someone took the lock off this window. He must have gone out from here."

Two of them ran downstairs and Josh went out the window looking for any trace of footsteps or someone on the roof.

There it was, the gutter had been pulled loose from the roofing at a spot near the lowest drop to the lower level. Josh jumped down to the first level and followed the tracks that shoes made in the roofing material along the ridge. One of the agents was now standing on the ground level and Josh hollered down to him. "He had to get out this way. When was the last time either of you saw him?"

"Last night when Benny took him his dinner and medicine."

"What time was that?"

"Maybe six or seven last night."

"Son-of-a-bitch, that was fifteen hours ago. He could be anywhere now."

He didn't want to make the call but knew he didn't have a choice. Once Chiarini requested him to visit the Professor at the safe house and go over the details of the bomb one more time he had to report it in.

Robert Chiarini stood in his office pounding on his desk when he got the news. "Get everyone out and find him, now!" He was still yelling when Josh took off with the other two agents. "Yes Sir, we're on it Sir," was all he could say. Chiarini placed a call to his man in Moscow. "Did you get the Professor's wife and daughter off yet?"

"They left yesterday and should have already made it to Seoul. I called it in and gave Jack the information. He said he'd pick them up and take them to the Professor." He was still talking in the phone when Chiarini had hung up and made another call.

The man picked up the phone in his office. "No Sir, I had a man waiting at the airport yesterday and neither one was on the plane.

No, I didn't call it in, thought they missed their flight or there was a change in plans. I sent him back out there today."

"I don't pay you to think, I pay you to do what you're told to. I want you to put every man on this now."

Robert Chiarini who had been toasted just a few days ago with his team's successes now had both the Professor and his family missing. Was the information about this so called explosive all bullshit? How was he going to tell the President? He needed to solve this first before telling anyone what happened. He contacted his men back in Moscow and told them to put an all points bulletin out for the Professor and his family. "Don't tell anyone why, just do it."

Josh and the two agents knew they were chasing the Professor who had at least a ten to fifteen hour head start. If he was meeting contacts he would be long gone. When Chiarini called Josh back and told him that the Professor's wife and daughter were also missing and never made it to Seoul it was clear that they had been fooled. Now they weren't sure what the bomb sent from Seoul looked like or even if there was a bomb.

Forty Three

The small motel room was dimly lit and Viktor stood in the corner as Ivan addressed the two men seated at the table. "How is the building guarded?"

"There is a surveillance camera on each floor and the guard makes his rounds once every thirty minutes. It doesn't seem like they changed anything from the usual schedule."

"And the crate?"

"We were surprised but once they put the crate in the storage building they returned just once to get stuff from it. One man took all the packing slips off the side of the crate and then he returned once more later."

"Your man is sure he can get the package and has the drop all set?"

"Yes, he said the cord was already in position to lower the package down. He was surprised they only took some of the marijuana from the crate."

"How long will it take for you to get our package out and into position?"

"The information you gave us from the Professor is that there is a sliding panel on one side that will give us easy access to it. Once we take it out and close it back up no one will know because there is a false panel. Our partner comes on for the evening shift and we're all set."

Viktor handed the man a burner phone. "Once you have what we need call me on the phone I gave you. It is important that it makes it to the spot we told you about."

"When do we get the rest of our money?"

"Not until I know the package is where I need it, we will wire the money to your account when I get that call."

Both men nodded approval. "We plan to disappear as soon as we have confirmed that our money has been deposited."

"Good," Viktor said.

Ivan handed them each a packet and told them they will be in touch. The two men got back into their squad car and headed back downtown to continue their scheduled surveillance of the route around the Staple Center.

"It is amazing how greedy these Americans are," Ivan said to Viktor.

"Money will lead to the ruin of the West," Viktor answered. The two men toasted each other with a glass of Vodka and smiled as their plan was coming together.

The Los Angeles Police Chief had gone over all the details with the lead Secret Service team. The FBI was completing plans at the Bureaus headquarters on Wilshire Boulevard. The Police Chief said his men would continue to make rounds around the Staple Center and adjacent area and they increased the patrols to every fifteen minutes instead of thirty minutes. He also said that his men would all be on duty and any leaves were cancelled until after the President's visit.

The Secret Service had a group of agents that would be scouring the auditorium for anything unusual and they planned to repeat this up to an hour before the event. The Chief said he had designated fifteen officers to do the same thing on Saturday evening. "I figure we can't be too safe so I will have some of my men checking out both the Convention Center next door as well as the Staple Center."

Tony Aued

"Good idea," the agents said.

Steve planned on assigning a group of his agents to ride with the President's motorcade to and from the airport and another group to work with the Secret Service at the Center. Although the Secret Service wasn't too keen on others than their personnel guarding the President they were good with the FBI having agents watching doors and entrances and exits. The meeting broke up and each entity tended to their assignments.

Steve headed back out of the conference room and his secretary said, "You had a call from Agent Adams, Sir." He had talked to Blair several times and she had given Booth the phone twice to talk to the boss. Steve had some time so he returned her call. "How's our patient doing today?"

"He thinks he is better and wants to get back to work. I told him until the doctor visit on Monday he needs to cool it."

"His best medicine is rest. How about you?"

"I'm okay and ready to get back to work. I appreciated the time off but I think Booth can be on his own now."

"Okay how about coming in to the office on Monday after you take him to the doctor."

"I was thinking more about helping with the Presidential visit on Sunday."

"I've got the whole team set up and we should be okay with the Secret Service and local police assisting."

"Yeah, I know, but just for my own sanity how about letting me jump in too?"

Steve wanted to ask Blair a delicate question but had been putting it off. "Before I answer I need to know something."

"Shoot."

"What's going on between you and Booth?"

"I'm not sure what you mean."

"The department policy forbids two agents working in the same office if they are related or in a, special relationship."

264

It was obvious that Steve was having a problem asking this line of questioning.

"I know that but I'm not sure where we're going with this. Can I get back with you on it?'

"Sure but we can't put this off too long."

"Okay."

"Don't tell Booth that you're coming in on Sunday to help. He'll be right there wanting to be a part of it all." Blair agreed and took the phone into her bedroom so Steve could talk to Booth. Once he finished he asked to talk to Blair one more time.

"Listen, you are both key players in our agency and there will always be jobs for both of you but we have to follow procedures."

"Understood Sir. What do I need to know for Sunday?"

"I'll have Kathy call you and give you a rundown of where we are going to be stationed. I'll let you know then where you'll be. The only thing they want us to handle is guarding entrances and exits."

Steve hoped he didn't make a mistake telling Blair she could come in but after all it was a plum assignment and if it made her feel better why not. When he talked to Booth, he told him if the doctor released him on Monday he could come back on desk assignment for a short time. Booth understood and was just happy that he was getting close to returning to work.

Blair returned to the bedroom after talking to Steve and Booth was sitting on the side of the bed. "By the look on your face something is wrong. What is it?"

"He asked about us."

"You mean, us!"

"Yeah, dummy, us!"

"What did you tell him?"

"I said it was too soon to say anything." She stared down at the floor and had a sad look on her face.

Booth took her hand and she looked up at him. "I have never met anyone like you in my life, Blair Adams. You are the most beautiful, strong and intelligent person in the world. I love you; I'm in love with you and will shout it from every roof top in the valley."

The two embraced and Booth pulled her toward the large king size bed. "Be careful," She said, as they kissed a deep lingering kiss and fell back on the bed with Booth wrapping his legs around hers. She ran her fingers down his side and kissed him. She whispered in his ear, "I love you Brandon."

Forty Four

The Los Angeles Police cruiser moved down Figueroa Street slowly and turned onto Chuck Hearn Court. The two officers had made contact with their partner, the night watchman at the Drug Task Force warehouse on West Pico Boulevard earlier and were going to meet at a designated area in an hour. The guard had done some preliminary work on the crate and removed four screws that held a secret panel in place. Once he had the assigned package out of the crate he would put the panel back together. The package was supposed to be small and easy to conceal in a carrying case or duffel bag. The guard carried a black backpack normally on his route which wasn't unusual. The guards had assigned rounds in the warehouse and would often have their lunch and or other key items on their person. The lockers for the personnel at the warehouse were on the main level and the guards were not supposed to leave the warehouse area once they clocked in. All backpacks and carry-on items were to be left at the guard station at the third floor entrance. Once he had the package he planned to lower it down the back side of the building from the window in the men's bathroom. He had concealed a bungee cord outside the window yesterday and checked to make sure it was still in position when he arrived. The warehouse, by design, had very few windows and there was only a bathroom window on every floor in the back of the building.

The plan was well thought out and each man knew they were about to be rich.

The two officers checked their watches and knew that they were just an hour away from being millionaires. They were promised half-a-million dollars to move the package from the drug unit to the Convention Center. It would be passed off to another man there and their task would be successful. They knew the package was important and if it contained the amount of cocaine that they were told, it was worth millions.

Instructions were clear; the package contained uncut cocaine and was extremely valuable. Once they handed it over to the Russian a contact would put the money into their accounts. "No one is going to know. Shit, with so many damn drugs coming in from Mexico how's this going to change anything." They had convinced each other that if they didn't do it someone else would. The local police force for years had been suspected of being on the take and if people suspected them they might as well get rich. It was common knowledge among cops that a pound of uncut cocaine would be worth over $150,000 an ounce cut five or six times. This was close to fifty pounds. Each man talked about what they planned to do with the money. They talked about big houses, cars and boats. They would both move from California in due time and made a pact that none of them would spend any of the money until the coast was clear. "We can't take a chance by spending too much money too soon. If someone sees we're spending too much money on a cop's salary it's the first way to get caught."

This was their third trip around the area and once they turned on Chuck Hearn they would go past the back of the West Hall and Convention Center then head back onto West Pico.

This wasn't the first time either man had been involved in something like this but it was definitely the biggest haul they were ever involved in.

When the partners got the message from their contact that there was big money to be made they jumped at the idea.

"I wonder how much this package is worth?" the first officer asked his partner.

"If it is truly uncut cocaine and high grade who knows what it is worth. You could be right. It could be fifty times or more than what we are getting." They turned the corner again and passed the front of the warehouse on West Pico. It would be on the next time around that their contact was to pass the package to them.

"On the next trip around I'll drop you off and wait at the corner while you collect our prize."

The guard in the warehouse planned on releasing the bungee cord so that all the evidence would be gone.

Air Force One banked to the left as the pilot got clearance to land on the special runway designated for the Presidential plane today. Los Angeles airport had cleared the air space for the plane and had three other planes in a holding pattern as they made the final approach. The landing was smooth and they taxied to the executive terminal that was heavily guarded by both the Secret Service personnel on the ground and key FBI people. President Morgan had brought his wife and two daughters for the evening's event. It was a Sunday thing and they would be back in time for school tomorrow. One of the many perks of the office.

Mrs. Morgan enjoyed these events and during the Presidents first term she had been to so many it was hard to remember them all. His popularity afforded her the chance to push her agenda.

Gloria Morgan was an avid supporter of early education and wanted more opportunities for those less fortunate.

She had grown up in a rough area of Chicago and her parents had gone to great length to see that she received a great education.

Gloria's mother was an Elementary School Teacher in the South Side of Chicago. Her father was a postal worker and both her parents loved reading and the arts. On weekends her parents took her to McCormick Place to see exhibits or to the Navy Pier to experience the educational things it had to offer.

Gloria wanted to be able to have those less privileged to have the same experiences. She had been on many television shows talking about the need for early childhood education and her husband had her on a council that studied changes that could be enacted to promote learning in pre-schools. Mrs. Morgan was well liked and many times her popularity exceeded that of her husband. The President knew this and whenever he could he touted his wife's attributes.

The President, Mrs. Morgan and the two girls made their way into the terminal and were greeted by the Mayor and a host of fans that had been cleared by the security team. People waved banners and signs that proclaimed four more years as Morgan and his family walked on by. One young Asian girl yelled to the President's daughters. "We love you both." The girls waved back and smiled at their dad. Trips to California had always been pleasant and there was great support for the First Family.

The Mayor moved in to shake the Presidents hand and hugged Mrs. Morgan. Morgan had made a few trips to Los Angeles during his first campaign and he and the Mayor became close friends.

There was a short presentation at the terminal and local television caught the President as he put his arm around the Mayor and made a short speech. "Together we can continue to make a difference. I ask you to vote in two weeks and get your neighbors, family and friends to the polls."

Yells of, "We love you," and "Four more years," continued to come from the crowd as the First Family got in their vehicle.

The Secret Service had the terminal checked out earlier and members of the FBI along with the Los Angeles Police team were going to escort the Presidential motorcade to downtown and the Staple Center. The route was marked out and they had not released it to the press as an extra precaution.

The line of black GMC Escalades stretched out for a quarter of a mile along the terminal parking lot. Morgan and his family would be put into the special bullet proof vehicle that was sent to LA earlier. Steve's team was taking the lead and would have two vehicles drive the route a few minutes before the rest of the SUV's followed. The Los Angeles Police team set up road blocks for two different routes so that no one was positive which one the President would be on. This was normal procedure for any Presidential or high ranking government visit. It was a straight ride out of LAX down West Century Boulevard to the 405 freeway. The L.A. Police division had the entrances on the 405 north blocked off as soon as the Presidential plane landed.

Once the Presidential motorcade made its way onto the Santa Monica Freeway from the 405, the 405 would be opened up to regular traffic. The Police Chief was glad that the President was going directly to the Staple Center and then heading back to Washington after the event. They would follow the same procedure in closing the Santa Monica Freeway, locally known as highway 10, when the motorcade was headed to downtown.

The event at the Staple Center was scheduled for four in the afternoon. It was normal for many west coast functions that were scheduled for live television to start early for prime time viewing. The Oscars, EMMY's and other Hollywood events were always early afternoon affairs often bleeding into the wee hours of the morning with parties and such.

It was odd at times watching them on television when it was seven at night in New York but only four in Los Angeles. The Hollywood press had once complained about this but due to the early scheduling it allowed sponsors to have many gala parties that would start at eight on west coast time.

Steve had his team already in position at the Center and another group in the Los Angeles Convention Area. The Secret Service had performed their second search of the Staple Center making sure nothing looked out of the ordinary or that someone or something hadn't been placed where it didn't belong.

South Figueroa Street was in the process of being blocked off at the exit off the Santa Monica Freeway all the way to the Staple Center. Once the motorcade made its way from the Freeway they would open the freeway back to local traffic. It was now three o'clock and the President was just a few miles away from his final destination.

Forty Five

The crowd that gathered in front of the Staple Center was huge and had been on Figueroa Street for close to five hours. It was like most Hollywood events with fans and paparazzi lining the street. People held banners and waited to see famous celebrities and the President arrive. The Los Angeles Police had set up temporary road blocks about two feet off the curb so that no one would accidently be too close to the cars that would be coming down Figueroa. Once President Morgan and his family got in front of the Center the plan was to have them enter just off the first driveway that led into the building. The Secret Service and FBI would flank the First Family as they walked maybe twenty feet into the entrance. President Morgan requested to be able to be seen by the fans that lined the street and the security team compromised and came up with this plan.

How the Secret Service hated these things. People had long telephoto lenses on cameras pointed toward the President and there was no way to check them. Once the First Family was in the limo they made Morgan put on a bullet proof flak jacket under his shirt. It was specially made for him and fit tightly covering his chest and upper torso. If there was an assassination attempt they knew a shooter would be aiming at his head. There was no way to protect someone from that.

The Staple Center was in a good location because there were no tall buildings across the street all the way to Flower and Hope Street. There was always a concern about snipers. The FBI had sharp shooters on the top of the Convention Center with lookouts constantly surveying the crowd and street below.

The two police officers were now making their final turn around the Staple Center and the large crowd was causing them some concern. "Where is the guy supposed to be for the drop off?"

"He is going to be just at the corner of West Pico and Figueroa and will be holding a red umbrella in his right hand. I'm sure the crowd won't be a problem because they are further down the street and it will only take a few seconds to pass the package off." It all was coming together.

The L.A. Police had men stationed along the barrier that lined the street. Three other units were circling the area and four cars were positioned across the street from the Center in front of the parking lots. Guests had been told to park in the garage at the Holiday Inn City Center. The organizers had made provisions for the arriving guests to be escorted across from the Holiday Inn to the side entrance of the Staple Center. Many of the guests were familiar with this because the Grammy Museum was on the next block.

The long line of black SUV's was coming into view and the crowd started to yell and wave their flags and banners. The police presence tightened their reins and held back people who were getting excited.

The two officers had set the time for retrieving their package and to make the drop to coincide with the arrival of the President. Everyone would be concentrating on the events on the corner of Figueroa and the Staple Center and no one would notice what they were doing. It was a perfect plan. The driver of the police cruiser slowed and let his partner out at the back of the warehouse.

He moved into the walkway between the garment warehouse and the Drug Task Force building and lifted the backpack off the pavement and rolled the bungee cord up. It took seconds and he headed back to the cruiser. "Got it," He said as he got back in their vehicle. Their car started moving back down West Pico and slowed at the opposite side of the street.

It was now three forty five and the area was packed. The organizers had placed a stage at the end of the floor normally used for basketball. The maple hardwood floor had been covered with carpeted panels for the event. Plans were to have President Morgan enter from the left side of the stage when he was introduced. A large screen was set up behind the stage and it covered almost half of the seats that would normally be at the far end of the basketball court. The stage was lined with flashing neon lights and the curtain behind wrapped around the temporary screen. Television cameras had been set up across the front of the stage near the orchestra pit. The Hollywood flare had transformed the basketball arena into a fully fledged movie theater.

The Secret Service had their personnel positioned both with the First Family that was seated in the front row and the President who was standing in the wings talking to other guests. Assignments had been handed out to the FBI personnel that were there in supporting roles. Agents from the Los Angeles Bureau flanked the wings of the stage as well as were stationed at every levels entrance and exits. Kathy O'Conner and Blair were in the mezzanine level at the point farthest from the stage. They had been on that level both checking guests that took their seats and watching the action below. "I guess this is what you would call being a glorified usher," Kathy said. The two smiled at each other and continued to keep a watch on everyone in their sections.

Each person had been assigned an area or section of the balcony to watch. Guests were not allowed any packages just small handbags that had been scanned at the entrance. Anything that appeared out of the ordinary was to be called in immediately.

The sections in the balcony were last checked two hours before the event. Once everyone had been seated in the areas assigned to the agents they were to make sure their presence was obvious. They were to walk down the aisles and check for anything unusual. The Secret Service team had been through the auditorium twice before anyone had been let in but due diligence was the best method to avoid any problems.

The master of ceremonies was taking the center stage. Billy Crystal opened the show with quick witted jokes and poked fun at some of the many celebrities in attendance. He was on for about ten minutes and had the crowd on its feet applauding and laughing. He then introduced a special guest and Harrison Ford took the stage. He received a standing ovation from the excited crowd and promptly bowed to the audience. Harrison Ford was not normally someone that would be chosen to do this but he was good friends with Spielberg and because he had played a President in so many films the organizers though it would make for a lot of funny lines. Mr. Ford was a big supporter of the President. When President Morgan was told that Harrison would be introducing him he was pleased. The lights were turned low and Ford entered from the west wing of the stage to a resounding thunder of applause. He received a standing ovation and once people began to take their seats again he opened with, "As your President I thank you all for coming here today." That received a loud roar of approval and another standing ovation.

Ford laughed and held his hands up in post election celebration style as the laughter continued. "I had a tough time getting here today, someone tried to hi-jack Air Force One and I had to toss them off my plane." It couldn't have been a better opener. Guest roared and the First Family in the front row loved it. The President's two daughters were shown on the big screen laughing with their mother.

Blair moved down the aisle. She thought she spotted a dark shadow under a seat halfway across the fifth row in the balcony. She radioed across to Kathy who was now near the top of her section. "We've got a problem. It looks like there's an item under one of the seats in row five in section 223. I'll head down this aisle and you come from the opposite direction?"

Kathy hurried down the aisle, "I'm on my way now." Blair decided to move down the sixth row behind the object. If someone had a something dangerous she didn't want to spook them. Kathy saw what she was doing and slowly walked down the fourth row. Everyone in the section was paying attention to the action on stage and waiting for President Morgan to be introduced. The two agents slowly made their way to the center of row and spotted a man wearing a dark coat. He was seated above the item on the floor. How did he get in with that Blair was thinking. She kept her eyes on the package as well as the man while moving through the crowd.

Five Secret Service Agents were now descending into section 223 of the balcony and quickly moving down the long aisle. Guests around the area were now aware that something was wrong and Blair had just made it to the seat behind where she saw the package. Suddenly the man who was seated turned and saw her. He jumped from his seat and turned in the opposite direction when Kathy tackled him sending the two over the top of the row of seats and sprawling into the guests in the sixth row.

Blair grabbed the package from under the seat. It was a dark colored backpack about twelve inches long and weighed less than five pounds. Secret Service Agents now surrounded Kathy and the man she held on the ground as patrons moved out of the way.

The action was far enough from the stage that no one on the first floor or along the sides noticed what was happening.

Blair moved from under the seats to the side aisle and Secret Service Agents took the package from her and hurried toward an exit. The other agents took control of the man from Kathy and jerked him out of the balcony toward another exit. People around the two sections wondered what had happened. Blair and Kathy quickly tried to calm them down. "Nothing more folks, he didn't belong here." As if they planned it, Harrison Ford now turned and introduced the President. Everyone in the two sections stood and applauded forgetting the scene that just took place. "Hell, we'll read all about it in the papers," one man said.

Kathy had moved to the top of the section and Blair moved over to see if she was okay. She radioed back to Steve what had just happened and he sent two other agents to section 223 to see how to help. "We need to know what was in the backpack," she asked Steve.

"I'll get with the Secret Service team and find out what I can."

Harrison Ford stood on stage with President Morgan and the audience was now giving their fourth standing ovation of the night. Morgan waited for the crowd to be seated and turned to Harrison. "Thanks for loaning us your plane but why did you throw the Vice-President out?"

That got another big roar from everyone and both men embraced. The evening was less than thirty minutes into the event and everyone was having the best time ever.

President Morgan now stood at the center of the stage and thanked everyone for their warm reception. He pointed to the front row and introduced his wife and two daughters. "I'm very privileged to be accompanied by three beautiful women tonight." That drew another applause.

The three of them stood to the fifth standing ovation of the evening. He then turned his remarks to Billy Crystal. After a few jokes about Crystal and the trip to California he moved to the front of the stage.

"We're here tonight to honor both a man of vision and a great film maker. Steven Spielberg's, *Lincoln* is a masterpiece. He captures a time in the history of this country that all men and women weren't treated equal and although he faced enormous odds he was able to change the path of our great country and show the world why the United States is the greatest nation on earth."

The crowd again jumped to its feet and applause rang out loud and long. "I am only humbled to follow in Mr. Lincoln's footsteps." This kept the audience standing and cheering. As things started to settle down President Morgan turned his remarks to Spielberg. He closed by introducing Mr. Spielberg. Once the two were on stage together Morgan presented him a Presidential Citizens Freedom Medal. The two men shook hands and President Morgan moved to the wings of the Center as the Secret Service was escorting his family backstage. The plan was that when he had completed his remarks Spielberg would re-introduce the President and his family.

Secret Service agents were pulled in tightly around the President and First Family as they stood in the wings off the left side of the stage. "Sir, we had an incident in the balcony that has been taken care of." The lead agent then relayed what had happened.

"The man, maybe in his early forties had a backpack that our agents along with local FBI personnel confiscated. We're checking it as we speak and I'll know a little more later on."

"I'd like to know who found the backpack and thank them myself," Morgan said.

"I'll find out for you Sir."

Steven Spielberg was concluding his remarks and turned back to the left side of the stage. "It is with great pleasure that I again bring you President and Mrs. Morgan and their two daughters."

The evening was like a rollercoaster for the audience. Up and down, laughing and applauding. President Morgan put his arm around his wife and held the hand of his youngest daughter while Mrs. Morgan held her eldest daughter's hand. The crowd was pleasantly surprised that it was Gloria Morgan that now spoke. "It has been a great pleasure to be here with you tonight and I'm looking forward to many more trips to Los Angeles after the election."

It was a fitting plug for the upcoming election and votes for her husband.

She continued, "I'm afraid that we'll have to leave a little early because the girls have school tomorrow and they need to finish their homework on the ride home." That brought out both laughter and applause. Gloria Morgan was a master on having her family being identified as close to the typical American family as possible. President Morgan thanked everyone and ended with, "God Bless America."

The First Family was shuffled off stage to their limo that was now in the parking garage under the Staple Center. The Secret Service wasn't going to take any chances when leaving. They had the motorcade take a different route back to the airport and Air Force One was gassed and ready to take off.

No one would be aware of what happened in section 223 of the auditorium and there would be no mention in the papers either. The man that was captured had been taken to the FBI interrogation room on Wilshire Boulevard. He would undergo a plethora of questions and any accomplices would be rounded up.

The evening was a great success and the Presidential family was just arriving at the airport as people filed out of the Staple Center. They would be safely in Washington in less than five hours.

Blair and Kathy were now standing with Steve Orrison at the front exit to the Staple Center detailing what had transpired on the balcony.

Steve asked, "What was in the backpack?"

"I'm not sure the Secret Service Agent took it from me and headed out of the Center in a hurry."

"I'm sure he thought it could be a bomb and wanted to get it out of there fast. Just then her phone rang. She looked at both of them and wondered who could be calling. "Hello," She said.

"Special Agent Adams, this is President Morgan." Blair had a blank look on her face and Steve and Kathy stared back at her. "I just wanted to call and thank you and your partner, Kathy O'Conner personally for your diligent work tonight. You both may have saved my life and the life of my family." After a second of stumbling she said, "Thank you Mr. President."

"Is your partner close by?"

"Yes Sir," and she handed Kathy the phone. After Kathy talked to the President she hung up and both women looked at each other with the widest grins on their face.

Forty Six

The man at the other end of the line was screaming and yelling in both Russian and English. "What do you mean the package never got to you? What are you trying to pull? I'll find you. You are dead!"

"I swear, the two cops never brought it to me. I waited just as we planned and there were many cop cars that passed by but none of them stopped."

Ivan was furious, "They were supposed to call and never did. I tried to trace the burner phone this morning but it is off line. Are you sure you were in the right place?"

"Yes, I'm telling you the truth. Why would I lie?"

"We need to find them. Where is our package? I will hunt them down."

The man was still trying to calm Ivan down. "Ivan, we know who they are. Something must have gone wrong. I will try to find out what happened."

"You have three hours, if you haven't got our package and why it did not get to the event I will find and kill them myself."

The message was clear and the man knew Ivan was going nuts. They had everything going just as planned but something went wrong, but what? He dialed the phone number that he had stored in his I Phone.

The number rang over and over but there was no answer.

The two officers had been told only that the package was important and in the Drug Task Force warehouse. They were never told what was in it. What happened?

The late model Chevrolet Malibu headed down the Pacific Coast Highway to the meeting place just outside of Long Beach. Terminal Island was north of Long Beach and close to the Port of Los Angeles. The area had many storage buildings that had shipments ready to leave Long Beach Harbor for foreign destinations. It was an area that had very little foot traffic and many spots that were desolate. The Cartel used an abandoned building just off of Highway 47 and W. Ocean Boulevard. It was the perfect spot to conduct business without any interference from the local authorities. Manuel Garcia was the notorious leader of the group. From extortion schemes, to vicious violent crimes, they worked with Mexican Street gangs and had strengthened their grip in Southern California. They had been responsible for smuggling vast amounts of cocaine, marijuana and heroin into the United States and were rumored to have many cops on its payroll. When Manuel got the call about pure uncut cocaine he agreed to meet with the two men.

The two off duty cops pulled off of Highway 47 onto Lomita Street. The directions said to head about a mile down Lomita and turn right at Willow. Willow Street was a short block lined with warehouses and storage buildings. It was often very quiet and only large trucks and men bringing items to store were usually seen. A vehicle coming down the lane was very unusual but there was hardly anyone around to see what was taking place.

The storage building they were to meet at was about a quarter-of-a-mile after they were on Willow on the left side with a large blue sign above the front entrance.

They were to come alone and bring the package into the building.

"Shit, I sure hope we can get what this is worth," one of the men said.

Once they made it out of downtown one of the officers stuck his knife an inch into the dense package and withdrew white power on the tip of the blade. He touched it to his lips and smiled broadly. "Pure shit, this is just pure shit. We got the real stuff buddy."

His partner laughed. "If the Russians were willing to give us a

Half a million dollars it must be worth a hell of a lot more. Why not get the big haul and then we can disappear." Neither officer had been married and knew that they could vanish pretty easily with millions of dollars. They had thought about this with every trip around the Staple Center yesterday. If the package was in a secret panel under a mountain of marijuana it must be very valuable. The street value of cocaine had escalated especially since the U.S. had worked with the Mexican government to stem the tide of drugs crossing the border. Drug dealers will cut coke with baking powder or baby laxatives and increase the value greatly.

"Garcia said that if we have that much uncut cocaine, it could be worth millions and he would pay us a few million for the package." This would be enough to disappear. The two officers were in their late twenties and had been involved a few times before in this type of activity but this was their biggest score yet. Last year they were investigated by Internal Affairs but nothing came of it.

There was the storage building just as the direction said. "Should one of us stay here?"

"Why?"

"I don't know what if something goes wrong."

"Hey, we know Garcia and he came through last year so what can go wrong."

They pulled to the side of the building and grabbed the package from the trunk. It was a normal Monday in the Terminal area with hardly anyone around.

It was the first time the two men had been down there and in the past they only had small amounts that they stole from the property room. This time they didn't want to involve anyone else. They were lucky that one of their high school buddies worked at the Drug Task Force warehouse. They walked into the storage building and waited at the front entrance. No one was seen at first. "Hope this is the right place."

Viktor and Ivan had gone over everything again and again. They knew the names of the two cops but not their partner who worked in the Drug warehouse but he shouldn't be too hard to find. They still had a dangerous explosive out there somewhere. The detonation device was in the briefcase that Ivan had in his possession. "If we do not find these men soon I'm going to blow the damn thing up," Ivan said. Viktor knew he would. "Maybe we can still use it. If we get it to Washington we can get another chance to succeed. We've come too far to fail now."

The extent of the damage the bomb would cause would be tremendous. Ivan could contract the private plane he'd used in the past to take him and the package to the Capitol. First they had to find it.

Manuel Garcia was a ruthless drug lord and waited in the small office on the second floor of the storage building. His lookout had signaled that the two men just entered and were standing inside the warehouse. "El gringo dos esta' aqui'." The two gringos' are here.

Manuel wanted to make them wait. He knew if they had to wait a little they would get nervous and he could get the package cheaper, if he paid them at all. He sent his men downstairs to greet his guests. Manuel didn't like either cop and in general distrusted American police. If they would sell out their people, why wouldn't they turn on him too?

Forty Seven

The investigation at FBI headquarters in Los Angeles continued with the man captured at the Staple Center. The backpack had been inspected and it contained a high power rifle that was in two pieces. It could have easily been assembled with one hand and the damage would have been catastrophic. The position of the man's seat was in a straight line to the stage and there were no obstructions in his way. With so many standing ovations he could have completed his act although he would have never made it out of the building. It wasn't unusual for a would be assassin to want to take his target out in front of a crowd. It had happened too many times before. History had shown six failed attempts on the life of a U.S. President. In 1835 an assassin tried to kill Andrew Jackson but his derringer misfired. Both Franklin Roosevelt and Teddy Roosevelt had attempts on their lives and in 1981 John Hinkle, Jr. stood in the crowd and tried to kill President Regan. Sadly, four Presidents didn't fare as well. The most famous of those assassinations were those of Presidents Lincoln and Kennedy. Both gunned down and died from the hands of an assassin.

Steve had conferred with Frank Fitzgerald and once an initial investigation was completed the man would be sent to Washington where he will be subjected to further examination and investigating by the Central Bureau of the FBI.

The local team checking into the background of the man had not uncovered very much conclusive information.

Sahar Wahidi had been in the United States for a few years and was an undocumented Afghan citizen. From everything they could find he may have come into the country from Mexico and was living off the grid in Los Angeles. There had been a small Afghanistan community just outside of downtown in the Mid-City area along Olympic Boulevard just past Koreatown. They didn't have an address and he stopped talking once they had him in FBI headquarters. The Agents had hustled him out of the Staple Center and Secret Service along with the FBI had made the initial attempts to question him. They had been able to get his name when he was pulled out of the Center and he kept yelling, "Infidels, you Americans killed my family."

"What family are you talking about," one Agent asked. "My brother and his wife were killed by your bombs." At that time he did give his name but since hadn't said anything else. The Bureau had men canvassing the area in Mid-City showing Sahar's picture hoping to find out more. Was he part of an organization here or was he on his own? Those were critical to their investigation.

The two cops stood nervously in the entrance of the warehouse waiting for Manuel to meet them. The two guys that stood in front of them held sub-machine guns and had only said wait here. "Oh shit, I hope this isn't a mistake," one of them said.

"It will be okay, we've done business with him before. They just want to sweat us out, probably trying to lower our price. We'll stick together on this, right."

They could hear loud footsteps coming from somewhere on the second level and then it sounded like more than one person coming down a flight of stairs.

"My two favorite Gringos," Manuel said as he came into view. "So what do you have for me?"

The package was heavy and being held tightly by one of the cops and he reluctantly handed it Manuel. "I tasted it, pure as snow," he said.

"I will see," Manuel took out his knife and pushed it softly into the package. He withdrew white power on the tip of the blade and touched it to his tongue. It was as they had said. He had a big grin on his face and said. "Well my two friends this is good, no!"

They both nodded.

"So where did you get such a big package?"

"We have a contact at the Drug Task Force warehouse and he got it from a recent stash that they recovered from France."

Manuel looked puzzled. He hadn't heard of any real drugs coming in from Europe and there was a lot of money to be made especially with pure cocaine. "France you say. I would like to check this out further." Manuel took the package and started to walk to the back of the building.

"Hey, wait a minute. How about our money?"

"I told you, I need to check it out."

The two cops didn't like what was transpiring. "We'll agree only if you give us at least a down payment before we leave it here."

"Oh I see. You want to be paid first, yes?"

"Well at least a portion of what we had agreed on."

"Okay, I give you your share now." Manuel turned to his two guards and spoke Spanish to them. "Matar a los dos Gringos y enterer sus cuepos en la espalda." It meant, Kill the two Gringos and bury their bodies in the back.

"Se Senior." With that the two opened fire on the cops and the bullets ripped their bodies in half. Blood and guts were all over the floor as the two men who completed the task laughed.

The bodies were scraped off the pavement and buried in a shallow grave inside the back of the building.

Their Malibu was brought inside and the plates were taken off. One of the men that just finished burying the bodies was told to junk the car in the Harbor.

Manuel took the package and headed up to the second floor of the warehouse.

Forty Eight

Josh and his team in Seoul were running out of options. The search for the Professor had widened and no clues had turned up. They had been to all the obvious places including the local coffee shop that was a known hang-out for Eastern Europeans. Josh had shown the picture of the Professor around but no one recognized him. The Professor's story was that he had been taken hostage in Moscow. They confirmed that his family was being held just as he said. Now they were missing too. New concerns were rising. Did the Professor and his family flee or were they abducted?

Agents had searched all night and soon had to call the bad news into their boss. The CIA Director didn't want to tell anyone what his agents discovered but the search needed to be expanded and his back was up against a wall. He had to tell the President that their initial information gathered from the Professor may have all been false. The chase through LAX may have all been drug related and no bomb may have even existed.

Chiarini thought about Tony Kim and that he was still out there and could pull the entire agency into question. He had dismissed all of that after giving the President and Chiefs of Staff such glowing news. Now it was all coming apart.

Where could the Professor and his family have disappeared to?

Calls went out to every International agency with their pictures and vital information.

This was quickly becoming a massive worldwide man hunt. If his people could find the escaped Professor before he had to tell the White House it all could be saved.

Rumors filled the halls of the West Wing with news of something important happening in Langley, Virginia. The Central Intelligence Agency had only said that their National Clandestine Service was finalizing the details of information gathered from those captured in Seoul. When the President's Chief of Staff asked Chiarini about the request sent to other world's agencies for help in finding the missing Professor he tried to dodge the question. Chiarini started answering questions with other questions. That was a sign that he was in trouble. He said that they were making sure no other group or faction was still operating in consort with those captured. His group was running a sting. That made no sense to anyone but sooner or later he'd have to come clean. Robert Chiarini knew he had less than twenty-four hours to resolve his problem or he would have to level with the White House.

It was now Monday morning and Viktor was losing all hope of finding the package. Not only had they failed in an attempt to assassinate the President but he had no idea where the bomb was. His contact had reported that he had tried to call the two cops but they were not answering. When he contacted their precinct he was told they had the day off. The man that was working in the Drug Task Force warehouse had also disappeared.

"Where in the hell are they." Viktor and Ivan knew that the two cops needed money that is why they were picked. The bomb was packed with uncut cocaine in case the FBI discovered the package hidden in the crate. It was all planned out, how did they fail?

Ivan now wondered if the cops double crossed them and found the layer of cocaine and took the drugs to sell. They had already given the two a hundred thousand dollars and figured the offer of half-a-million would make sure they came through.

"We need to end this now," Ivan said.

Viktor now agreed with the harsh line that his partner took. He reminded Ivan one more time that they might still recover the bomb. "If we could find it, I will and take it to Washington." Ivan knew that was just hopeful thinking. He opened the briefcase he had brought on the plane and he was determined to stop anyone that ruined their plans.

The building on Willow Street stood about twenty yards off the road. The street came to a dead end just past the storage warehouse. Garcia's men had moved the two dead cops from the entrance and dug a hole in the back of the building. They were laughing as they kicked the bodies one more time before pushing them into the shallow grave.

Garcia had taken the package the cops delivered to a room upstairs and was waiting to hear back from one of his contacts in San Diego. He would take the cocaine there and they would cut it with baby powder. It would then be distributed to his many drug peddlers throughout southern California. He told them on the phone, "We would be pushing weight today brother." When one of the men asked about the rock, he said, "This crack is gator," Signifying that it was the highest quality.

Manuel Garcia was smart and controlled a large cartel that had made significant inroads in California. He also knew he needed to confirm the quality of his crack. Once he secured the package and confirmed its contents, his men in San Diego were prepared to cut it. He planned to deliver the package himself. It was resting on the corner of the table in front of the large print couch that Garcia now sat on.

He had a Dos Equis in his right hand and laughed so loud while telling his men a story that his two front gold teeth caught a beam of the sunlight that shown through the small window. There were now all five of his men standing in front of the couch and chuckling about the two gringos that thought they would be rich.

Garcia stood and pointed to the package and held his hands out wide. "Te hare' todo Rico." I will make you all rich, he said. Everyone was cheering in the room and toasting each other with beer and Tequila.

Suddenly, the room erupted in a ball of fire that rose eighty feet in the air pulling everything in the vicinity into the flames that engulfed buildings along Willow Street. The Red, yellow and blue flames could be seen from as far as twenty miles away. Ships moored in the Port of Los Angeles and Long Beach Harbor rocked in their slips as the ground shook. People were sure that it was an earthquake.

A dark cloud covered the entire harbor as people from the Maritime Museum across the Channel ran for cover. Debris landed all along the buildings and ships off of Ocean Boulevard and even the Queen Mary rocked as tourists grabbed for railings to steady themselves. Sirens could be heard from every direction and fire engines and police cars rushed to the scene. It was impossible to get very close to the blaze as the heat from the blast baked the paint off of anything for miles around it. The air had a foul odor that made everyone cover their face along the harbor.

Emergency vehicles were now arriving along Harbor Freeway but unable to cross the bridge that led to the warehouse district. Ports O'Call Village and Fisherman's Village had people lying on the pavement overcome from the smoke and stinging of the blast. People tried to help those affected and panic filled everyone's face.

Palos Verdes was close to thirty miles from the action but because it sat high above the harbor people from homes and business could see the flames and feared the worse.

"Has there been an attack," some asked each other. Communities along the coast responded with every emergency vehicle available.

News teams rushed to get people close to the action so that they could report what had happened and calls were coming in from all over with eye witness reports.
As in many of these types of incidents some were filled with misinformation and conjecture. Helicopters moved to the scene but had to fly around the damaged area due to the heat and height of the flames that erupted. The blast found additional strength from the cargo that was stored in adjacent buildings and with so many flammable items in the warehouses it was impossible to get anywhere close to the area.

Information was sketchy but the FBI office in Los Angeles was getting initial reports that terrorists had blown up the harbor at Long Beach. Steve and his team had automatically linked it to the missing bomb. But why Long Beach? Was that the target? Agents were dispatched to the action and Steve wanted to get down there as quickly as possible.

Already accounts of dead and injured numbered in the hundreds. News was just coming into the White House and President Morgan who had hoped to enjoy the moments of the past weekend saw all of that wash away with dire news reports.

Forty Nine

Once news of the magnitude of the damage had been confirmed, President Morgan ordered the National Guard and United States Marine Corps stationed at Camp Pendleton, to take every action necessary to help people in need and determine what had transpired. Frank Fitzgerald had conferred with his Bureau Chief, and said that they would be leading the investigation along with the California Bureau of Investigation. The ATF and Drug Task Force sent their evidence response team to oversee the investigation and see if there was any involvement of a foreign entity.

On Tuesday morning, twenty four hours after the explosion flames still rose some ten feet above the buildings along Willow Street and fire departments from as far as Torrance and Lakewood helped spell those from Long Beach and Terminal Island. Fire fighting ships used cannon hoses to send volleys of water to the affected area hoping to quell the blaze. Investigators from every agency continued to concentrate on the center of the action and had narrowed the blast to have originated from warehouse row. The Drug Task Force released details that they had a building under surveillance in the past that may have been a haven for cartel leaders but never confirmed it. So much effort was on saving lives that finding out who was responsible was taking a back seat.

The blast and its location were totally confusing to all the agencies involved. Why here, what was the game plan? There wasn't any key national security positions involved. Damage to the harbor and the ships was minimal and wouldn't affect its operation for more than a week. This certainly wasn't compared to the events of 9/11 or the Oklahoma City bombing. If terrorists were involved they would have wanted to make a statement that brought the United States to its feet. Bombing in the Long Beach Harbor wouldn't accomplish that.

Steve Orrison had his Special Agents Blair Adams and Kathy O'Connor working the case along with Brandon Booth who was back in the office manning the desk doing research on the type of bomb and who owned the buildings involved. Agents from the CBI worked along with the FBI on the case and it was now suspected that the bomb fragments recovered resembled the one used in Oklahoma City bombing of the Federal Building. Many pieces were being recovered and sent to the forensic team that would dissect them and determine the actual chemical make-up.

West Ocean Boulevard and the Harbor Freeway were closed from Highway 110 and the Channel Bridge all the way to Highway 710 leading to San Pedro Bay. Many tourist attractions had been damaged and closed. The Port of Los Angeles has suspended ships from loading or unloading until the flames were fully under control. All the local police and fire departments were working 24/7 to put the flames out and help those who had been killed or injured in the blast.

Brandon Booth worked the new computer screen that the Bureau had set up in the Wilshire office and plotted information as it came in from the field. He was thrilled to be back in action even if it was only in the office. He fielded reports as they came into the headquarters and he, along with two members of the CBI, updated the details.

The investigation into the explosive was taking a turn with each piece of information that arrived. The forensic team started to put together a beginning idea of what chemicals had been discovered. When the list included radiological dispersal everyone from Washington to Seoul knew it was the make-up that the Professor had told the CIA agents. This is a device that is designed to destabilize a community. This may be one of the reasons why so many of the dead were found as far as a mile from the explosion. Many people had damage to their eyes and throats. Beyond the massive blaze and thunderous effects this bomb was meant to kill and maim many Americans. Thank God it wasn't detonated in a highly populated area was all the Bureau could say.

Everyone was now only wondering what would have happened had this been at either the Kennedy Center or Staple Center event. The FBI would be busy for months working on this endeavor. Agents had been dispatched from all over the Western half of the country to work on this. Orrison reported hourly back to Fitzgerald and in turn Frank kept the White House informed.

Blair had been in Long Beach for almost a full day along with Kathy when they stumbled on traces of cocaine and bomb fragments along the shore line. How could they have survived such an enormous blast? The piece of plastic and metal had melted together forming a seal around the coke. The cadaver dogs that were working the scene with the teams of agents sniffed it out. They bagged the evidence and sent it by courier to the forensic lab. Maybe this will give the teams back in the lab some clues.

In Washington things had gone from bad to worse for Chiarini and the CIA. More questions started to arise about the information the agents in Seoul got from the Professor. When a request for another round of interrogating him came up Chiarini had to come clean.

"We lost our guy," he started telling the Chief of Staff and John Martin.

"How in the hell could you lose a man you had in custody? Damn, you even had his family too."

"Well, they're gone too!"

John Martin was furious. "When were you going to tell us?"

"My agents had the Professor under guard in a safe house but somehow he either was taken or got out sometime Sunday night. We've put out a B.O.L.O. with every international agency and thought he would still be in South Korea and he would be found."

"Son-of-a-bitch Robert, you can't keep this shit to yourself. I need to know what is going on." Martin's face was red and he stomped around the room shaking his head. He knew this would reflect badly on him too.

"We've got to tell the President," his Chief of Staff said. "Where are you in the search for him," Martin asked Chiarini. "He's nowhere to be found. His family is gone too." Robert Chiarini knew he was in trouble and there was no way around it now.

"We're going to the White House together," John Martin told him.

The Chief of Staff knew if anyone was going to take the fall it would be Chiarini.

"Get your shit together because it's all on you, buddy, let's go." John turned and headed toward the door.

Fifty

Frank Fitzgerald was meeting with President Morgan in the Oval Office discussing the events in Long Beach and that his team was putting details together. "It appears that the same chemicals that we were told existed in the dirty bomb sent to LAX are the ones used in the Long Beach explosion Sir."

The President was sitting behind the Resolute desk and Frank was flanked by the Secretary of Defense and Secretary of State. They had just heard that John Martin was on his way with Robert Chiarini. Morgan would have all his key men together as they sorted this all out. Frank cleared his throat and added. "We have some disturbing news that our agents uncovered during our operation in California." He opened his briefcase and handed Morgan a package. "Here is a burner cell phone that we recovered while chasing a suspect. It has orders from the CIA Director to derail our FBI investigation. There is also an admission of him still operating his Black ops Silverstone group."

The President was furious. "God Damn him, who in the hell does he think he is." Everyone leaned back toward the couches and Morgan pounded on his desk. "I personally gave him the order to disband that group. He told me it was all handled." He handed the evidence that Fitzgerald brought in to the Secretary of State.

The election was only ten days away and the President didn't need any of this to come out, not now. He was riding a wave of euphoria after the events at the Kennedy Center and in Los Angeles at the Hollywood event.

"I'll take care of all this for you Sir," the Secretary of Defense said.

"Chiarini is on his way in with the Homeland Security Chief. I'll let him handle it, but thanks Jim. Once they get here I want all of you to stay for a short meeting then you can leave. Nothing about this leaves this room."

A chorus of "Yes Sir" filled the air.

President Morgan told everyone to be seated and he moved to the large winged chair across from the two sofas. His secretary informed him that Martin and Chiarini had arrived. "Send them in."

Robert Chiarini looked like he had been sentenced to the guillotine. Martin stood tall and after exchanging pleasantries with everyone he addressed the President. "Sir I have some disturbing news. Robert has informed me that his team has lost both the Professor and his family in Seoul. They have been searching for him but have come up empty."

Morgan turned his head toward his CIA Director, "Is that so Robert?"

This was bringing back every memory anyone had of being called to the Principals office after breaking a window in school or something similar. Robert shuffled his feet and looked down on the carpet before answering. "Well my team did a great job breaking this whole thing wide open and stopping the bombing of the two flights to Paris and London."

Morgan jumped in, "This isn't about your team and their work; and it's about you and your handling of this investigation."

"Yes Sir, I understand."

"I'm sure you don't fully understand all the ramifications that go along with this."

Morgan stood up and excused everyone but John Martin and Robert Chiarini. Robert stood in the center of the room and waited for the others to leave. The President moved behind his desk and motioned John Martin and Robert to come closer.

"On January 20th I took the oath of office, the same oath each one of you took to defend this country and preserve, protect and defend the Constitution of the United States. I hold that oath and the words I spoke on the steps of the Capitol as sacred. Robert, today I found out that you had not held up your oath as promised."

Chiarini could not have hung his head any lower. "John, I plan to take the oath again this year after my victory and at that time I will expect Mr. Chiarini to tender his resignation. We will say he wanted to spend more time with his family. I'm also going to tell the Secretary of State to give you a package that has come to light that Mr. Chiarini is still operating his Silverstone group. I want it disbanded today. If it is not I will expect your resignation too!"

Both men were speechless. The President now stood again and turned to the flags behind his desk. "I hold this office and the tenets of it sacred and expect every representative of this administration to do the same. Until January 20th of next year the under-secretary of State will operate in Mr. Chiarini's place. We'll tell everyone that he has had a medical condition that required rest. If I hear any different I will release exactly what you have done Robert and hold you for trial as a conspirator."

John Martin said, "I'll accomplish everything you have requested Sir and report back to you when it finished."

"I expect nothing less John."

Robert started to talk and Morgan held up his hand. "Not now, not anywhere, not anytime do I want to hear from you."

Morgan pointed to the door and both men turned and left. The President paged his Chief of Staff and slumped back into his chair behind the desk.

Epilogue

Fifty One

A month had passed since the Bureau's Evidence Response Team had completed its investigation. Steve was in his office with some serious looking guys and they had maps laid out on his desk. Two men from the California Bureau of Investigation detailed that the explosion had been the work of a drug cartel. Competing cartel members must have planted an explosion that triggered flammable materials stored in other warehouses along Long Beach. It just didn't add up to Steve.

Regardless, it was the information that the Federal Government wanted released. They couldn't tell the public that another unsolved bombing had taken place. Especially since the bomb may have been the work of a terrorist organization. No group had taken credit for the actions which only made the case muddier.

Steve Orrison and the L.A. Bureau were applauded for their work on the case. Frank Fitzgerald told him better things were on the horizon. The L.A. Bureau team was stronger than ever. Special Agent Brandon Booth was fully recovered and back at work. He was meeting in the conference room with Blair and Kathy going over the material that the CBI had given them. "It just doesn't add up. Why would the Cartel blow up all the drugs too?"

The Bureau members all agreed however that the Department of Homeland Security had the lead on this and had handled the press release along with the CBI.

The man with the gun that was captured at the Staple Center had been sent to Virginia and was being questioned there by members of a special task force assigned to handle possible Presidential attacks. The press never found out the details and only knew that people in the second level had said a man was taken out of his seat by authorities. When the L.A. Times reporter called the Bureau office he was told they had no news of any such thing taking place.

The election wasn't close. President Morgan won the five key battleground states that had been called a toss-up just a few weeks ago. Robert Chiarini, in a surprise, had announced that he was leaving his position in the CIA citing personal health reasons. The Washington Post had done a story on the administration's cabinet members the week after the election and had been told by John Martin that he was considering a position in the private sector. That surprised many political insiders because John had been pegged as a key member of the Presidents staff. It wasn't unusual for there to be cabinet changes in a second term but the names of Chiarini and Martin came as big surprises to everyone.

Frank Fitzgerald was heading up an investigation along with the Deputy Director of the CIA on events in Seoul and the whereabouts of the man that the Agents had captured that gave them information on a massive bomb. This information would never be released to the press.

Meanwhile in Moscow, Ivan and Viktor waited for the Professor to arrive. It was a cold and blustery day in Moscow as he and Viktor watched out the window for their friend. They would develop new plans to attack the United States and kill the President. He and Viktor agreed that they would succeed this time.

"We will have another chance," he told Viktor. The Professor had been valuable in the first plan and he would be again. "This time we will build the bomb in the United States and not worry on how to get it to our destination."

The Professor had made sure that his wife and daughter were safe and would not be compromised. He would be critical to this new plot.

"We will do it right next time," Viktor agreed. "We cannot trust any of the Americans to help." They both were still disappointed that the two Los Angeles Police officers failed to deliver the bomb to the Staple Center.

They waited in the small room behind the local café,' close to Red Square. It was once used by the KGB as a secret meeting place. Famous Kremlin buildings were in a short walking distance. They sat at a small round table toasting their new endeavor with a bottle of Stolichnaya Vodka. The two men clinked their glasses, "Za oos Pyeh" to future success!

Fifty Two

Steve was meeting with his two Special Agents in his office. "I talked to the President and Fitzgerald earlier and they have a request." Booth and Blair looked at each other. "When President Morgan was told about the event in the upper level of the Staple Center he wanted more information on the Agents involved. I gave him Blair and Kathy's names and all their background."

Booth interrupted. "Sir, we came in here to tell you that we set a date. I asked Blair to marry me."

Steve smiled. "I'm glad to hear the good news. I understand your concerns," Steve said.

Blair jumped in, "Sir, I understand the rules and will tender my resignation effective today."

"I appreciate that, but about that resignation, I can't accept it."

The two Special Agents gave each other puzzled looks. "But Sir, the rules," they said.

"Well, I talked to the Director and you know that the President was thrilled with our action here during his visit and once he saw your and Kathy's pictures he had an idea. He wants to get more women interested in joining the Bureau and hoped either one of you would be willing to become a spokesperson for us.

It will be a national campaign and would require you to handle the talk shows and a lot of traveling.

I talked to Kathy and she wasn't interested. How about it Blair, will you take the job?"

Tears welled in her eyes. She loved what she did and the opportunity to grow the ranks of women in the FBI with a chance to stay as an agent was great news. She looked at Booth and he shook his head up and down. "Yes Sir, I'd be proud to be the Bureau's representative in this endeavor."

"You'll still have an office in this building but it will be upstairs in public relations. I'll talk to Bill tomorrow once the Director finalizes the change of venue for you. Until then you're still assigned to my office and I couldn't be happier for both of you."

Booth turned to Blair and smiled. "You deserve every opportunity sweetie, and we'll make this all work for us."

"So when's the date?" Steve asked.

"We're working on that. Maybe in the spring," Blair and Booth were holding hands and Steve smiled as they got up from the chairs in his office. "Can we tell the group?"

"Absolutely," Steve said.

Tony Aued

Acknowledgements

To Carl Virgilio, your work on the cover was outstanding and the suggestions on the plot were valuable;

To Joshua Eli Smith, your research and photography in Seoul was important in making the events and geography of South Korea come alive;

To the members of the Shelby Writers Group, you're the best group ever, thanks' for everything;

To Beverly Styles, your editing work was great and you helped make the story much better;

To Charles Allen, your FBI insight was very helpful. You will always be remembered;

To my special friends Tony Kim, Robert Chiarini, Frank Fitzgerald, Steve Orrison, John Martin, Rusty Nelson, Manny Ramos, Leonard Herrman and Joshua Eli Smith. I hope you enjoyed your roles, and the various characters that you played in this novel.

To my daughter, Blair, you have given me great material to work with and the character of Blair Adams will continue her exploits. I love you little kid!

The Blame Game is the fourth novel in the Blair Adams Series. Mr. Aued's FBI Thriller Series has gained many fans. Inspiration for the series had been developed after a family tragedy. The series has sold many copies throughout the United States and Canada. Mr. Aued has had many newspaper reviews and appeared in a special television interview in 2012.

"Aued weaves a riveting tale that reads more like a motion picture than a novel," according to reviews by Sheila Yancy of The Times Herald in Port Huron, Michigan.

He is a retired teacher, and also had a corporate career that took him across many cities in the South and Midwest. He currently resides in Michigan with his wife Kathy and their dog Baxter.

Photo's of Seoul and Suwon Korea

Tony Aued

The Blame Game

Made in the USA
Charleston, SC
16 September 2015